Emotional Geology

Linda Gillard

Other titles published by transita

Elissa's Castle by Juliet Greenwood
Forgotten Dreams by Doris Leadbetter
Pond Lane and Paris by Susie Vereker
Scuba Dancing by Nicola Slade
The Waiting Time by Sara Banerji
Turning Point by Bowering Sivers
Uphill All the Way by Sue Moorcroft

transita

Transita books reflect the lives of mature women.
Contemporary women with rich and interesting stories to
tell, stories that explore the truths and desires that colour
their lives.

To find out more about transita, our books and our authors
visit **www.transita.co.uk**

For the Book Crossers!

Emotional Geology
Linda Gillard

With best wishes

Linda Gillard.

transita

Published by Transita
3 Newtec Place, Magdalen Road,
Oxford OX4 1RE. United Kingdom.
Tel: (01865) 204393. Fax: (01865) 248780.
email: info@transita.co.uk
http://www.transita.co.uk

British Library Cataloguing in Publication Data
A catalogue record for this book is available from the British Library

Map drawn by Nicki Averill
Cover design by Baseline Arts Ltd, Oxford
Produced for Transita by Deer Park Productions, Tavistock
Typeset by PDQ Typesetting, Newcastle-under-Lyme
Printed and bound by Bookmarque, Croydon

This novel is set in real places, but the events and characters exist only in the
author's imagination, and any resemblance to real people is purely
accidental.

ABOUT THE AUTHOR

Linda Gillard graduated from Bristol University and trained as an actress at the Bristol Old Vic Theatre School. For eight years she pursued an acting career, the highlight of which was sharing a table in The National Theatre canteen with Sir Michael Gambon. (The lowlight was playing a fairy for four rainy months in an open-air production of *A Midsummer Night's Dream* in London's Regent's Park.)

Whilst under-employed at the National Theatre, Linda accidentally became a successful freelance journalist and wrote many articles based on her self-sufficient "Good Life" in rural Cambridgeshire. For twelve years she had a humorous column in *Ideal Home*. Linda ran her two careers concurrently for a while, then decided to give up acting to raise a family and write from home. Twelve years later she retrained as a primary teacher and taught in Norfolk, specialising in English and Art.

A further rethink entailed giving up teaching and down-shifting to the Isle of Skye, realising a long-held dream to move to a Scottish island and write full-time.

Linda now lives with her teacher husband in a big house overlooking the Cuillins, a mountain range featured in her novel, *Emotional Geology*.

For more information about Linda and her work visit www.transita.co.uk

ACKNOWLEDGEMENTS

I would like to thank the following for their help:
Carcanet Press Ltd. for permission to quote from
Sorley MacLean's poem *An Cuilithion /The Cuillin*
printed in *FROM WOOD TO RIDGE*
(Carcanet/Birlinn, 1999)

Roger Sanderson for his advice on mountaineering.
(Any errors are mine, not Roger's.)

My writers' e-group for their enthusiasm and support,
with special thanks to Sheree, Elie and Wendy.

My agent Tina Betts and publishers Giles Lewis and Nikki
Read for believing in the book.

My daughter Amy Glover for her unmerciful, but always
constructive criticism.

A NOTE ON PLACE NAMES

Uist is pronounced 'Oo-ist'.

The Cuillin (pronounced Coo-lin) mountain range on Skye is referred to usually as 'the Cuillin' (a plural noun and anglicisation of the Scots Gaelic *An Cuilithionn*) or sometimes as 'the Cuillins'. 'Cuillin' is usually used as a plural noun but occasionally as singular, depending on whether it refers to a collection of peaks (eleven of which are Munros, over 3000') or a mountain range.

What is not in dispute is that the Cuillin are the finest mountains in the British Isles.

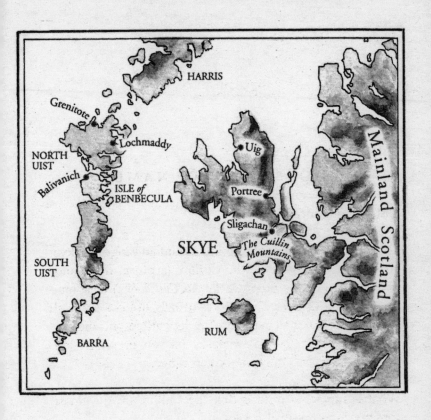

'O the mind, mind has mountains; cliffs of fall
Frightful, sheer, no-man-fathomed.'

Gerard Manley Hopkins

PROLOGUE

I TALK TO THE ISLAND. I don't speak, but my thoughts are directed towards it. Sometimes it replies. Never in words of course.

I miss trees. You don't notice at first that there are hardly any trees here, just that the landscape is very flat, as if God had taken away all the hills and mountains and dumped them on neighbouring Skye. But eventually you realise it's *trees* that you miss.

Trees talk back.

In the hospital grounds there was a special place where I used to stand, where I went to feel safe. It was my magic circle, my fairy ring. There were three slender pine trees in a triangular formation, only a few feet apart. I used to stand within that space, sheltered, flanked by my trees, like a small child peering out at the world from behind grown-up legs.

Once, when the air was very still and a brilliant blue sky mocked my misery, I stood between my trees, head bowed, not even able to weep. I placed my palms round two of the tree trunks, grasping the rough bark. I begged for strength, support, a sign. Anything.

My trees moved in answer. Quite distinctly, I felt them move. As my palms gripped them they shifted, as the muscles in a man's thigh might shift before he actually moved. The movement was so slight it was almost imperceptible, as if their trunks were flexing from within.

I knew then that the doctors were right, I was indeed mad. I threw up my head and cried out. Above me a light

1

breeze played in the treetops, a breeze I had been unaware of on the ground. It tugged at the branches with a sudden gust and I felt the trunks flex again, bending to the will of the wind.

I *wasn't* mad.

At least, not then.

CHAPTER ONE

A WOMAN ALONE IN A LIGHT, WHITE ROOM. A glowing stove, a scrubbed pine table. No mirror, no clock, no photographs. A sewing-box lies open on the bare wooden floor. On a window-sill a still-life: driftwood, shells and a sheep's skull. The woman – not old, not young – lays down her pen and shifts her weight in the chair. The screech of wood on wood shatters the silence. She folds sheets of paper with great care, pushing them into the envelope with hands that tremble slightly.

Grenitote
North Uist
Western Isles

January 11ᵗʰ 2000

My dear Megan,
The days are very short, very dark and the wind is almost constant. My new home – my doll's house! – is small, but I like it that way. (For a start there is very little to keep clean.) I have a sitting room and a workroom downstairs, a minute kitchen extension out the back and a bedroom and bathroom upstairs, all of a monastic simplicity. I can see the sea from the sitting room and from my bedroom. The holiday-home buyers didn't want this one because it's too close to the sea, or so my neighbour Shona McAskill says. (Dear Shona, fount of all wisdom and a great many outrageous Gaelic proverbs. There seems to be one for every occasion – all of them gloomy.) If there's a freak

high tide I shall have seawater round my ankles apparently, so I haven't bothered with a carpet. The floorboards are bare and I have put my oldest, most faded quilts over the furniture to hide the suddenly-garish colours I've imported from my former life. (I like the idea of having a Former Life. It makes me sound intriguing and romantic, doesn't it? Or does it make me sound reformed, like a criminal? Perhaps I shall tell the locals that I have moved here in an attempt to go straight. In a way, I have.)

I try to go for a walk every day, whatever the weather – that is if the wind allows me to stay perpendicular. I see very few people on my walks. There are no tourists at this time of year and the locals are sensibly installed by their firesides, watching daytime TV. (Not an option for me as I don't have one.) The radio has been my constant companion and the shipping forecast has taken on a new meaning. I don't pretend to understand it but I am beginning to get the gist. The prognostications for 'Mallin, Hebrides, Minches' always sound vague but dire. (Rather like Shona's proverbs.)

Today I walked very fast to get warm, then I sat on some rocks to watch gannets dive, which made me cry. I can never watch gannets without thinking of how they go blind in old age and die of starvation. They hit the water at God knows what speed with their eyes open, looking for food. How can their eyeballs withstand the impact? And how do ornithologists know gannets don't sneakily shut their eyes at the last minute? (Maybe gannets don't have eyelids? I will ask Shona. I am sure she will know.)

The silence and the long expanses of uninterrupted time are Heaven. ('When God made time, He made plenty of it.' The Gospel According to Shona.) I think it's affecting my work already. I seem to be using less colour and more texture and when I do use colour it tends to be colours from the natural world. I think this place will be good for my work, good for me. I hope so.

Apart from the fact that they have made it clear that they think I am a) mad and b) unlikely to last six months, the locals have been kindness itself. I am sure they regard it as their Christian duty, although I doubt that duty prevents them from repeating (and probably embellishing) every snippet of personal information that I am foolish enough to let fall. But I don't mind – I didn't come here expecting privacy. I realise I am an event. I am what passes for entertainment on an under-populated Hebridean island. I am an anomaly – a woman alone, too young to be widowed and too old to be looking for a mate. I occupy that no man's land – no woman's land – between youth and old age.

Write soon, darling, or phone if you can. I'm not at all lonely but would love to hear your news.

With love,

Mum

P.S. I am keeping very well – no nightmares and I have not had to increase my dosage so far. You do not need to worry about me at all!

She seals the envelope with a sigh and picks up her pen again. Gazing down at the blank white space, her memory shuffles, deals another blank white space. The pen hovers, dashes off a name, then skids across the envelope. She concedes defeat, replaces the cap on her pen and walks to the window where she rests her head against the cold glass.

***

The comfort of glass. The attraction, the seduction of breaking glass and the quietus it will bring. No effort, just push, push until it cracks, breaks, then peels back your skin, letting the blood, letting the pulsing blood flow, cleansing your body, emptying your mind, letting life ebb away like the tide, leaving the beach clean, flat, blank.

No one will ever know you were here.

I lie in my bed, the bed I used to share with Gavin. Tiny pieces of fabric are flying round the room, a flurry of multi-coloured snowflakes, a rainbow blizzard. They cascade down until the floor is covered, inches deep in brilliant fragments, and still they fall. I watch the pieces flutter round the room, see them settle on the duvet, settle on me, piling up until I am buried like the Babes in the Wood by a mountain of multi-coloured leaves. And still they fall. My face is covered and I cannot breathe. I call out to Gavin but my mouth fills with pieces of cloth...

I wake, sobbing, sweating, the duvet over my head, my mouth full of hair. In the dark I turn to Gavin's side of the bed and reach across, terrified.

He isn't there of course. He hasn't been there for five years.

But still I reach.

***

When I wake I think at first that it is silent. I lie in bed quite motionless, thinking 'Is *this* what it's like to be dead?' Gradually sounds impinge – the rumble and hiss of the waves on the shore, the whingeing of gulls, the tick of the clock.

I wonder – do I really need a clock now? Here I have all the time I need. Once when I was researching a project, I saw a strange clock in a museum, a clock used by early American pioneers, a clock with only one hand. They only ever needed to know the hour. When they boiled an egg they used an egg timer.

When God made time, He made plenty of it.

Sometimes it requires a great act of will to get up, not because I am reluctant to resume my new routine, simply that I feel suspended, outside time, in a white space, here at the edge of the world. I do not move, I cannot move.

Then I remember being in the hospital.

It is in the end the memory of feeling drugged that induces me to move. I move to prove to myself that I am not drugged, that I have willpower and can use it. See me – I can move. I exist. I am me.

The first battle of the day is fought and won.

Brushing my teeth, I stare out the window but a cobweb catches my eye, a cobweb slung across the corner of the rattling window frame. I raise my hand with a housewifely impulse to brush it away, then feel a sudden reluctance to destroy the web, so perfect, so mathematical in its construction. A small spider waits in the centre for its prey, looking not sinister, but pathetically vulnerable and exposed. The cobweb billows in the draught, like a sail.

Who is there to pass judgement on my slovenly house-keeping? I am prepared to share my bathroom with this tiny spider. We shall endure the draughts together.

So now I have company. A lodger. I shall call him Bruce. After Robert the Bruce, of course.

We both dangle by a thread, Bruce...

A spider splayed on a limestone rockface.

Not a spider. A man. A vertical impossibility.

He is still, spread-eagled, waiting to make his move. Then, sudden as an insect but with more grace, he moves diagonally upwards, jamming claw-like fingers into invisible cracks, folding grasshopper legs beneath him ready for the push, the swing, the gymnastic counterbalance as his body grazes the rock and takes up another perilous, temporary foothold on a crumbling ledge. He gathers himself, rests, an insect basking in the sun.

Below at the foot of the cliff, a woman watches.

When I think back to life with Gavin it was always as if he had just moved in. Or was about to move out. Boxes, cases, rucksacks, boots, jackets, sleeping bags, bivvy bags, crampons, ice-axes, harnesses, maps and hundreds of bars of chocolate.

In my bitterest moments I used to ask myself if it was me Gavin needed or just my house as a place to store his gear.

Was it love, Gavin? Or was it just need?

The climber descends, sliding easily down a gaudy rope. He walks towards her, the glossy lycra shocking, revealing as nudity. He is not tall, but good-looking, with a dazzling thatch of white-blond hair and the old-young face climbers have: bright-eyed, tanned, prematurely wrinkled by the sun. He coils rope slowly, his large hands white with chalk.

'Do you climb?'

'No. But it fascinates me. It's so beautiful to watch. Like dancing... Dancing on a rock-face, defying gravity.' She gazes up at the amphitheatre of bleached limestone. '"Death-defying". That's what they say about circus acts, isn't it? Is that what you're doing? Defying death?'

I never asked if you were faithful. I didn't want to know. I had no illusions about your appetite for adventure, for risk, for novelty. With your charm and looks, your reputation in the climbing world, you must have had women throwing themselves in your path. Moral scruples – as I later discovered – were unknown to you, so I don't doubt you availed yourself of whatever there was going.

Ours was a very modern relationship, very grown-up, based on trust. Or so I thought. You had no idea what I was up to back in Fort William while you were freezing your balls off halfway up a Dolomite. For all you knew I was screwing your best mates. Except that you knew I wasn't. I wouldn't. Because I loved you. Because I loved *you*, Gavin. And attractive though Dave and Andy and Simon were – especially darling Simon who had a thing about older women and whose chat-up line (and I've heard worse) was that I reminded him of his mum who died when he was six – I would never have succumbed, in case you found out and were hurt and finished the relationship.

And that is surely what you would have done, because you of all men wouldn't be able to hack it if your girlfriend bedded any of your mates. Dear me, no. If a bloke has to climb a sodding Himalaya to prove he's a man, he's hardly likely to take a philosophical view of a mate shagging his woman. And the thing for you, Gavin, the thing that you would have killed to know, would have been whether Dave or Andy or even little Simon were any better at it than you. Had they scaled my North Face any quicker? With any more expertise, or with less gear? Or even without oxygen?

So I didn't screw around. And you knew I didn't.

But *you* screwed around. And – eventually – I knew that you did.

Then I got angry.

'Why do you climb?'

He laughs, flings the coil of rope to the ground and takes a large bottle of water from his rucksack. He drinks deeply, ignoring her, then wipes his mouth with a chalky hand.

'It's like a drug. The adrenalin. The high. There's nothing else like it. Booze, speed, sex... They're all an impure form of the experience you get up there.' He tips the bottle up over his head and lets the dregs trickle down through his hair and over his sunburned face and shoulders.

'It sounds like a dangerous form of escapism. Do you escape up there?'

'What makes you think I'm trying to escape from something?'

'Isn't everybody?'

Looking away, disconcerted by her frank stare, he gestures upwards. 'There's no escape *here*... Too many fucking tourists. It's different in the mountains.'

'How different?'

'Persistent, aren't you?'

'I'd like to know.'

His broad shoulders sag and he exhales. 'I need a piss.'

'Tell me. Please...'

He runs a hand through his damp hair, suddenly tired, exasperated. He shuts his eyes and turns his face up to the sun. 'You stand on a ledge and you're safe, you know you're okay. Your foothold is secure, you've got a good grip, you can even rest for a while... You want to stay there forever. The last thing you want to do is move, lift that foot and place it down somewhere else, somewhere that might give under your weight. But you have to move because if you don't you'll die of exposure... So you move.' He opens his eyes suddenly and fixes her with a stare, unsmiling. 'That's your ultimate reality, that moment when you decide to risk it. You lift one foot and put it in front of the other and you just don't know... In that moment you are fully alive, because you know you might be about to die. But you just put one foot in front of the other.' He shrugs, embarrassed by his avalanche of words. 'That's how it is. You can't explain.'

'I think you just did.'

He pulls a bright fleece jacket from his rucksack and puts it on, tugging violently at the zip. 'That's our world and it's more real than all this – the tourists, the picnickers, the weekend hikers... This isn't real at all, it's a fucking nightmare! The nine-to-five and the suit and tie, traffic jams and shopping in Tesco's... You wheel your trolley but your mind is planning the next climb, your body is rehearsing the moves. You're just killing time till the next climb.'

'And your next fix of reality...'

He glares at her but she is gazing up at the rockface, her head thrown back. 'What do you do when you come down... to earth?' She smiles. 'I mean, how do you cope with all the... *un*reality?'

'Drinking. Fucking. The groupies are usually very accommodating. Climbing turns some women on, you know.' He runs his eyes over her breasts in an appraising, professional way.

'Really? I'm surprised you find the energy... I suppose it must be in the blood.' He looks puzzled, momentarily at a disadvantage. She extends a hand and touches the damp, blond thatch. 'The Viking ancestry. Rape and pillage as a not very subtle way of celebrating the fact that you're still alive.'

***

I dress like a bag lady. The only sensible outfit to wear in this climate is wellies, thermal underwear and several woolly jumpers. No make-up – what use is mascara in perpetual mist and rain? I slap on moisturiser and lip-salve as often as I remember but my complexion still resembles stewed rhubarb. My long hair is proving inconvenient and resembles the heaps of seaweed that are washed up here after a storm. When I go outside I can't see unless it is tied back in a heavy-duty elastic band and the constant tangles are beginning to annoy me. I suppose I could have it cut. I notice none of the younger women on the island have long hair and the elderly have theirs scraped back with vicious hairgrips.

Am I becoming de-sexed? Most of the trappings of townie femininity have gone by the board – shoes with heels, tights, perfume. I live now in my unadorned state, shapeless and colourless; I no longer engage in anything David Attenborough would construe as a mating display. But then as I recall, in Nature it is the male of the species who is supposed to make all the effort – the female just sits back and waits to be entertained. It is rather like that here as there are so few young women. The ones that have resisted the lure of jobs and education on the mainland seem unimpressed by their male peers but the men and boys are polite, eager to please and take trouble over their appearance on social occasions.

I notice such things but they are other, they do not concern me.

But I shall buy a bottle of industrial-strength conditioner next time I'm shopping in Balivanich.

***

I popped into Shona's today to ask about the mobile bank. We sat at her kitchen table drinking coffee. She has the most wonderful job. I wish I had it for the sheer pleasure of telling people how I earned a crust. Shona counts corncrakes. She counts them for the RSPB and in summer she goes out at night and counts the number of corncrake calls she hears. She logs the calls and ventures into fields with her torch to locate the birds so that the RSPB can work out what corncrake numbers are doing. The money's pitiful but I think Shona quite likes having time to herself, albeit in the middle of the night. She doesn't appear to sleep very much. She says ten years of getting up to children in the night have cured her of needing anything more than catnaps.

She appears to have four children but it may be fewer, or indeed more – I haven't been able to do a head count as they don't often assemble all together and when they do they tend to rush about, shouting and squealing, making their number seem larger. If Shona and I ever manage to have an uninterrupted conversation I think we'll find we get along just fine.

Every available surface in her kitchen was strewn with toys, felt-tips, newspapers, books, bills, letters, half-eaten biscuits, brown apple cores, hair-slides, exercise books, screwdrivers, spanners, knitting, mending and seed packets. Shona surely never needs to dust as no surface can ever be exposed long enough for dust to accumulate. When the children came in and needed room to eat their snacks and do their homework they swept the table slowly with their arms in what looked like a practised gesture, until they had cleared some space.

Not surprisingly, Shona is always lamenting that she cannot find things, but Aly, the eldest, a cheerfully precocious ten-year-old with a face like a currant bun, can usually find anything within a couple of minutes. 'Lost Property Office' is apparently the name of a game the children play, a variant of Kim's Game, invented by Shona's younger brother, whom she refers to with obvious affection as 'wee Calum'. Aly always wins. When I got home ('home' – it still sounds strange) it struck me for the first time how odd it is that my house is so tidy apart from my workroom, which always looks as if a particularly chaotic jumble sale has just taken place. I couldn't bear for the workroom to be tidy and I couldn't stand disorder in the sitting room. (The disorder of my mind is quite enough.) The chaos of the workroom is only an illusion in any case. The clutter is controlled. When it reaches a certain height and depth I sweep it aside, as Shona's children did. But I know what is there, hidden under the heaps of scraps, stashed away in shoeboxes and carrier bags. I can put my hands on a gold sequin, a piece of felt or a fragment of antique silk kimono within minutes. Just like Aly.

There's method in my madness.

Two dark curly heads, one large, one small, are bent over an exercise book at the kitchen table. Without lifting her eyes from the ironing Shona announces briskly: 'You've a new neighbour, Calum.'

'Oh, aye?' The man points. 'That's not how you spell "because", Aly.'

The boy gapes, first at his book, then at the man with the red pen. 'It is too!'

'Trust me. I've been spelling that word for over thirty years and it's never had an "o".'

'She's bought poor Lachlan's house.'

'Who has?'

'Your new neighbour. Rose Leonard.'

Aly sits back in his chair, arms folded, truculent. 'Well, how *do* you spell it then, Mr. Clever Clogs?'

Shona and the iron hiss. 'Alasdair, you'll no' speak to your uncle like that! I'm sure he has better things to do with his time than help you with your homework.' She smooths a shirtsleeve carefully, then smooths her voice. 'You should drop by some time, Calum.'

'B-e-c-a-u-s-e.'

Aly makes an indeterminate choking noise. 'You're kiddin' me!'

Calum spread his hands and shrugs. 'Would I joke about *spelling*?'

Shona persists, unregarded. 'She's English, mind, but she seems very nice.'

Calum leans back in his chair and announces, 'Big elephants can always upset small elephants.'

His sister bangs down the iron. 'And what's *that* supposed to mean?'

'Och, I was talking to Aly... That's how you remember to spell "because". You take the first letter of all the words in that

16

sentence – big elephants can always upset small elephants. Because. Easy.'

'Cool!'

'Sausage.'

'*What*?'

'That's your next spelling.'

Aly groans and bows his head over his book. Dragging another shirt from the overflowing wash-basket Shona continues, 'She's an *artist* of some sort. But then they usually are... No doubt you'll have a lot to say to each other. She's a real intellectual, mind.'

'You managed to establish that over a quick cup of Nescafé, did you, Shona? What did she do – offer to lend you her back-numbers of *The New Internationalist*?'

Shona sniffs. 'It was obvious.'

'How, obvious?'

'She has a room full of books and no TV.'

'*I've* got a room full of books and no TV.'

'Aye... But *you* come over here and watch ours.'

'So what does that make me, Shona?'

'A *pseudo*-intellectual.'

Aly sighs and prods his uncle with his pencil. 'If you don't hurry up and finish testing me on ma spellings we're gonna miss *The Simpsons*.'

Calum places a hand on his heart. 'Et tu, Brute?'

Aly frowns. 'That's no' one of ma spellings, Uncle Calum...'

***

I discovered today with something like relief that, no, I am not quite neutered. I finally got to meet 'wee Calum', Shona's brother. Wee Calum is six foot if he's an inch and seemed to take up a lot of room in Shona's kitchen. His designation as 'wee' would appear to be merely a concession to her seniority. He appears to be mid-thirties – could be older I suppose, which means Shona is older than I first thought, but probably still younger than me.

Calum, like many island men, seems to be a jack-of-all-trades, one of them climbing. He teaches at the high school on Benbecula and, in the summer holidays, at an outdoor activity centre on Skye. With the characteristic black curls and startling blue eyes of the Celt, he looks like one of the models in the Hawkshead catalogue, only not so self-absorbed. From the way he moves you can tell – and I think perhaps I would rather not have known – that underneath the layers of wool, fleece and ancient denim is a rangy, athletic body.

My decision to abandon mascara and all other artificial improvements was perhaps precipitate. Could eyelash dye be procured by post, I wonder?

Collecting pebbles on the beach I fill my pockets like a would-be suicide. So many shades of grey, beige, brown, oatmeal, ivory. The odd faint tinge of orange and pink. My eye is caught by some dazzling lime-green seaweed, dramatic against Rastafarian black bladderwrack. I wish I knew the names of the different types of seaweed... I could check in the library. Somewhere new for me to venture. An expedition.

I bring the pebbles indoors to study their colours, sorting them, arranging them in piles. Playgroup play. I reject the more colourful stones and settle for a monochrome selection of greys, browns, taupes, creams and a dazzling white.

Feels right...

Looks wrong...

I pull out fabrics in a similar colour range, drape them, twitch and fiddle, irritated. They look dull, colourless. Like the men's wear department in Marks and Spencer. But the pebbles *don't*. Something is missing. A colour? A texture? Maybe silks would work better, have more life?

I abandon the pebbles, leave them heaped on my work-table, like a memorial cairn.

White sand, crystalline, colourless, slithering between my fingers, dusting my boots; castaway seaweed; scattered shells like broken beads, precious and useless. Elephantine lumps of rock, humbug boulders, striped and stratified, like a pile of collapsed deckchairs.

So much sky...

So much space...

I shrink, entirely irrelevant. My soul expands. Tears mix with salt spray on my cheeks.

A running figure, male, tall, wet hair slicked back by the wind, running easily, naturally, leaving deep, ridged footprints as his trainers bite into the wet sand. He slows down as he sees another figure: female, dressed in a waxed jacket and wellingtons. Her long thick hair flails around her head, Medusa-like. She scrapes it back behind her ears, bows her head, unaware of the man's approach. She bends down, turns over a few pebbles, picks one up, discards it.

The man jogs to a halt beside her and says something. She looks up alarmed, takes a step backwards. He smiles. 'Hi... I didn't realise it was you, Rose.' She still looks confused, almost distressed. 'We met yesterday. Calum Morrison. Shona's brother.'

The woman peers at him. She registers wet, tanned skin stretched taut over prominent cheekbones; a long, straight nose pinched with cold; eyes of a glacial, glittering blue. She remembers the eyes.

'I'm sorry! I didn't recognise you. You look different today. Your hair's so wet. I remember it as shorter... and very curly.'

'Aye. It was raining a wee while back. But it's no' so bad now.'

'No... Well, not bad for January, anyway!'

'Have you lost something?'

'Oh, no, I'm just beachcombing. Collecting material for my work. Seeking inspiration...'

'I'll leave you in peace then.'

'Don't worry, you're not disturbing me. I was about to call it a day anyway. I'm rather cold so I think I'll head for home...' She smiles. 'It still seems odd to call it that... I have to keep reminding myself I'm not on holiday.' A vicious gust of wind whips long strands of hair into her eyes. She tosses her head back, laughing. 'Some holiday!'

She gathers up all her hair with both hands and whoops with excitement as the wind buffets them. He sees that her head under all the hair is quite small, her face heart-shaped, not young, but firm and unlined. The smile she turns on him is sudden, dazzling, a bright slash across her face. 'It's so beautiful here, it makes me *ache*! Even on a day like this... the space, the scale... Oh, I can't describe it!' She lets down a cascade of hair. 'And you certainly can't photograph it.'

'Aye... You really need a wide-angle lens.'

She rakes the dunes with narrowed eyes, then stares out to sea. 'Actually, I think you need a wide-angle *mind*...'

'We can ease the pain, Rose, you know we can... and you can make something out of it, something positive. You of all people will know how to make a silk purse out of this particularly nasty sow's ear.'

'Ha, ha, very funny.'

'You will survive. You will grow as a result of all this. I've seen it happen many times. Your illness is a terrible gift. It makes you see things differently, it makes you create. Without it you would probably not be an artist, a maker. And if you didn't make things, who would you be? After all, isn't that the reason you stopped taking your medication?'

'But the pain in my head...'

'It will pass, believe me. But you must let us help you.'

'If a dog or a horse suffered like this you would put it down!'

'The fact that you can articulate that thought shows how far you are from being a dog or a horse.'

'But why should I have to suffer more than them?'

'You don't. You have choices, Rose. Very hard ones.'

'What do you mean?'

'You could have killed yourself. If you had slashed your throat instead of your wrists I doubt you would have survived.'

'I wanted to die!'

'You no longer wanted to live.'

'Is there a difference?'

'Oh, yes, a great deal of difference... We can do very little for those who want to die.'

I lay awake for some time last night thinking about Shona's brother, Calum.

It appears I am not going gentle into the good night of a contemplative, blessedly celibate middle-age since I spent some considerable time trying to imagine what it would be like making love with Calum. Having imagined this in various locations and positions (in a tent on a mountainside on Skye, in the dunes with the Atlantic breakers crashing around us, on Shona's kitchen table) I came to the conclusion that it might be very nice indeed.

This will not *do*.

Tomorrow I am going for a long, exhausting walk on the beach. Sexual frustration is not a complication I wish to incorporate into my new simple life. I am surprised and dismayed. I had thought all that – 'all that'? Oh, Gavin, *listen* to me! – was long dead. My passions are for my work, for causes (preferably lost), for poetry, for landscape.

My body has slept.

But now Sleeping Beauty wakes...

Is it possible to feel such an animal attraction to a man you have met only twice, who says very little, some of which is in a language you don't understand?

It's not just my body that stirs. Memories too.

When I look at Calum I remember Skye and why I chose to live here instead. The landscape here on North Uist is female: pale, undulating, yielding. There are no cliffs or mountains, no wide rivers, no great heights or depths, not even many trees. There are sparkling lochans like jewels, wild flowers scattered on the dunes like bright beads, burns that chatter and gurgle like Shona's children. I feel safe here, even in the teeth of a gale. To be sure, the wind and sea seem male, gnawing away at the land, occasionally beating her into submission, but they come and they go, like the fishermen.

When I stayed on Skye the world seemed very different. I walked in a masculine country of hard edges and angles, of ridges and gulfs. The upward thrust of the Cuillin mountains, the perilous cliffs and precipices seemed male and exciting. Disturbing. Sexual. I felt small and helpless, excluded and overwhelmed, but that too was exciting. I was alone on Skye but I wanted desperately to make love. I tried to think who it was that I wanted to love. Certainly not Gavin.

Then I realised there was nobody. No body. I wanted to fuck the land. The whole fucking island.

But instead I came here.

Damn you, Calum. I had almost forgotten.

CHAPTER TWO

January 18th

Dear Megan,

I was thinking today that there is a difference, isn't there, between being lonely and being solitary? I'm enjoying the blessings of solitude here but I have to admit that there is no one on the island to whom I feel I am remotely connected. There is no one in whom I think I could confide, should I feel the need. (I don't.) I think I feel impelled to write to you to create intimacy – or at least the semblance of it. Perhaps that will be superseded by friendships eventually, or at least some sort of an inter-dependence. I have offered to baby-sit for Shona to give her a break but she hasn't taken me up on my offer yet. Perhaps she thinks I won't cope with her brood? (She could be right – motherhood was never my strong suit, was it?)

The social life here is awkward for those not used to it. If you fancy some company you just turn up on people's doorsteps, preferably with a half-bottle of whisky, and you sit round a fire and chat. (It's called ceilidh-ing and the connection with music dates from pre-TV days, though I think people do still pull out a fiddle or an accordion and have a sing-song now and again.) Cynics say it's a way of saving on your heating and food bills since visitors must be offered food, preferably home-baking, but I prefer to give the islanders the benefit of the doubt.

No one has turned up on my doorstep yet (maybe they've heard about my baking?) and I'm wondering whether to issue a specific invitation (a coffee morning?!), but that isn't the done thing. I'd like to ask Shona's advice, but I think that might sound as if I am lonely, which I'm not. It would just be nice to 'fit in', be one of a crowd or feel part of the community now and again. I suppose I am just a little bit jealous of Shona and her extended family, something you and I never had...

Sagamartha. Mother of the Universe. The Sherpas' name for Mount Everest. I think it was Dave who first coined my nickname and it stuck. But at times I felt like Snow White with the seven dwarves. Not that there was anything dwarfish about Gavin and his climbing friends. God, how they *ate...* I seemed to spend entire weekends standing over the cooker frying bacon and eggs, listening to them seated round my dining-room table, arguing, jabbing their fingers at maps, shouting at each other in a mixture of profanity and impenetrable jargon, laughing uproariously at any mention of potential disaster.

Megan used to sit at the kitchen table, pretending to do her homework, pretending to be irritated by a house full of men, but really she was entranced. She idolised them. They were father, brothers, heroes, gods to her.

After one expedition Gavin brought her back a piece of Everest. (He said it was Everest. Knowing Gavin, it might just as well have come from Glencoe.) Megan wept and kissed the rock, flung her arms round his neck and kissed him. Gavin had no idea what such a present might mean to her, nor what his giving such a present might mean to me. It was really his way of boasting.

The lump of Everest sat on Megan's bedside table till she left home. She would have taken it with her then had I not already hurled it through her bedroom window. It landed deep in the shrubbery and there it remained, lost, forgotten.

By then of course Gavin had gone.

And I was alone.

I like to think that one day in the distant future my act of vandalism will give geologists pause: how did a lump of rock from the foothills of the Himalayas come to be embedded in Highland topsoil?

January 19th

Forgive my handwriting, my dear, and the dis-jointedness of this letter. It's 3.00am and I have drunk far too much whisky. (I didn't think I even liked whisky very much but I find it grows on you if you drink enough of the stuff.) I have had such a wonderful evening I don't want to go to sleep, so I'm eking out my pleasure by sitting up in bed with a mug of tea and a hot water bottle, determined to finish the letter I started yesterday.

I was very brave and went ceilidh-ing! I just presented myself at Shona's this evening and asked about the Burns Supper on the 25th, what contribution to the catering I could make. (Wasn't I brave?) And of course they asked me in. I finally got to meet husband Donald who fishes (like most of the island men) and evidently drinks (ditto). He is a handsome, red-faced, red-haired man, inclined to fat, thanks no doubt to the fibre-free zone that is Shona's cooking. Donald had poured me a hefty dram before I'd registered that they already had what seemed like a houseful of guests. In fact it was only the children, the minister's wife Jean, and Calum, Shona's brother. They all made

*me feel very welcome, as if I were an old friend. I think they were
actually a bit surprised to see me but far too polite to say so...*

As I come into the sitting room Calum stands up to vacate
a chair for me. Shona eases her considerable bulk from the
fireside armchair and insists I take it. She looks delighted to
see me. One of the twins, Eilidh, proffers a plate of scones
with such a smug expression I know she must have made
them. There is much commotion about the whereabouts of
another chair; Calum asserts repeatedly that he is quite
comfortable perched on the arm of the sofa but Aly is
dispatched. A chair appears and since the only remaining
space is next to me, Calum takes up a position beside me,
which unfortunately largely deprives me of the pleasure of
looking at him. The conversation is general (the Burns supper,
the ceilidh afterwards, the weather, the fishing) in both
English and, occasionally, Gaelic – sometimes a mixture of
both in the same sentence. Calum apologises for this but
explains that the house rule is that the children must speak
Gaelic in the evenings. He translates for me so I don't think I
miss much.

They are warning me again about my house's proximity to
the high tide line. 'The gales just come from *nowhere*,' the
minister's wife informs me in shocked tones. She is a tiny,
bird-like woman, white-haired but clearly once a beauty.

'Aye, but the fishermen know...' Donald says with a wink.
Misty-eyed, he beams at me over his glass, nursing his sizeable
belly like a cat in his lap.

'They can look up into a cloudless sky, stare out across a
calm sea and *smell* it,' Shona says with relish. 'Then before you

know, the wind freshens, the sky turns black and the island will be lashed by a gale. It might last minutes or days,' she says, picking up her knitting, a large lacy garment of an eye-popping pinkness. I trust she isn't knitting it for herself but fear the worst. 'Sometimes the rain is so constant you forget what it's like to be dry and warm.' She shivers theatrically. 'But the wind – och, the wind drives you *mad*!' Shona clicks her needles, and shakes her head. As the whisky goes to mine, Calum speaks in a low voice.

'Aye, we lie in our beds, listening to the howling and banging, waiting for a window to blow in – like shell-shocked tommies in trenches.'

Eilidh giggles and bounces on the sofa. 'Once the shed roof blew off! We found it half a mile away!'

Aly looks up from his Gameboy momentarily and exclaims to me in Gaelic. Calum smiles and translates: 'He's telling you that's why my caravan is tied down.'

'When it's all over and the skies are blue again you'd think you'd dreamed it, if it weren't for the trail of *devastation*,' says Shona, making the most of the four syllables in her sing-song voice.

'Aye.' Calum refills our glasses. 'Every so often the island throws a cosmic tantrum and reminds us of our place in the scheme of things...'

'Pretty near the bottom!' Shona puts the pink confection down and throws another peat on the fire. Calum asks if I am finding it a little too warm. I realise that one side of my face is indeed very hot and so we all move round, like musical chairs, with the minister's wife being 'out'.

...Jean was delighted to recruit another neep-basher (that's swede-masher to you) for the Burns Supper preparations. Calum and I ended up on the sofa with little Aly (and his infernal Gameboy!) but we managed to hold a conversation over his head. Like so many people on the island, Calum speaks quietly, in a restrained – perhaps I mean contained? – way, as if exhibiting too much facial expression would somehow be unseemly. It was probably the whisky beginning to take effect, but I found the Hebridean accent quite hypnotic. Occasionally one of the children spoke to him in Gaelic and he would answer, then translate for my benefit. It's such a musical language. I am determined to try and learn some. I think there are evening classes and that would be another way of getting to meet people...

Listening to Calum speak Gaelic, I am stirred by the different-ness of him. The guttural sounds seem to me to emphasise his otherness, his maleness. But he listens to the children intently and answers at length in a way that is rare in men – southerners anyway. I gather that he is explaining things to them, also that he is very fond of them...

...Calum eventually asked why I had moved to the island but by then I was half-cut thanks to Donald's ministrations with the whisky bottle, so I don't quite remember what I told him – the truth mainly since, with the awful clarity of drunkenness, I realised that I had nothing left to lose by doing so...

But I do remember how Calum listened... I deliver most of my monologue to the fire but whenever I look at him, I meet an unblinking, unnerving stare and am momentarily distracted from my story. When I finally grind to a halt he merely nods, toys with his almost empty glass. Eventually he says, 'You've done the right thing, Rose. If you have it in you to be happy, there's no better place to be than these islands. And if you do not...' He looks around the room at his family. 'There's plenty folk here ready to catch you if you fall.' My eyes swim. It's just the whisky... He smiles and raises his glass to me. '*Slàinte mhath!*'

...With a little prompting Calum told me about himself. He teaches English and Gaelic at the High School on Benbecula, the island between North and South Uist. (There are causeways linking all three islands, like beads.) He climbs and works on Skye in the summer holidays...

I wonder, did he ever meet Gavin?

...He is trying to get a bi-lingual community magazine off the ground (an expansion of the school magazine for which he is responsible.) He has an ex-wife in Glasgow...

Oh God, what must I have asked to elicit that nugget of information? 'Are you available for fucking?'

...and he's come back to the island to live after many years on the mainland. He writes but wouldn't be drawn on what he writes, so it's probably poetry. He has a semi-derelict crofthouse about a mile away which he's doing up with Donald's help, meanwhile he's living in a caravan on site. Donald brings him home every so often for a square meal and to thaw out. While Shona cooks, Calum entertains the kids

and helps them with their homework. The arrangement seems to suit everyone...

Shona's generous application of peats to the fire eventually causes Calum to shed some layers of clothing. His white tee shirt reveals brown arms almost bare of hair, odd for such a dark man, but I've noticed this is often the case with Celts. He has the typical climber's physique, top-heavy with muscle, particularly on his shoulders and forearms. His legs are by contrast slim and elegant (I think of Jeremy Fisher on his lily pad.) When he bends to tend the fire I try to drag my eyes away, but the combination of gently-strained denim and moving fire-lit muscle proves too alluring. Aly lets out a yell of triumph as he scores on his Gameboy. Calum straightens up, slightly unsteady on his feet. He smiles at Aly, then at me.

The Scots are right – whisky is *indeed* the best drink in the world.

Eventually the Gameboy is confiscated and Aly is packed off to bed, protesting. Shona rounds up the other children and shoos them upstairs, leaving me with the men, but by now Donald is asleep. When Calum returns to the sofa we sit in companionable silence listening to snores from Donald, shouts and giggles from upstairs. After a while I say, without a great deal of conviction, 'I'd better be going... Donald obviously needs to get to bed.'

'I'll see you home.' A statement not an offer. I make feeble noises of protest, which Calum ignores. 'It's on my way.'

Shona reappears, sees her sleeping husband and is aghast. 'Och, Calum, will you shoogle Donald awake now!'

'Let him sleep, Shona. I'm seeing Rose home anyway.'

'Will you no' stay and have some tea, Rose?' I decline and stand, unsteadily. 'You see her right to her door, Calum,' Shona says briskly, as if I am no longer in the room. 'She's no' used to the whisky and I don't want Angus the Post driving up tomorrow morning, telling me that the poor wee woman's been found upside-down, drowned in a bog!' Upstairs a child begins to wail. Shona mutters something in Gaelic, raises her eyes heavenwards and ushers us out the front door. 'Cheerio just now, Rose!'

The cold hits like a slap in the face. As Calum and I walk away from the house, darkness enfolds us and seems absolute, apart from the odd square of light in crofthouse windows and the distant flash of the lighthouse, but there is a shaving of moon, obscured at times by cloud. No stars. The air is wet with the finest drizzle, the kind of non-directional rain they have in the Highlands that makes you feel as if you're walking through a cloud of vapour. I stumble into a hole in the road and Calum puts a hand under my elbow to steady me. 'There's a few more of those... Would you be happier taking my arm?'

'Yes, I would – if you don't mind.'

'No bother.'

His leather jacket feels old and soft, yielding, like flesh. But cold. The flesh of a corpse. I say, conversationally, 'I suppose if we were walking home through Glasgow we'd be stepping over broken bottles and puddles of vomit.'

'Oh, aye... Pools of blood, used hypodermics and the odd, dead heroin addict... Och, there I go again, getting nostalgic...'

'God, I'm glad I live here and not there!'

'You think you'll make a go of it here?'

'I hope so. I don't see why not. I can't stand cities.'

'Me neither.' We walk on. 'You pay a price for the beauty and peace, mind.'

'How much?'

He pauses. 'They cost me my marriage. Alison wouldn't come back and I couldn't stick it in Glasgow.'

'She made you choose?'

'She didn't have to. It was all taken out of my hands.'

'What happened?' Calum doesn't reply. 'Sorry – are you okay talking about this?'

'Oh, aye. It's ancient history now... I was teaching in a big tough Glasgow school... Head of English... One day one of my wee head-bangers went for me with a knife.'

'Oh, my God!'

'I was trying to break up a fight in the yard... Probably a drugs deal.'

'Were you hurt?'

'Not badly. But I couldn't carry on after that. I'd had enough. I was fair sick of being a social worker instead of a teacher, you know? A teacher can't put the world's problems to rights.'

'No... But you tried anyway.'

A silence. In the darkness I feel him smile. 'Aye, I did... But enough's enough. I've come back home and I'm teaching again. The divorce was neat and tidy, we'd no children... And I'm happy here. It's not some kind of Hebridean holiday camp – we have our problems too, mind. But somehow they're manageable, you get *support*... In Glasgow folk seemed to have lost the meaning.'

We arrive at my front door. As I unlock it I say over my shoulder, avoiding his eyes, 'Would you like a coffee? I'm afraid I don't have any booze.'

He hesitates. 'I'd love a coffee, and God knows I *need* a coffee, but if I sit down I'll talk you into the ground. That's teachers for you – love the sound of their own voice. I'd rather leave you wanting more...' He pauses, hears himself, sways a little. 'Do you?'

'Do I what?'

'Want more?'

'What've you got?' The words are out before I realise that this ill-considered response is open to a variety of interpretations, all of them compromising. 'Sorry, Calum, I'm treating you like a doorstep salesman.'

He laughs. 'And I'm behaving like one. I must away home...' He doesn't move. Drops of moisture have collected on his dark fringe, now clinging to his forehead. They dangle briefly, like jewels, before dropping onto his nose. He pushes his hair back out of his eyes. 'There's something I've been wanting to ask you, Rose. A favour.'

Yes. Whatever it is, the answer is 'Yes'. Darn your socks, sew on your buttons, undo your buttons, help you off with your wet clothing...

'Shona's been telling me about your work... I wondered, will you come and show some of it to my pupils? I'm trying to encourage them – well, *goad* would be a more accurate term – into writing poems about their environment. I want them to think about the problems for visual artists, the kind of decisions they have to make – choosing a colour instead of a word... you know, an empty canvas instead of the blank page. I

35

thought it might get them going... Would you do it?' The dancing eyes cloud suddenly. 'There's no money in it, I'm afraid, but they're a great bunch of kids. They'd make it worth your while.'

You'll make it worth my while. 'Yes, I'd love to. I'm very flattered that you should ask, especially when you haven't seen my work.'

'I have.'

'Where?'

'Glasgow. Alison taught art. She dragged me to a textile exhibition – bloody *feminist* textiles! – at some tiny, God-forsaken gallery.'

'Good heavens, did you go to that? I was exhibiting with a group of very right-on women artists.'

'Aye, as I recall there was a quilted *vagina* – and a pink satin foetus attached to an embroidered placenta.'

'There was no placenta! Don't exaggerate!'

'Honest to God, there was! I had nightmares for weeks! Yours was the only work I could take seriously.'

'I don't remember now what I was exhibiting. It was years ago.'

'It appeared to be a landscape, just a beach with dunes, but as you looked at it you could see the figure of a woman...'

'Dunes, Luskentyre.'

'Aye, that's right! The dunes formed the reclining body of a naked woman... She had tufts of marram grass embroidered in her armpits and between her legs... and I think there were bunches of pink thrift for her nipples... There was a great mass of bladderwrack for her hair and she was just lying there on the beach with her legs apart... being pleasured by the watery fingers of the incoming tide... Fantastic.'

'I can't tell you how many people have looked at that wall-hanging and never even seen the woman.'

'Seriously? Alison had to drag me away... It had never occurred to me that textiles could be an erotic medium – tactile obviously, sensual maybe – but *erotic*? It was pure dead brilliant!' He grins, school-boyish. 'That's what I wrote in the visitor's book. Alison wrote a short thesis, I seem to remember... Your work changed the way I looked at a landscape I'd grown up with. And I remembered your name. Teachers remember names... So you'll maybe come and talk to my pupils then?'

'After that superb review I think I have to! No, really, I'd love to. When?'

'Can I give you a call?'

'Yes. Let me give you a card with my number.' I turn away to fetch one from my desk. I turn back and see him framed in the doorway, wet and cold. I hand the card to him, touching his chilled fingers briefly.

'Thanks...' He still doesn't move, but looks at me, studies me almost, as if I have just shifted into focus. 'Shona said you're thinking of cutting your hair.'

I remember that I complained to Shona about the wind's ravages and asked for the number of the mobile hairdresser. 'I thought I might... It's really not very practical.'

Calum lifts a hand towards my damp, unruly head, thinks better of it and gestures vaguely. 'Don't. It's beautiful. Wild... Like seaweed.' He takes a step towards me. 'Can I change my mind about that coffee?'

I inhale a mixture of rain-soaked hair, peat smoke, whisky and arrant male-ness that translates itself in my head into the kaleidoscope of greys, browns, taupes and creams I was working with this morning. They need blue. It doesn't work because I need blue, an electric blue, the exact shade of Calum's eyes now as they reflect the light from the interior of my house. The rush of excitement, the exhilaration is all to do with my *work*. Of course it is.

'Come back when I'm sober, Calum – I'd hate to miss anything.'

He cocks his head on one side, confused. 'Did Shona warn you about me?'

'No... Did she warn you about me?'

'Aye, she did, but I took no notice.' A silence in which I both dread and pray he will touch me. 'Another time then?'

'Yes, another time. Thanks for seeing me home.'

'No bother. Goodnight.'

I shut the door firmly before I can change my mind.

...Calum saw me home, which was just as well as I'd forgotten to take my torch. He's asked me to go into the high school to work with the kids in a sort of cross-curricular way, which sounds very exciting. I take back what I said at the beginning of my letter – maybe I am going to fit in here.

Guess what – Calum saw the 'Sisters in Stitches' exhibition in Glasgow and still remembers my work!! ('Dunes, Luskentyre'. You hated it and thought it was smutty, but then you were only 16.) Calum thought it was 'pure dead brilliant'! I think I'll have that engraved on my tombstone.

Must sleep...
Love,
Mum

Pure

Dead

Brilliant

My eyes were brilliant, you said so, Gavin, brilliant, dancing, faceted like diamonds. The mania turned you on, didn't it, like the mountains, you loved the danger, you didn't know what I might do, and I might do *anything*, kill myself, kill you.

And I was pure, pure like the snow jewelled with my blood, pure like a corpse, bloodless and white, the wounds whitening under the hospital shift, under the white hospital sheets, starched and crisp, like a fresh fall of snow, covering me, burying me...

Dead? Not yet, Gavin.

Not yet.

CHAPTER THREE

I 'M WOKEN BY SHARDS OF GLASS being driven repeatedly into my brain.

The telephone.

I pull the duvet over my head but the noise is still unbearable. Hauling myself out of bed, I stumble towards the door and stagger down the stairs clutching the handrail, wondering where the hell I left the phone.

'Hello?'

'Good morning... I was about to hang up. I thought maybe you'd died of alcohol poisoning. Sorry if I got you out of bed.'

'Who *is* this?'

'Calum Morrison.'

'Oh, Calum! Sorry.' I rearrange my scowling face. As if the damned man could *see*.

'I was ringing to ask how bad, on a scale of one to ten, your hangover was, and to ask if you could come into school next Wednesday?'

'School?'

'Aye. We talked about it last night – d'you no' remember? Showing your work to my pupils. To help them with their creative writing...' He pauses. 'Maybe it wasn't such a grand idea – the whisky talking. I'm sorry I disturbed you.'

'No, Calum, don't hang up! I remember! I'm just being rather slow... I *do* remember, and yes, of course I'll come! Wednesday, did you say?'

'Aye. I'll meet you in Reception – about ten, if that's okay? I'll give you a hand unloading your stuff.'

'Thanks. And in answer to your first enquiry – my hangover is pretty bad – six going on seven – although I have to admit I haven't actually puked yet.'

'Well, that's a good sign!' he says cheerfully. 'What you need is a bowl of porridge to settle your stomach.'

My innards turn over in protest. 'Like hell I do!'

'No, honest to God, nothing better. Come on over and I'll make you some.'

'Is this some weird local custom – ringing people up and inviting them for breakfast? The ceilidh-after-the-night-before?'

'Well, it's almost midday, so I suppose sophisticated urban folk like yourself would call it brunch.'

'But the menu is still porridge?'

'Aye, 'fraid so. But cooked by my own fair hands.'

'How can I resist? Look, I need ten minutes to shower and drink several pints of coffee. Where is your caravan exactly?'

'Are you on a cordless phone?'

'Yes.'

'Stand outside your front door and face left.'

'Calum, I'm in my nightie!'

'It's okay – I won't be able to see you.'

'I mean, I'll freeze – it's January!'

'Oh, aye, sorry. Well, if you stood on your doorstep and turned left you'd see in the distance a caravan standing beside a dilapidated croft house. That's me.'

'Dilapidated?'

'Very.'

'Okay, I'll see you in ten minutes. But Calum, I don't think I even *like* porridge...'

'You'll like mine.'

Yes, I probably will.

At the sound of shuffling feet the man in the kitchen looks up from his frying pan. A thin, pale girl of maybe eleven or twelve stands in the doorway, inside a pair of plush polar bears. She isn't smiling. Gavin, veteran of many a bar-room brawl, smells trouble.

'Hi! I'm Gavin. I thought I'd make breakfast – would you like a bacon sandwich?'

The child winces. 'I'm a vegetarian.'

'Fried egg sandwich?'

'No, thank you.'

There is an awkward silence. Gavin switches on the radio and tunes in to Radio 1. The girl walks over to the worktop, pours herself a bowl of cereal, then re-tunes the radio to Classic FM. 'Mummy prefers soothing music in the mornings,' she announces.

'Oh, yeah... Right... Does she drink tea or coffee?'

'Tea. Earl Grey.'

'Would you like some? Or there's coffee in the pot...'

'I drink orange juice.'

'Naturally,' says Gavin under his breath, filling the kettle and putting a tea bag into a mug. He sits down at the table with his bacon sandwich, keeping a tactful distance. The girl eyes his plate with disgust. 'Pigs are very intelligent animals, you know. Much more intelligent than dogs.'

'Yeah,' says Gavin, his mouth full. 'They taste better too.'

The girl gets up from the table, would perhaps have flounced had the polar bears allowed it. She pours herself a glass of orange juice and sits down again. Gavin breaks a long and painful silence with 'So you must be Megan!' and then wishes he hadn't. She looks up slowly from her cereal, narrows her eyes, then looks down again. Increasingly desperate, he adds 'Your mum's told me a lot about you!'

'She hasn't told me anything about *you*.'

'Well, what would you like to know?'

'Nothing in particular... I just thought she might have mentioned you. For all I know you could be a burglar... or a child molester who's broken into the house.'

'I can assure you I'm not!'

'Well, you'd hardly *tell* me if you *were*, would you?'

Gavin can see the logic of this and feels he is losing ground. 'I'm... a friend of your mum's. I stayed over last night. I... missed my train.'

'What time's the next one?'

'Umm... I'm not sure...'

'Don't you have a timetable?'

'I lost it.'

'You don't seem very well organised. The number of the station is on the board by the 'phone. It's under S,' she adds. 'For station.'

The kettle comes to the boil and Gavin springs to his feet, glad of an excuse to avoid his inquisitor's stony gaze.

'She drinks it black. No sugar.'

'Right. Thanks. You've been very helpful. It must be great for your mum to have such a helpful little girl...' As the adjectives fall from his lips Gavin realises biting off his tongue would have been a better idea. 'I mean – I bet you do a great job of looking after her!' He turns his flashiest smile on her, a smile that has been the ruination of many a virtuous woman. Megan isn't looking. She is scraping her cereal bowl, noisily.

'The man who was my father ran off and left us when I was a baby. Mummy and I look after each other.' She pushes her bowl away and stands up. Drawing herself up to her full height she says, 'We don't need anyone else.' She turns abruptly and the polar bears carry her back upstairs.

Gavin scowls and lights a cigarette. 'Bloody hell... Give me the north face of the Eiger any day.'

It's like walking into a mobile library. Calum's caravan is full of books and on the few surfaces not colonised by books sits the sordid, accumulated clutter of a single man living alone in a very confined space. I step gingerly over several piles of exercise books and laugh.

'It looks as if you've just been burgled.'

'Och, you should see it when it's in a *mess*... Clear yourself a space and make yourself at home. Tea or coffee?'

'Coffee, please.'

'With or without aspirin?'

'I've already taken some thanks. Are you hungover too?'

'I was feeling a wee bit fragile earlier on but I went for a run on the beach and that blew the cobwebs away.'

'I don't usually drink whisky... Actually, I don't usually *drink*.'

'You'll get used to it. It's part of island life, especially in winter.'

I sit down next to an overflowing box of books while Calum busies himself in the kitchen area of the caravan. There are ominous bubbling sounds coming from a saucepan, which I take to be the porridge. I wonder briefly why I am here and then decide not to pursue that line of enquiry. 'I see you've got a lot of poetry in your book collection.'

'Aye. Do you like poetry?'

'Very much. I used to read a lot when I was convalescing... after my illness. I told you about that last night, didn't I? My memory's a bit hazy...'

'Aye, you did.'

Suddenly nervous, I scan the books, asking randomly 'Do you like Ian Stephen?'

'Aye, you'll find his books there somewhere. Do you know *Providence II*? It's illustrated with some of his own photos – colour and texture studies. Your sort of thing, maybe?' Calum puts a mug of coffee on the floor beside me. 'Porridge is on its way.' He looks down at the jumble of books and shakes his head. 'There's no' much system to it, I'm afraid.'

'We could do with Aly.' Calum looks at me, puzzled. 'You know – Lost Property Office. He'd be able to find it for us.' A slow smile. I remember now why I am here.

'Did Aly tell you about the game?'

'No, Shona did.' I rifle through a few more volumes. 'Your sister thinks the world of you, you know.'

'Aye, well, the feeling's mutual, but don't tell her I said so.' Calum returns to porridge-stirring and my eye is caught by a familiar-looking paperback. 'I see you're a fan of Malcolm John Morrison.'

'Fan?'

'Well, you've got one of his books.'

'I've got them all. You know the poems?'

'Oh, yes... Is he any relation?'

Calum laughs as he spoons porridge into bowls. 'Aye, in a manner of speaking... *I'm* Malcolm John Morrison.'

'Oh...' My mind changes gear as I reject my image of an elderly Hebridean bard with a passion for geology, and substitute Calum in jeans and red and white striped rugby shirt. 'Why do you use a pen-name?'

'It isn't really, no more than any English name is for a Gael. My name is Calum Iain Moireasdan. That translates into English as Malcolm John Morrison. As I was writing in English I preferred to publish under an English name... Here's your porridge. Don't look so worried – I haven't salted it. I even added some sugar in view of your enfeebled state.'

'Thanks. Do you write in Gaelic as well?'

'Aye, but there's no' much of a market for Gaelic poetry, as you can imagine. Well, any kind of poetry in fact. I'm always fascinated to find out what kind of person pays out good money for books of poetry.'

'Me.'

'Well, on behalf of all poets, struggling or otherwise, I'd like to thank you for throwing your money away in such a reckless fashion.'

'On the contrary, it's me who should be thanking you. *Emotional Geology* was a book I read and re-read during a very dark time. It really spoke to me.'

'Aye, I suppose it would. Our experiences have been similar... in some ways.'

'You know, this porridge is actually rather good once you get over the unappealing colour and texture.'

'You overwhelm me...'

'Sorry! Can I ask a silly question?'

He shakes his head. 'The recipe's a closely guarded secret.'

'I'd like to know why you write poetry.'

'Why I bother, you mean?'

'No, of course not! You know what I mean. Or is *that* a closely guarded secret too?'

He pushes a spoonful of porridge round his bowl, silent for a moment, then he announces, *'No one has ever written, painted, sculpted, modelled, built or invented except literally to get out of hell.'*

'Who said that?'

'Antonin Artaud.'

I consider the probable truth of this statement. 'What was your hell?'

He rests the bowl in his lap and is silent. He rubs the stubble on his chin with his fingers. I hear the rasp in the long silence. He is rubbing a thin white scar, three or four inches long, which runs under his chin, following his jawbone. I remember words from last night. A fight. A pupil. A knife. When Calum finally speaks his voice is thin, barely audible. 'Mindless violence... the death of idealism... the deaths of friends.'

'Climbers?'

'Aye... Five in two years.'

'Jesus... I'm sorry.'

'No need. They knew the score.' He shuts down again, putting up the screen of his usual composure. 'More coffee?'

Gavin puts down the phone. He does not look at her.

'Please don't go, Gavin...'

'Rose, you might as well ask me not to breathe!'

'Not this one, Gavin, please, this one's a death trap, you've said so yourself! You don't need to do *this* one – you've been before, for God's sake!'

'But this time it's a different route! A first ascent, Rose! I can't turn this one down! And I can't disappoint my mates.'

'But you can disappoint me.'

'That's not fair! You knew what I was when we got together, I told you how it would be. Didn't I?'

'Yes, you did.'

'But you thought you could change me, make me settle down.'

'No, I wasn't that naïve! I just hadn't realised the extent of your... *obsession.*'

'It is an obsession, I admit it, and it means more to me than you, than Megan, than anything.'

'I know. We can't bloody compete.'

'Nobody could! If it's any consolation, I do feel bad about going. Your miserable weeping face at the airport will definitely take the gilt off the gingerbread... But I can't not go. You have to accept that, Rose. Accept me as I am.'

'If you really loved me you wouldn't go.'

'Well, if that's your definition of love, then no, I don't love you.' She flinches, as if he has struck her. 'If you really loved me, you'd *let* me go. It would mean a lot to me to have your blessing.' He puts his arms around her. 'I've always hoped that the times we're together compensate for the times when we're apart.'

'What could possibly compensate me for your death?'

He is silent for several moments. 'Knowing I died happy... Doing what I wanted to do.'

She struggles out of his arms. 'You just don't get it, do you? I don't want you to die happy – I want you to live! Live and be miserable – like the rest of us! Stay *alive*, Gavin!'

He shakes his head slowly. 'This isn't alive for me, Rose. It's just... a different kind of death.'

'Why poems? Why not novels? Or plays?'

'Good question.' Calum pours himself another mug of coffee. 'I suppose because I'm a sprinter, not a distance runner. A novel would not be my natural form. It's a question of scale, too, I suppose. I've never been an Everest sort of climber. I'm happiest climbing the Cuillin on Skye. They're technically challenging, world-class mountains – if a bit on the wee side. And they're never boring. Folk die every year because they think the Cuillin are some kind of climbers' playground,' he says scornfully, 'A warm-up for the real thing. But any experienced climber will tell you that Everest is just a long, boring slog. And now there's rich tourists and company executives queuing to pull themselves up on fixed ropes, breathing bottled oxygen. If you can afford the guide and you can jumar, you can climb Everest. But what's the point?'

'Well, forgive me, but I always thought climbing was the ultimate pointless activity. I mean, it's *heroically* pointless, isn't it. Mallory summed it up for all time.'

'Because it's there?'

'Exactly. Rather Zen, isn't it?'

'I preferred Sherpa Tenzing's comment.'

'Which was?'

'We've done the bugger!'

I laugh, perhaps more than the remark merits and Calum relaxes a little. 'You know about climbing, don't you, Rose?'

'Yes, I suppose I do.'

'But you're not a climber?'

'No. I've been hill-walking and scrambling, but not serious climbing. How did you know I know?'

'You don't ask questions. You didn't ask what jumar meant.'

'No need. I've lived and breathed climbing without ever doing it myself. The man I lived with for five years was a serious climber.'

Calum hesitates. 'Is he dead?'

'I've no idea,' I say briskly. 'I threw him out and he never made contact again. I know he was alive for about a year after that. I heard through... another source.'

'Why did he climb?'

'Oh, to escape, I think. He loved the big mountains, the snow, the whiteness, the purity of it all. He said he found it *cleansing*. It was his penance and his absolution. But it was also a very effective way of avoiding people, family life, commitment – all the messy stuff he couldn't cope with down here in the real world.'

Fuck you, Gavin.

Fuck you and thousands of others who littered the pure white holy wastes of Everest (and countless other mountains) with your empty oxygen bottles, your abandoned tents, your lost ice-axes, your broken ropes, your unwanted rucksacks, your cameras, your film canisters, bog roll, faeces and the odd unclaimed dead body.

And for *what*? What did you achieve? You fucked the mountains – so fucking what! You got off on getting higher, faster, quicker, better than your rivals, than yourselves, high on adrenalin, your risk-charged, pumped-up bodies screaming, throbbing, swelling with oedema, and for what?

Thrills. Expensive thrills. Deadly thrills. An addiction.

You messed up the mountains, Gavin, and you messed up me...

Trails of blood in the snow.

Snow white.

Rose red.

'Why did you throw him out?'

'He was sleeping with another woman and I found out. Usual story. Oh, when you put it like that it sounds so... *banal*. It wasn't really like that. I mean, I didn't think he'd been faithful to me all those years – in fact I knew he hadn't. But this was... too much. I couldn't cope. It had to end.'

Calum is silent for a while. 'So you'll be giving climbers a wide berth in future then?'

His gentle irony pulls me back from tears towards laughter. 'Thank you.'

'For what?'

'For not taking me too seriously. It's all ancient history. Very painful at the time... but I'm over it now,' I say brightly.

In the long silence that follows we both hear the lie.

You were the rock I clung to, Gavin, the tree that rooted me to the ground, stopped me from blowing away, floating into the stratosphere, buoyed up by panic and my own hot air and the limitless, terrifying possibilities of my ideas. You contained me, stopped me from shattering into a thousand fragments, tiny, sharp as glass.

I believed it was possible, it was simply a question of effort, of work, of crystalline honesty, of giving, of openness, for fear and defensiveness can only corrode, corrupt.

I gave you all myself, Gavin, and that was more, a lot more than you bargained for. And far more than you ever wanted.

Calum is watching me. Waiting. My mug is empty but I don't remember drinking. I dread him asking more questions, know I will have to leave if he does. I don't want to leave, I want to sit here, cossetted by the cosy fug of the caravan, exposed to this man who is not Gavin, who is nothing like Gavin, who is dragging my mind and my body away from Gavin to another place if only I have the courage to go.

Eventually he speaks, carefully, after a lot of thought. The incision is gentle, not very deep. 'Do you mind talking about your work?' The slight emphasis on the last word tells me he has understood. No doubt my face reflects my relief. Encouraged, he pursues the enquiry. 'It's such a different medium... How do you get started? A visual idea presumably, not verbal.'

'Oh, no, it can be both. But I think I translate verbals into visuals automatically. I think I experience everything visually. I feel emotions in terms of colours and textures... I see music – I mean I *hear* it – like that too. I used to think everybody saw things that way.'

'No, they don't, but folk who do tend to agree on how they see things – what colour the key of C major is, and so on.'

'Really? How amazing... But verbal or visual, it's all much the same to me. But the traffic is one way. I suppose if the traffic is going the other way you're a poet?'

'Aye, I suppose so. The brain must be wired up differently. Tell me about your creative process, I'm fascinated... Do you start with a grand design?'

'Good Lord, no. I've never had the time or the space to work big – or even think big.'

'Or the confidence? I'm thinking of how women's art has always been sidelined. Still is.'

'That's true. I've always worked in small chunks, pieces that can be put together to make something bigger. I started with patchwork quilts when my daughter was born, traditional stuff that developed my love of textiles and then I moved on from there... But it was always 'portable' art, something I could pick up and run with if the house caught fire – baby on one arm, work on the other. It also had to be *concealable*. I didn't really want to make a statement about what I was doing, I wanted people to think it was nothing serious, just a hobby.'

'Like Jane Austen writing novels in a corner of the drawing room, hiding pages under her blotter.'

'Exactly! Nothing I had to say was important enough to be said loud. Or large.'

He nods. 'My ex-wife was an art teacher, did I tell you? She used to give her pupils huge pieces of paper to draw on. She said if you gave them a piece of A4 cartridge they'd do a careful, matchbox-sized drawing in the centre of the paper. If you gave them a giant sheet of coloured sugar paper and a stick of charcoal they'd loosen up and let go. They didn't believe in their drawings until it was 'play' and the quality supposedly didn't matter. It's the same getting kids to write poetry... They're all writers at primary school, they know what they think and how they want to say it, but gradually all that shrivels up and dies. It's really sad. And it's bloody difficult trying to resurrect that confidence, that belief in what they want to say and their ability to say it.'

'But you manage to do it?'

'Aye, sometimes... It's a question of building up their confidence, so I use Alison's trick – I give them big pieces of coloured paper and felt-tips and get them to work in groups, make word collections, then write a group poem. No problem... You can't hear yourself think for the arguments! After that experience, they mostly want to write their *own* poems because they're fed up with having to write by committee.'

'And what are their poems like?'

His eyes are alight, excited. I watch his mouth, want his mouth, know what he is going to say.

'Pure dead brilliant!'

The rain is horizontal and the caravan strains at its guy ropes occasionally, threatening to topple the columns of books on the floor. While Calum washes up I re-read some of his poems. They are short and dense, as if each word stands for many more. I have to read them slowly so that I can absorb them, bit by bit.

I've never read poetry written by anyone I know. It's a strangely intense and intimate experience. I feel as if I have seen Calum naked, but in an unerotic context. He makes toast and Marmite and we picnic on the floor by the stove. The windows weep with the condensation that was our words, our breath, the warmth of our bodies.

Calum waves his piece of toast. 'So when you're working, do you have a blueprint in your head?'

'No, not really. I don't need to know how it will all end, I only have to be able to begin, to see an opening. It might not amount to anything or it might become huge and important, it doesn't matter a great deal. It's the detail that matters to me as much as the overall concept... *more* than the overall concept.

There is only detail really, if you look properly. The beach is made up of shells, pebbles and grains of sand, bits of driftwood, rubbish... It's only when you stand back that you see a coastline, stay uninvolved, uncommitted – that's a climbing term isn't it? With the same sort of meaning?'

'Aye.'

'But I can't stand back from my work. If I do it disappears. I have to be right in there with it... You'll see me peeping out from behind a scrap, some threads, a smudge of colour – I'm in there! I'm not sure I exist anywhere else, apart from inside the work...'

'And you've come here to find out.'

'Yes... I suppose so...' My breathing is too rapid and I detect a familiar metallic taste in my mouth that has nothing to do with the Marmite. I should leave. Peace of mind is sitting, forgotten, in a bottle on my bathroom shelf.

'Does it matter to you what the whole looks like, in the end?'

'Yes, of course, but it doesn't really matter *until* the end, until you stand back and see what you've made. It's the making that's important to me. Process, I suppose. Sounds a bit posey.'

'No, I know what you mean... For me it's a question of imposing order on my thoughts, selecting particular words out of thousands, to make a poem. I'd *like* folk to read it, for sure, but it doesn't really matter if they don't. The poem exists, I've *made* it exist. That's the main thing.'

'And the meaning of the poem?'

'Well, that's no' for me to say. It means whatever you want it to mean. My meaning won't be the same as yours and mine

56

is no more valid. Once I've written it, a poem has a life of its own, I have to let it go, like a child... What about your work? What does *Dunes, Luskentyre* mean?'

'Do you mean what does the *title* mean or what does the work itself mean?'

He smiles. 'Chinese boxes! It's harder for visual artists isn't it? I hadn't realised. The encumbrance of words...'

Something bursts, pierced by his words; a stream of images gushes into my brain and out of my mouth and I speak, not looking at him. 'What a brilliant title for a poem! Or a series of poems... an *exhibition* even – of textiles and poems!' My hands flutter in the air trying to channel my thoughts into words. 'The textiles could have *poems* to explain them and the poems could have *pictures* to explain them – except that they wouldn't explain exactly – they would just be signposts, clues... or maybe just translations into another medium, another language, you know, like those captions you get for tourists, in French and Italian and Japanese... *The Encumbrance of Words*... The poems and the textiles could be chained together in some way... *linked!* Oh, God what an awful pun... but each link could be made of a word and so the chains *themselves* could be poems... It could be interactive maybe! There could be a textile-poem at the end, lots of different pieces of fabric with a word on them, you know, like fridge poetry, and people who came to the exhibition could make up their own poem and hang it up on the wall!' I clutch at Calum's hand, his bony fingers, his knuckles cool and smooth, like pebbles in my palm. 'We could do it together, Calum, at the Arts Centre in Lochmaddy, it could be a joint exhibition called *The Encumbrance of Words*... What do you think?'

When I finally stop speaking, his face comes into focus and I think at first that he is giving me a blank stare but then I notice that he is scarcely breathing, that he is thinking, considering. He narrows his eyes. Brown skin folds into tiny, delicate pleats as he looks into an imaginary distance.

I let go of his hand. 'You think it's a stupid idea.'

'No! I think it's... fantastic! It would be beautiful – colours and pictures and textures and text!'

'Textures and text! Oh... oh... I can see something using calligraphy there... No – words carved on tombstones! But the stones are eroded and encrusted with lichen...'

Calum shakes his head, laughing. 'I'm never going to be able to keep up with you – my mind's on overload already!'

My heart is thudding now, my throat tight. 'You think we could do it?' He nods. 'Do you think we should?'

'I think we *must*!'

Curled up, hugging my knees, rocking back and forth, my mind still racing, I cannot contain the excitement. It escapes as a kind of groan: 'Oh, this is better than sex!'

The words tumble into a gulf of silence. Calum appears to be studying the laces of his trainers. When he looks up he isn't smiling any more.

I gabble. 'That's just something I used to say to my girlfriends... We used to list all the things we thought were better than sex... you know, hot chocolate fudge cake with ice-cream, buying hardback books, breast-feeding, Mahler's Tenth... You know...' I am laughing. He isn't.

'I'm not sure I do. Sounds to me like you and your friends were having sex with the wrong men.'

'We were. Our husbands mostly... Occasionally each other's.'

'Ah...' Calum is thoughtful. 'I don't see it as an either/or proposition, necessarily.'

'Sorry?'

'You seem to think working together, our exhibition, would be better than sex. The two are not mutually exclusive.'

'Oh, that was just a manner of speaking... It was a silly thing to say. I'm sorry.'

'So that would be a "no"?'

'No?'

'No, you don't want to go to bed with me.'

I am about to try another evasion but he skewers me with unsmiling blue eyes. Behind his cool, clever words lies need. 'No, Calum, that would be a "yes".'

'Yes?'

'Yes, I do want to go to bed with you. But I'm not going to. Not yet anyway. But I'm terribly flattered that you've asked.'

'No, I'm sorry, I shouldn't have asked, but it just seemed a natural thing to say... Talking like this, about poetry and climbing, laughing so easily with you... It really turns me on, all this bouncing ideas off each other. I've hardly ever experienced that... Well, with climbing pals maybe, but never with a woman...' He answers the question I would not dream of asking. 'Alison was a lovely woman, a gifted teacher, and she knew her stuff but... I suppose we didn't talk a great deal.'

'I don't think you do if the sex is good. You think you don't need to. Sex with Gavin was amazing, *Wagnerian* – God, that man was fit – but he couldn't hold a conversation. Attention span of a fractious two-year-old. On the ground anyway. I suppose it must have been different in the mountains otherwise he'd be dead, wouldn't he? Maybe he is dead by now... Although I somehow think I would know...' Calum is watching me intently. 'Oh dear – this is *awful!* I've said I want to go to bed with you and here I am reminiscing about an ex-lover. I'm sorry, Calum...' He is laughing again. 'Why are you laughing?'

'You are a piece of work, Rose! I don't know what it is about you – you seem so vulnerable but at the same time you are totally your own woman. There's no front to you. You're so... exposed.'

'Skinless.'

'Aye, that's it!'

'People like me, they say we have one less skin than other people. It means we are more open and honest perhaps – I could have pretended I didn't want you – but it also means we are... more easily hurt.'

'Which is why you're saying no?'

'At this point in time, Calum, I don't know why I'm saying no...' His face brightens and he opens his mouth to speak. I lift my hand to his face, spread my fingers and lay them on his lips, silencing him. 'I just know it's the right thing to say. Right for *me.*' He opens his mouth wider and closes his lips around my fingertips. His hot, wet mouth shocks me. I withdraw my fingers and resort to cliché. 'After all, I hardly know you.'

'You know my poetry.'

'Well, you don't know me, then.'

'I know enough to know that I want you and that making love to you would be the natural extension of all the things we've talked about. It would be another way of getting to know each other.'

'You make it all sound so uncomplicated!'

'Do I? I don't mean to, because I know it isn't, especially for you, Rose... Och, maybe I'm barking up the wrong tree and you're just too polite to tell me where to get off!' The smile is sardonic, but his eyes betray him.

I lift one hand to his head, cup his ear and bury my fingers in the tangle of dark curls. 'Calum, don't move. *Please*...' I lean forward and press my lips gently against his, then slide my other hand along his thigh, registering the sudden, involuntary clench of muscle, and on into his lap. There I cradle the mound in his bulging jeans.

'Christ, Rose!' As his mouth moves my lips are grazed by stubble and I inhale his breath. I feel him tense, about to move in response, then he remembers. He mumbles something in Gaelic.

After a long moment in which we are both quite still I release him and lean back. 'Thank you for not jumping me.'

'It's me,' he says faintly, 'who should be thanking you.'

'Well, I think I made my point. I'm not saying no because I'm not attracted to you. I wanted to feel you... to taste you...'

'Please – any time,' he says in a hoarse whisper. 'Don't bother to ask.'

'It's been a long time, you see. There's been no one for five years. Not since Gavin. I've spent five years murdering what I felt for him, starving my need for him, purging my memory. But somehow it still feels... too soon. They say time heals, but –'

'They lied,' he says simply, then shrugs. '*Geological* time, maybe...'

'You wrote a poem about that, didn't you? The slow healing process?'

'Aye.' Calum looks uneasy.

'*Stalactite*?'

He nods. 'You've done your homework... Tell me why you came to Uist of all places. I'm curious.'

'You're trying to change the subject.'

'No, I *am* changing the subject. Why Uist?'

'Gavin was never here.'

Calum laughs softly. 'No mountains...'

'That's right. No mountains, so no Gavin. Just Gavin's ghost... Calum, if – if we did go to bed, I'd like to be certain it was about *you*, and nothing to do with him. I don't want there to be three people in the bed.'

'Is he here for you now?'

I actually look around the caravan, as if he might be. 'No... There's just you and me.'

'Well, that's a start...' He takes my hand, tentatively, checking me with his eyes to see he is not off-limits. 'The thing I don't understand – I mean, it just doesn't make any sense to me – why would Gavin *want* to sleep with another woman? The man was obviously an *eejit*.'

Tears start into my eyes but I'm laughing. 'Oh, Calum, you don't know the half of it!'

***

'You're lying, Gavin.'

'Why would I lie, for Christ's sake?'

'You wouldn't do this to me... Even you wouldn't do *this*...' Rose slowly shakes her head from side to side.

'Well, I did!' Gavin throws back the duvet and starts to get dressed. She watches his naked body, tries to feel revulsion and fails.

'Did you do it in this bed?'

'For God's sake, Rose – what does it matter? It's done.'

'Is it over?'

'Between us?'

'Between you two.'

Gavin's head is bent over socks and trainers. He doesn't answer.

'Gavin... Is it finished?'

He sighs, straightens up. 'I don't know.'

'*Christ*, Gavin!'

'I just don't know, Rose! I didn't plan for it to happen. I didn't set out to – to *betray* you. It was just one of those things.'

'How *could* you?'

'Because I'm a bloody selfish bastard, that's how, because I'm a man and therefore a lower form of life! And because I can't bloody say no if it's offered on a plate – which it *was*.'

'I don't believe you.'

'You want more details?' he says nastily.

'No! I just can't believe... that you... I can't...' Rose starts to cry. Gavin yanks a holdall out of a cupboard and begins to throw clothes in, randomly, savagely. Rose stumbles towards him.

'You're going?'

'Well, I can hardly stay here, can I?'

'Where are you going?'

'Dave's. Or Simon's. I don't know...'

She grabs his arm. 'Why did you do it, Gavin?'

He wheels round on her, his eyes blazing, glittering with tears. 'Because she was there!'

'I mean why did you *tell* me?'

His chest is heaving as he tries to steady his voice. 'Because... I was angry with you... and because – oh, Rose, you'll love this – because I felt such a shit lying to you.'

'But you didn't feel a shit sleeping with her?'

'Not at the time, no – I had other things on my mind!' Rose recoils as if he has slapped her.

'I didn't deserve that.'

Gavin is pale, his mouth moving as he struggles to retract, apologise. 'No, you didn't. You don't deserve any of this. I'm getting out, Rose – I've done enough damage.'

Gavin lifts the holdall and stalks out of the bedroom. Rose follows him downstairs, into the sitting room. He gathers up maps, correspondence, his address book. A fat stone Buddha sits on the desk, Rose's Christmas present to Gavin two years ago. She studies the Buddha, notices how his smile has turned into a fatuous smirk. She moves away.

Standing in front of the French windows she stares out at the moonlit garden. Snow is falling again. The scene looks like a Christmas card. Rose spreads her palms and rests her forehead on the icy glass. Behind her she can hear Gavin making a phone call in the kitchen.

She wants to sleep.

Sleep in the snow.

Lie down in the soft, clean, perfect snow and forget about all this. Fall asleep as the snowflakes settle around her. The cold will slow her racing thoughts, still her pounding blood. The cold will bring peace, stop the thudding in her head.

She looks down for the key to the French doors but it isn't in the lock. Panic seizes her until she realises with a great surge of relief that she doesn't need to unlock the doors. She picks up the stone Buddha from the desk, weighs it in her hand, grips it tightly then swings her arm back. She smashes one of the glass doors. The hole isn't big enough yet for her to walk through so she smashes more glass.

The rush of freezing air is bracing, exhilarating. Rose squeezes through the doorway, her nightdress snagging on the glass shards, her thighs and arms tearing as she struggles through the opening. Stepping through the broken glass she walks across the snow-covered patio, her bare feet leaving bloody footprints behind her. She walks into the middle of the lawn, kneels and then lies down in the snow.

Rose feels slightly better now. The dreadful pounding in her head has stopped. She feels at peace. She can't quite remember... There was something, something very upsetting... Something to do with Gavin... No matter. She will sleep now and sort it out in the morning.

But she cannot sleep. There is too much noise. Someone is screaming. Someone is in terrible distress. A man is yelling, sobbing, calling out for help.

Poor man. Rose wishes she could do something but she really is too tired to move.

Gavin will deal with it.

Gavin is good in a crisis.

***

Rose and Calum stand awkwardly at the door of the caravan, she huddled into her waxed jacket. Darkness is already falling even though it is barely mid-afternoon. Calum ducks back inside the caravan and emerges again on the threshold with a fleece jacket and a small book.

'Let me see you home.'

'No, Calum, it's okay – I mean, thanks, but there's really no need.'

'It's no bother.'

'I know, but actually I'd quite like a walk on my own... ' She scans his face for disappointment. There is only a nod. 'I need to calm down. There are too many thoughts... I have to be careful.'

'Aye, I know.' He holds the books out to her. 'You said you wanted to learn more about geology. That's a kind of beginner's guide.'

'Oh, thank you... You've been very kind, Calum. And understanding. I do appreciate it.'

'Aye, well, as you now know, I have ulterior motives.'

'You mean you're really a bastard like all the others?'

'Aye,' he grins, 'But I'm a *canny* bastard.'

'I'll see you at school on Wednesday then? 10 o'clock?'

'If you need anything – I mean, if you want to see me before then – och, you know what I'm trying to say. I'll not give you any more hassle, Rose, but I'm here if you need me. My door's never locked.'

'Go inside, you're getting cold. I'll see you Wednesday.'

She sets off along the track, narrowing her eyes against the onslaught of wind, rain and sand that reduce visibility to a few yards. Resisting the temptation to look back at the glowing windows of the caravan, she wishes she'd left a light on at home to welcome her. Calum's book digs into her ribs and she steps up the pace, eager to be indoors again.

She opens her front door. At least there is no fumbling with house keys – no one locks their doors here, day or night, and Rose has learned to leave hers open during the day. The night is another matter.

She switches on the kettle and shrugs off her dripping coat, removing the book. She examines the contents briefly but then reaches down from a shelf her own copy of Calum's anthology, scanning the contents page for *Stalactite*. The wood-burning stove is still alight but languishing, so she opens the doors, shoves in some driftwood and then curls up on the sofa with one of her anaemic, much-loved antique quilts. She finds the page and reads Calum's poem of lost love.

When, some time later, she has finished crying, Rose reboils the kettle, makes a pot of tea and retreats to bed, trying to decide whether she is angry with Calum or grateful. The question defeats her. She swallows a tablet and eventually she sleeps.

I lie straight in the hospital bed, face down, suffocating. My fingers creep out across the coarse darned sheets until they grip the hard edge and sink into the flesh of the mattress. Pinioned like a butterfly, my eyes tight shut, I cling to the cool solidity of the sheets, then lift my head to breathe great gulps of stagnant, antiseptic air.

I roll onto my side, sweating, crushing lacerated arms and legs, glad of the distraction of pain. I am suddenly conscious of the length of my limbs, how they flex, slipping and sliding over each other and across the sheets. I curb them and lie still on my back, listening to the thudding of my heart.

God damn you.

God damn you to hell, Gavin. You should be in my bed not hers.

CHAPTER FOUR

SUNDAY. GOD'S DAY.

It seems impossible that the Hebrides could ever get any quieter, then Sunday comes around and even the wind abates. (Not the rain, however, which is a law unto itself.) The few people who are about are on their way to church, or visiting relatives. Even here there is a certain amount of traffic during the week – cars, a few lorries, the odd flock of sheep – then on Sunday everything stops. All you can hear is the wind and the sea and – if you're close enough – sheep urinating. It's peaceful but eerie. Time staggers to a standstill.

God would not approve, but I have been working hard today, buried under one of my periodic landslides of ideas.

I am playing around with some ideas from Calum's book of poems, *Emotional Geology*. Geology is not a subject I have given any thought to before. The book he lent me is illustrated with beautiful aerial photographs of Scotland and brightly coloured diagrams. I realised the patterns formed by landslides and folds in rock would lend themselves to a quilted wallhanging. I've made a few sketches and lots of notes. I can make something in three layers, then slice it into sections and re-assemble them – bingo, instant earthquake. Maybe some of the filling could protrude? (Or *ex*trude as the geologists say.) And then of course the fabrics could be distressed for erosion.

My mind is buzzing with ideas – cross-sections, layers, pleats, folds, distortions...

I am alive again. I can work, my senses are functioning, I'm noticing things. It's as if I have woken up after a long sleep. A nightmare.

I am *me* again.

Calum's little book has explained geological vocabulary to me, so I now understand the significance of the titles of his poems. Boiling rock, while still underground, is called magma. (His poem of the same name describes the suppression of grief-stricken rage.) Lava which cools slowly becomes a black rock called basalt. (Calum's *Basalt* is a poem of numb resignation and defeat.)

I know so little about the earth on which I walk – know little and understand less. The mountains of Harris (visible from the north end of this island) are gently rounded hills, barely in the Munro category of three thousand feet, but apparently they were once as tall as the Himalayas. They are unimaginably old, some of the oldest rocks in the world, but they have been eroded by the elements until they are now gently curved, mere stumps of a once gigantic mountain range.

A timescale I cannot possibly comprehend, a meaning, a purpose perhaps, that is beyond my understanding. It's somehow reassuring that there is something bigger out there, bigger even than the mountains.

I'm not sure what it is. Not God.

Time, maybe?

***

By eight o'clock on Wednesday morning Rose's bedroom is strewn with clothes. Sitting on the edge of her bed wrapped in a damp bath towel she sifts through a pile of clothes, casting each garment aside as variously, too smart, too casual, too sexy or too small. Her judgement is clouded by the knowledge that – much as she despises the idea – she is dressing to meet a man she finds attractive and wishes to impress. However, since she does not wish to look as if she has spent any time or energy grooming herself for the encounter, she is aiming for 'casually stunning'. Or even 'stunningly casual'. She will settle for either but doubts whether, at her present rate of progress, either state can be achieved in the two hours remaining before she is due to meet Calum at school.

Gavin, a man who had a limited understanding of the subtleties of sexual allure, had favoured short skirts and low-cut tops. Whenever Rose dressed to please him she felt like a barmaid. Despite possessing a decent figure, Rose inclined toward a retro/hippy look, choosing clothes for their feel, colour or the way they moved. So, for old times' sake as much as anything, Rose selects the outfit that she always knew she would wear, the one that Gavin hated: a black velvet Edwardian jacket, tight-fitting with tiny jet buttons fastening up to a high neck and a long burgundy skirt. Both items were flea-market finds and Gavin was unimpressed. When she insisted on wearing them to the theatre he requested that she wear no underwear to give him 'something to think about' during what turned out to be a very dull production of *Lady Windermere's Fan*. To further spite Gavin she selects sensible rather than pretty underwear and holds her breath as she tries on the jacket and skirt, unworn for more than six years.

They still fit. To be sure, the jacket is tight now – Gavin would have approved – but the buttons do not actually strain. She piles up her red-brown hair with tortoiseshell combs. Standing ankle-deep amidst discarded outfits she looks anxiously into the mirror, more anxiously still at her watch, then decides that she will do.

At 9.45, having driven over the causeway onto neighbouring Benbecula, Rose is wrestling with the wind and the heavy glass doors at the high school entrance. Already she is regretting her flamboyant outfit. Passing students stare at her as if she were Mary Poppins, just blown in on an east wind. She approaches Reception cautiously.

'Good morning. I'm here to see Calum Morrison... of the English department.'

'Is Mr. Morrison expecting you?'

'I hope so. I'm giving a talk to his class.'

'Will you take a seat please?'

'Thank you.'

Rose sits and stares gloomily at the toes of her lace-up boots.

I am nervous. For no reason. No reason other than that I am about to see Calum again after a gap of three days. No reason other than that I am inside a building I have never visited before. But there is a familiar school smell, a mixture of chip-fat and chlorine, laced with glue and a faint whiff of locker-room cheesiness.

I remember the many Parents' Evenings, all of them attended as a single parent. Perhaps that's why I am nervous. I am bracing myself for the bad news...

'She doesn't mix very readily...'

'Of course, she could achieve more if she made the effort...'

'She's very *quiet*, isn't she?'

As if taciturnity were the eighth deadly sin. Poor Megan. You said I talked enough for two. And so, God knows, did Gavin. And you were such a good listener.

Did we ever give you a chance to *talk*, Megan?

Calum appears and strides towards me. He looks tidy, smart even, in a denim shirt, navy cords and a Simpsons tie and looks as edible as I remember him. I deeply regret my Lillie Langtry outfit.

'Rose! Thanks for coming. Sorry if I've kept you.'

'No, I was early. It's not 10 o'clock yet.' His welcoming smile fades. He is staring at me. 'Is something wrong?'

'No... I'm just... stunned. You look fantastic!' He winces and lays a hand on my sleeve. 'Sorry! I was going to be Mr. Cool-and-Professional, not give you any more hassle, but... you look amazing.'

The long, splayed fingers on my arm are white with chalk dust. My stomach lurches as I remember Gavin's hands coiling rope, chalky, damp with sweat, his knuckles bleeding from hand-jamming. Malham Cove. Ten years ago. As if it were yesterday.

'D'you want a coffee? Tea?'

'No, thanks. Lets's get my stuff in shall we?'

'Okay.'

He reaches the heavy glass door before I do and pushes it open, seemingly without effort. As he holds the door open for me he looks me up and down again appreciatively. Obviously not a legs man then.

'The kids will be very impressed.'

'You don't think it's too... theatrical?'

'Not at all. Anyway, you want them to sit up and take notice. They will.'

'I like the tie.'

He pats the yellow-faced family on his chest. 'It's a form of silent protest against the school's dress code. I have Mickey Mouse for more formal occasions.' He hails a couple of senior pupils. 'Fiona... Rory... Will you give this lady a hand unloading her car?'

As the pupils shuffle into the classroom Rose busies herself unwrapping quilts and canvases. Calum stands at his desk watching as each child deposits homework in his marking tray. It is a class of twelve and thirteen-year-olds and they stare curiously at Rose as they wander to their desks. Some of the girls smile shyly.

A pale, under-sized boy approaches Calum's desk empty-handed. Calum is marking a register and does not look up.

'Morning, sir.'

'Good morning, Kenneth.'

'That homework, sir – '

'Let me guess, Kenny...' Calum does not look up from the register. 'You haven't done it *this* time because you won the Lottery on Saturday and you've been busy consulting with your financial advisors trying to decide how best to spend three million.'

The boy blinks and swallows. 'No, sir...'

'Detention, Kenny. I'll see you upstairs at lunchtime. Your essay subject will be 'What do you buy the man who has everything, or what I will buy Mr. Morrison when I win the Lottery.' 200 words.' Calum looks up from the register and beams. 'I look forward to reading it.' The boy's shoulders droop and he turns away. Calum throws down his pen. 'Och, no, I'm in a good mood today... Write a letter to your granny telling her you've been selected to play for Aberdeen.'

Kenny gapes. 'But I havna', sir!'

'You're not going to let a wee bitty thing like *truth* stand in the way of your literary career, Ken, are you? It's called fiction, man, and *you* wrote the book.'

'Aye, sir. Thank you, sir.'

'Any time, Kenny. Aberdeen has one B, mind.' Calum stands up and with a certain theatrical flourish produces a kitchen-timer from his drawer. A hush falls, pupils open jotters and rifle through pencil cases. 'Okay everybody... It will not have escaped your notice that we have a visitor this morning. Ms. Rose Leonard is a textile artist who has recently moved to Uist and later on she's going to talk to you about her work and you, I hope, are going to talk to her about *yours*. Jean and Helen, I already have one lad in detention at lunchtime, but if you want to make it *really* worth my while missing my lunch-break you just carry on chatting, okay?' There is a deathly silence and Calum continues. 'Timed writing, then. You know the rules but Ms. Leonard doesn't. Who'd like to explain? Mairi?'

A bespectacled girl in the front row turns to Rose, smiling. 'Mr. Morrison sets us a topic and we all write as fast as we can for five minutes, sometimes ten. We mustn't cross out, we mustn't correct and we mustn't stop until the timer goes. That's the hard part, keeping going! We just write whatever comes into our heads. If we get stuck we write 'What I really want to say is this...' and usually something comes. And we don't have to worry about spellings.'

'Very good, Mairi. And why do we engage in this exhausting activity? Alex?'

'It's a warm-up sir. It develops our writing muscles.'

'Indeed, it does. And it's a great way of tapping into the subconscious where all your best ideas live. You get down to the bare bones of your thoughts and you can write without all the usual inhibitions. What happens to these timed writings? Ken?'

'Nothing, sir.'

'Explain, Kenny, for our visitor's benefit. Do I mark them?'

'No, sir, because they're private. We can keep them or we can bin them.'

'But sometimes we *use* them, Miss,' Mairi pipes up again, her face shining. 'We use them for poems and stories. They're our *raw material*.'

'Aye, that's right, Mairi. Okay – enough explanation. Down to work...' The pupils bow their heads and hold their pens poised over their jotters, like runners on starting blocks. Calum too opens a notebook and unscrews a fountain pen. Setting the kitchen-timer he announces, 'Ten minutes timed writing, please folks, on...' He pauses for effect. 'Lost in the desert.'

Twenty pens, including Calum's, start to move across the page. Even little Kenny is writing, albeit slowly. I become aware of a texture of sound: the scratching of pens; feet shuffling; a persistent sniff; high-heeled footsteps in the corridor, first approaching, then receding; the flap of turning pages; a heavy sigh from Mairi; a sudden chesty cough that shatters the silence like a gunshot.

Calum looks up at the timer, then back at his notebook and continues to write. 'You've had five minutes. Keep going...' Some of the children write even faster, as if they are worried that the timer will go before they have finished writing what they want to say. Kenny is flagging now, his head down on the desk, but he's still writing. The timer rings, loud and long, accompanied by a communal groan, a mixture of relief and frustration.

'Finish off your sentence, everyone. Time's up.'

The pupils sit up and stretch, flex their fingers, pull faces at each other and laugh. Several look back over what they have written, counting the pages. Mairi is still writing.

'I said finish your sentence, Mairi, not the page.'

'Aw, sir...' She scowls at Calum who is grinning at her. He turns to me, the smile intended for Mairi still on his face. I see a different Calum. A man transfigured, completely happy, replete, so in his element that he has become the element and the element is joy.

'We're ready for you now, Ms. Leonard.'

I am not ready for them but I know I never will be, so I stand up anyway.

'Hello, everyone. My name's Rose Leonard and I'm a textile artist. Before I tell you about my work I just wanted to say how... *exciting* it was to see you all writing like that. It reminded me of when I was at art school. You could walk into a studio and all the students would be drawing or painting the same thing, a model or a still life and there would be a working silence. I think it's a wonderful sound! And that's what I was listening to just now – a working silence. Except that it isn't really silence, is it? It's a texture of small sounds that we register as silence unless we listen really hard... I'm fascinated by textures which I suppose is why I became a textile artist. Now, I don't know if you know what I mean by textile artist so I've brought some of my work along to show you... I'm not going to tell you anything about it – not yet, anyway – I just want you to look at it. Mr. Morrison, could you give me a hand?'

Calum and Rose arrange wallhangings and the contents of a portfolio around the room and as they do so a whisper builds to a buzz. Rose looks anxiously at Calum and mutters. 'Oh, dear, I think they're going to be bored.'

'No way. They're just simmering nicely. Relax. If there's any problems I'll step in with a big stick.'

Rose takes a deep breath. 'Right, everybody, I'd like you to get up and take a closer look. If you have very clean hands you may touch gently.'

Calum looks alarmed. 'Are you sure? They *will*.'

'Yes, of course. I don't believe in making textiles that can't be touched. What's the point?'

As the children gather round, Calum raises his voice above the excited murmur. 'If you need to go and wash your hands, go now.' Kenny stands beside him staring at his palms, in an agony of indecision. 'They look okay to me, Ken, but check with Ms. Leonard.'

Kenny thrusts his hands in Rose's face. 'Yes, they're fine. Grease is the killer. Grease attracts dirt, you see, then the dirt eats its way into the fibres.' Kenny lopes off and pushes his way to the front of a group gathered around a vivid three-D rainforest scene. Rose has selected a traditional patchwork quilt, several fibre landscapes, an abstract wallhanging and some working designs, complete with fabric swatches showing the gestation of a piece. For several minutes the children mill around, pointing, touching tentatively, then with more confidence, exclaiming, discussing. Calum joins them, shadowing a couple of the livelier boys who clearly don't know

79

what to make of it all. He looks back at Rose and asks, 'Would you like them sitting down again for questions?'

'Yes, please.'

At a word from Calum the groups disperse and sit at their desks again. Rose stands at the front of the class, nervous, exposed, hoping that they liked something. She clears her throat. 'Are there any questions?'

A forest of hands. Rose points.

'How long does it take you to make one of your pictures?'

'What qualifications did you have to get?'

'Why don't you use paint?'

'Do you cut up your old clothes?'

'Why aren't there any people in your pictures?'

'Do you make a lot of money?'

'Where did you get your jacket?'

When there is a lull in the questions, Calum asks, 'What kind of choices do you have to make as a visual artist, Ms. Leonard? As writers we choose the words, the order we put them in, how many of them...' He turns to the class. 'Can anyone remember the poet Coleridge's definition of poetry?' A few hands go up. 'Alex?'

' "The best words in the best order," sir.'

'Aye, that's right. Makes it sound pretty straightforward, doesn't he? D'you think the guy was maybe out of his head on opium when he wrote that? *We* all know writing poetry's not that simple. Choosing – that's the hard part. Tell us about the decisions *you* have to make, Ms. Leonard.'

'Well, I suppose there are quite a few... I have to think about scale – I might be making a miniature or something huge for a cathedral. I have to think about colours, of course...

Context, by which I mean where the work will be seen. I wouldn't make a cream and white wallhanging with dangly bits for a nursery school foyer for example! It wouldn't be practical or appropriate... I have to think about texture and that involves all sorts of decisions – there are so many possibilities with modern materials...'

'What's the hardest decision?' Calum asks.

'One of the hardest decisions is knowing when to stop! You can overdo something, work it to death, add too many colours, too many textures, so that the person viewing ends up with visual indigestion.' Some of the children laugh. Rose is thrown, but continues nervously. 'But I suppose the absolutely hardest decision is knowing when to *wait*...' She swallows.

Calum prompts gently. 'Can you explain a bit more, Ms. Leonard?'

'Well, sometimes you think nothing's happening... You think you're blocked. Everything you try doesn't work, or you think it's complete rubbish.'

'Aye,' Calum says ruefully, looking round the class, 'I think we've all been there...' Kenny, his eyes fixed on Rose, nods.

'I think sometimes you just have to wait. You have to accept that something *is* happening but it's happening on the inside. You go for walks, doodle in your sketchbook, drink too much coffee, turn out boxes of fabric scraps and swatches, but you wonder all the time if you're really getting anywhere, or if you're just wasting your time. It can be really miserable! But when you've been doing it as long as I have you get to recognise patterns. You know there are certain times of day – times of year even – when you can work well and others when it is hopeless. You get to know your moods and what things

81

inspire you, what gets your creative juices going... You learn to look after yourself as an artist. I can't work on dull, dark days. I need a lot of natural light – which is one of the reasons I came to live here. I also know now that I operate a bit like a computer – I feed in all the data, all my ideas, sketches, colours, samples and scraps and then when I'm ready I press a sort of mental button and it all starts to print out. When I'm up and running like that I might work eighteen hours at a time. Sometimes I'll work right through the night and into the next day – although I wouldn't recommend that, especially not if you use sharp cutting tools like I do. You can have horrible accidents if you're tired.'

'Is that what happened to your arm, Miss?'

Mairi points. A button from the cuff of Rose's jacket has popped off while she has been handling the quilts. The tight black sleeve has ridden up exposing the slug-trails of silvery white scar tissue criss-crossing her inner arm and wrist. In the silence that follows Mairi's question Rose is aware that Calum has stood up and is about to say something. She tugs her sleeve down.

'Oh, damn, I've lost one of my buttons! They're made of jet, you know, a semi-precious stone... No, it wasn't a work accident, Mairi, it was a car crash. I was in the passenger seat and there was a head-on collision. I put my arms up to protect my face and they were showered with broken glass. It was awful.'

'You're lucky to be alive, Miss,' Mairi says solemnly.

Rose's voice falters. 'Yes... I suppose I am... Very lucky.'

Calum steps forward. 'Could you all have a quick look now under your desks for that button? Helen, would you fetch

Ms. Leonard a glass of water, please.' He smiles at Rose with his mouth, his eyes concerned. 'You must need it after all those questions.'

There is a general commotion in which Rose retreats to her chair. Calum stands over her, placing himself between her and the children so they cannot see her. 'Are you okay? Do you want to leave now?'

'No, I'm fine. I just wasn't expecting... Do you think she believed me?'

'Oh, aye, you didn't miss a beat.'

She stares up at him. 'I'm not ashamed, Calum. I mean I would have told the truth but it would have spoiled the lesson! The truth wasn't *relevant*. It would have been terribly... distracting.'

'Aye, well, I think truth often is. '

'Sir!'

'What is it, Ken?'

'I've found Miss Leonard's button.'

'Kenneth Angus MacNeill, you are a man of many talents. I tell you, Aberdeen would be lucky to get you... Right, everybody, settle down, the button's been found. Listen carefully to what I want you to do next...'

After the lunch-time bell Calum helps Rose load the car allowing Kenny, hero of the day, to assist. When everything is packed Calum turns to the boy. 'Thanks, Ken. You've worked hard this morning so I'm letting you off your detention. But

I'd like to see that letter to your Granny in as homework tomorrow morning, first thing, okay?'

'Aye, sir. 'Bye, Miss. Thanks for showing us your pictures. They were *brilliant*.'

'Thank *you*, Kenny, for finding my button. Good luck with your essay.' He saunters off, hands in pockets, in search of chips.

Calum turns to Rose. 'Will you let me buy you lunch?'

'Thanks, but I don't think I could cope with the noise of the canteen. I'm feeling a little wobbly.'

Calum looks aghast. '*Canteen?* What kind of a cheap date do you think I am? I meant The Stepping Stone, round the corner. D'you know it? It's not exactly the Savoy Grill but it's pleasant enough – and quiet.'

'Have you got time for that?'

'I don't teach on Wednesday or Friday afternoons. That's when I do my shifts in the Poem Factory.' He clutches his temple and adopts a pained expression. 'But I feel a severe case of writer's block coming on...'

The Stepping Stone is bright and cheerful, the musak not too loud, the seating comfortable. Sitting opposite Calum at a secluded corner table Rose begins to relax.

'The timed writing is a brilliant idea.'

'Not mine. It's derived from Zen Buddhist meditation. A climbing pal of mine was into that sort of thing. But children can do it too. They love it.'

'Evidently... Your Kenny is a dear.'

'Aye, he's a good wee spud... Wee Ken's had some hard knocks, but he's one of my success stories. He used to be a school-refuser but now he comes in most days. I just had to persuade him that coming into school was more fun than sitting in the dunes with a half-bottle of whisky. Which wasn't that difficult. He told me recently that he can't decide whether to become a professional footballer or a writer.'

'What did you say?'

'I told him to relax, sit back and wait for the offers to come rolling in.'

'You must feel very proud.'

'Aye, sometimes. Christ knows, there are few enough perks in this job. Turning round the Kennies of this world is one of them. Are you wanting more coffee?'

'No, I'm fine, thanks.'

'I hope you'll come in to school again. I'd like to do some follow-up work on their reactions to your work. They've all made Word Banks this morning. Using them to write poems will be the next stage. Maybe you could come and hear them read their poems. They'd like that.'

'So would I... We could maybe include them in our exhibition?'

'You're still up for that?'

'Yes. Are you?'

'Aye! I'm really excited about the whole idea.'

Rose laughs. 'You *are*, aren't you? Excited, I mean. The kids excite you too... and teaching... I don't think I've ever seen anything quite like what I saw this morning. Was it like that in Glasgow?'

'It was more like being a stand-up comic there. I once suggested we get Billy Connolly in to do a training-day on classroom management. And I wasn't joking... You had to keep their interest, stay ahead of the game and not be afraid to come down hard sometimes. Och, the boys were all pussycats underneath the "hard man" exterior. The girls were tougher in a way. Lots of them had no resident father, some had never known anything other than an abusive relationship with men. They weren't used to a guy being nice to them, treating them with respect. Some of them thought I was after sex. Some of them *offered* me sex... '

'The boy who knifed you – '

'Davy didn't knife me, I just got in the way! He didn't mean anything by it. I don't think he even saw me. He was out of his head. I didn't press charges.'

'But you had to stop teaching.'

'Aye, for a while... Look, can we change the subject? We're getting into an area of discussion where I'd need the best part of a bottle of whisky to continue.'

'Sorry, I didn't mean to pry.'

'I'll tell you about it sometime. Not now, I'm enjoying myself too much. Did you enjoy yourself this morning?'

'Oh, yes, thoroughly... Apart from the hiccup. Did it go all right – the lesson, I mean?'

'They were eating out of your hand. You relate very easily to young people but you also take them seriously. It's a good combination.'

'I have a twenty-two-year-old daughter. Not so very long ago I had a house full of teenagers. It was fun.'

Calum looks surprised. 'You must have been very young when you had her.'

'Twenty-five. Not particularly young.'

Calum frowns. 'So you're...'

'Mental maths is obviously not your forte. I'm forty-seven.'

'You look years younger! I thought you were about the same age as me.'

'Which is?'

'Thirty-nine... Forty next month.'

'Really? I thought you were younger too.'

'Well, this is *Tir nan Og* – Land of Eternal Youth.' Calum leans forward and peers at Rose. 'You look as if you're doing a major mental adjustment in there... Have I just become more eligible? Or less?'

'I thought you were about thirty-five... What is it about climbers? Why do you all look like wrinkled adolescents?'

'Because we are?'

'I'm still a *lot* older than you, Calum.'

'Not as much as you thought!'

'A lot more than *you* thought.'

'Does the age thing really bother you?'

'Yes.'

He spreads his hands. 'Just "Yes"? You won't be drawn into a feminist critique of ageism?'

'Yes, given half a chance, I could work myself up into a good old lather about that! But now is neither the time nor the place.'

'When would be?'

'Calum – '

'Sorry. I'm hassling you again. I'd just like to spend more time with you, that's all. Talking. About the exhibition.'

'We'd need a chaperone – the last time we sat and talked about it I ended up groping you.'

'*Exactly*. So I've decided to give you another chance, an opportunity to prove you can keep your hands to yourself.'

'And if I disgrace myself again?'

Calum sighs. 'I daresay I'll survive. I have a very forgiving nature.'

Rose leans forward, grabs the Simpsons tie and pulls him towards her. 'Do you know what is absolutely lethal about you, Calum? It isn't the big blue eyes or the curls, it's the way you somehow manage to convey that going to bed with you would be *fun*, would be... a real *party*.'

'You know, you may have a point there. I remember once, Alison was laughing so much we fell out of bed. And I fell out of Alison.'

'Thanks for lunch.'

'You're welcome. I had a really good time.'

Gavin fixes her with his eyes, unsmiling, defying her to look away. 'I'd like to see you again.'

'That's a bit difficult...'

'Why?'

'I'm on holiday... with my daughter. She's eleven. We're staying with friends in Skipton.'

'I live in Leeds.'

'Oh...'

'It's not far.'

'No.'

'Where is she now? Your daughter.'

'My friends have taken her to York for the day. They're doing the museum and the shops. Touristy things.'

'So there's no one at home now?'

'No.' Rose swallows, tries to keep her breathing even. 'They won't be back till after supper. They're taking her for a pizza.'

Gavin lets loose his havoc-wreaking smile. 'Very obliging, your friends.'

'They wanted to give me some time to myself... I got the bus here from Skipton. This is my treat.'

'I can give you a lift back. If you want.'

'Now?'

'Yeah, come on.' He grabs her hand and pulls her across the road.

'But – it seems a shame to go home when it's still such a fine day.'

Gavin wheels round. 'There's rain forecast for later.'

'Really?'

'Yeah, heavy rain... high winds... a freak storm, in fact. Possibility of a blizzard, they say.' Rose starts to laugh. 'We should get going.'

'You don't give up easily do you?'

'Get in the car.'

On the drive back to Skipton they say very little. Rose watches Gavin's hands on the wheel, turns occasionally to look at his sun-lit profile.

'No sign of that rain.'

'Any minute now...'

She directs him to the cottage where he parks with more panache than accuracy. He gets out of the car and follows Rose to the front door. Her hand trembles as she tries to insert the key. Gavin takes it, opens the door and ushers her inside.

They don't get as far as the bed. By the time they reach the bedroom door Gavin has removed some of Rose's clothes and most of his own. Stumbling, he pinions her against the closed door and pushes into her hard, almost lifting her off the ground. Spread-eagled beneath him Rose remembers momentarily her first sight of Gavin on the rock face. She thinks she knew, then, exactly what was going to happen. Another rib-crushing thrust from Gavin and she yells loudly, but not in pain.

CHAPTER FIVE

THEY DRIVE HOME IN THEIR SEPARATE CARS, Calum with the reckless speed of the local used to empty roads, Rose with care, peering through the windscreen in the failing light for passing places. She is glad to be spared another doorstep conversation, not least because she realises she has a raging headache, the result no doubt of tension and the morning's exertions.

As she unloads the car she begins to sweat, despite the freezing wind coming in off the sea. She also remembers that she meant to shop at lunchtime – supplies are low. Lunch with Calum drove such mundane thoughts – and most others – from her mind. She checks the fridge. No milk. No juice. An unopened bottle of wine. She sighs and looks in the bread-bin. A heel-end of a loaf and a packet of flapjacks. Her head is now pounding to the point of nausea. She goes up to the bathroom to look for paracetamol. There is only one left. Rose never keeps more than a handful of tablets in the house.

She swallows the single paracetamol with a glass of water and 5 minutes later she is sick. Getting into bed she resigns herself to misery. Just before she falls into a fitful sleep she realises that if she'd brought the phone upstairs she could have rung Shona or Calum, or even a doctor.

On Thursday morning Calum is running late and swears when the phone goes.

'Calum, it's Shona.'

'I can give you two minutes, Shona. Short ones. What's up?'

'Och, nothing, probably... I just wondered, was Rose okay yesterday at school?'

'Aye, the kids loved her and I think she had a good time.'

'No, I mean afterwards.'

'We had lunch at The Stepping Stone, then we went our separate ways. Is anything wrong?'

'I don't suppose so, it's just that she's not answering her phone. And there was no answer last night either. She and I were going to have a session peeling tatties for the Burns Supper – I was ringing to check she'd remembered... It's awful dreich this morning – she surely wouldn't be out walking?'

'I'll call in on my way to school.'

'That'd be grand, Calum. I expect her phone isn't working, but if it isn't, she needs to know. I'd send Aly but that boy's such a noodle – as well try to talk to a post! And I daren't leave the wee ones. Donald's away out just now and I don't know when he'll be back.'

'No bother, Shona. I'll give you a ring if there's a problem.'

Calum knocks loudly on Rose's front door and listens for an answering shout. There is no reply so he goes in. The house is dark and cold. He lays a hand on the stove. It has been out for some time.

'Rose... It's me, Calum. Are you upstairs?'

Not waiting for an answer he takes the stairs two at a time.

***

'Rose, it's me... Gavin.'

Rose opens her eyes and squints. 'Fuck off, Gavin. Who the hell let you in?'

'I've brought you some flowers.' He lays a large bouquet of white roses on the hospital bed. A nurse materialises and whisks them away. 'What beautiful flowers, Mrs. Leonard! Shall we put them in a vase?' Rose ignores her.

Gavin sits awkwardly on a chair by the bed and says nothing.

Rose looks away. 'White roses, Gavin... How very tactful! You could hardly turn up with *red*, could you? Did Megan tell you what to buy? Where is Megan?'

'Staying with a friend. Katie Ferguson... Rose, I never meant for you to – '

'Shut up, Gavin! Whatever you want to say, I don't want to hear it. I realise it's not *your* fault I walked through a bloody glass door.'

Rose looks at him properly for the first time and sees a two-day growth of beard frosting his face, now as pale as his hair. She is confused. A few hours ago they were in bed together and he was clean-shaven, she was sure of it. There are dark circles under his eyes and he looks thinner, shrunken somehow, his broad shoulders drooping.

'How long have I been in here?'

'Three days.'

'Jesus!'

'You've been heavily sedated. I tried to see you earlier but they said there was no point...'

'Too bloody right. I want you to leave now, Gavin. Get your stuff out of my house and leave. And get someone to fix the broken glass. The sitting-room will be full of snow by now.'

'I've done all that. I've cleaned up. I just came to say – I'm sorry and... goodbye.' Gavin has tears in his eyes. Rose is appalled. She has never seen Gavin cry, Gavin who receives news of the grisly deaths of former climbing partners with stoic calm, with little more than a nod.

'Gavin, don't. Please... I can't bear it.'

'I'm sorry, Rose.' He lays his head down on the bed and buries his face in the blankets. She stares at the untidy tufts of blond hair and the fair down on the nape of his tanned neck. Her hand hovers then settles gently. She slides her fingers over his neck, inside his collar and rests them on the enlarged shoulder muscles, touching his warm, smooth skin for what she knows, with absolute certainty, is the last time.

'Goodbye, Gavin. Thank you for dealing with all the mess. You're well rid of me, you know. A bloody liability...' She withdraws her hand as she sees the cheerful nurse returning with Gavin's bouquet arranged in a vase. 'Go now, Gavin. *Now*.'

Gavin gets up, smears his hands across his eyes, turns and walks out of the ward without looking back. Rose watches him go, fixing him forever in her mind – the cocky, spring-heeled walk that even grief and exhaustion cannot quite suppress.

The nurse presents the vase at Rose's bedside. 'There! Don't they look lovely, Mrs. Leonard?'

'It's *Ms*. Leonard and no, they don't – they look like a bloody funeral arrangement. Throw them away – I'm still alive! More's the pity...'

Rose's bedroom door is open. Calum knocks and enters. The bedside light is on and he sees that, despite the cold, she is bathed in sweat, her tawny hair plastered to her forehead. She has kicked back the duvet and a voluminous Victorian nightdress clings to her body. As Calum bends and rearranges the bedclothes Rose opens her eyes and peers into the semi-darkness.

'Gavin?'

'Calum. You're ill, Rose. Will I fetch Dr. Kerr?'

She tries to sit up but falls back on the pillows, whimpering. 'Who let you in?'

'Your door wasn't locked. I knocked and called up, but you were asleep.'

Her eyes close again. 'You can get in but you can't get out... Everything's locked. Everything! The doors... the cupboards... Even the sewing-boxes. You can have a needle, but not scissors...' She throws her head from side to side. 'I'm thirsty... Gavin, get me a drink... Where's Megan?'

Calum lays a hand on her forehead. 'Rose, I'm going to get you something to drink and then I'm going to ring Dr. Kerr.'

'No! No more doctors!'

'Rose, you're running a high temperature and you're delirious. You need a doctor.'

Rose grabs his hand and begins to weep. 'Gavin, don't go! Don't leave me! Please don't leave me!'

Calum sits on the bed. He cups her face in his hands and stares into her half-closed eyes. 'Gavin isn't here, Rose... It's Calum. Listen to me – I'm going downstairs to get you some water, then I'm coming back up with the phone and I'm going to ring Shona, then the doc – okay?'

Rose is asleep again. Calum looks at his watch, swears and runs downstairs.

He opens the front door to Shona who arrives bearing milk, fruit juice, Lem-sip and a half-bottle of whisky. Calum raises an eyebrow at the whisky.

'Och, it's one less for Donald to drink,' Shona says, flapping her hand.

'Shona, I've got to go. I've rung the surgery and they say it's probably 'flu, in which case there's not much they can do. Dr. Kerr says he'll try and drop by later. She's to have plenty of fluids and keep warm – not too warm, mind. I've lit the stove – keep an eye on it.'

'Aye, but I can't stay all morning – I'm doing the playgroup run.'

'I'll be back at lunchtime. I've a free period after lunch – I've got time to get here and back if I drive fast.'

Shona snorts. 'When did you ever drive any other way?'

'Where are the weans now?'

'Jean's looking after Fergus. Aly's taken the others for the bus. They've strict instructions to hold his hand.'

'Poor Aly... I've *got* to go, Shona.'

'I'll manage fine. Away wi' ye.'

'You'll find her a wee bit delirious, maybe. She'll probably blether on about Gavin.'

'Who's Gavin?'

'The bastard she's in love with.'

'There's a man in the kitchen.'

'Mmmn?..' Rose sits up in bed. 'Sorry, Megan – what did you say?'

'I said there's a man in our kitchen. He's making himself breakfast.'

'Oh... Yes, I know. He's – a friend. He's called Gavin. He lives in Yorkshire. You know – where we went for our holiday with Penny and John.'

'Why is he here?'

'He's come to see us.'

'But I don't know him.'

'Well, he's come to see *me*... And to do some climbing. That's his hobby. He's meeting some friends in Glencoe tomorrow.'

Despite herself, Megan is impressed. 'Has he climbed Mount Everest?'

'No, but he wants to. He's saving up his money to go. Expeditions to Everest are very expensive, apparently. Thousands of pounds.'

'Did he stay here last night?'

'Yes.'

Megan's lip curls. 'So he's your boyfriend, then?'

'Yes, I suppose so...'

The child is silent for a moment, considering.

'He's not very tall.'

Rose laughs. 'No, I suppose not! But then neither am I, so it doesn't bother me. He's very nice. I think you'll like him when you get to know him.'

'Did he sleep in your bed?'

Rose looks down and smoothes the duvet, blushing. 'Yes, he did, as a matter of fact... ' She looks up at her daughter, asks nervously 'Does that bother you, Megan?'

Megan considers, then heaves a long-suffering sigh of theatrical proportions. 'No, not *really*...' She pads towards the bedroom door, then turns back suddenly. 'But if he stays again could you please ask him to put the loo-seat *down* when he's finished. I got up to pee in the middle of the night and I nearly fell down the toilet.'

When, a few moments later Gavin arrives with a breakfast tray, he finds Rose alone, with the duvet over her head, convulsed with silent laughter.

There is a knock at the front door. Rose struggles to sit up. She hears footsteps climb the stairs, then Calum's head appears round the door.

'Calum! What are you doing here?' Her voice is faint and she is breathing heavily. 'Did you know I was ill?

'Aye, Shona told me. She was looking after you earlier...'

'Yes, I think I remember. Was it you who called the doctor?'

'Sorry, but you were in a pretty bad way earlier. You were delirious so I overruled you and called him anyway.'

'Delirious? Oh, God – what was I saying?'

'Och, rubbish mostly. Well, nothing I could make any sense of anyway.'

Rose looks relieved. Calum fishes in a carrier bag. 'I've brought you some invalid stuff – Lucozade, some grapes and a box of tissues. No flowers, I'm afraid. Not that easy to come by in the Western Isles in January.'

'You are sweet... Thank you. But you shouldn't hang around, you know. I think I'm over the worst, but I might still be infectious.'

'I'll take my chances. Are you wanting anything to eat?' Rose shakes her head. 'Then do you mind if I sit and eat my lunch?'

'Of course not! Pull up that chair.'

As he pulls a chair over to Rose's bedside Calum glances around the light, orderly bedroom. There are small pieces of china and bric-a-brac on shelves, paintings and prints on the white walls and a faded Victorian sampler, but no photographs. A side-table in front of the window is crowded with pot-plants and a faint scent of pot-pourri emanates from a lidless Chinese teapot. Calum sits and admires the intricate patchwork quilt on Rose's bed. 'Is that an antique?'

'No, it's one of mine.'

'You made it?'

'Yes. Years ago.'

'There must be hundreds of pieces.'

'Probably near enough a thousand. The pieces are quite small. I call it my penance quilt.'

'That sounds like a story,' Calum says, unwrapping his sandwiches. 'I like stories.'

'Yes, but it's not one I'm proud of.'

'Shameful stories? Even better. Confess, child.'

Rose smiles wanly. 'I had one of my manic attacks... before my condition was sorted out with medication. It was what they refer to as a "major episode". Sounds like a cliff-hanger in a long-running serial, doesn't it? I chopped up a load of clothes with my dressmaking shears. I made a very thorough job of it and cut them into tiny pieces. I was beside myself.'

'What provoked the attack?'

She looks away, avoiding his eyes. 'Oh, I was angry with Gavin I suppose.'

'Was it his clothes you shredded?'

'No... Mine.'

'That's a pity. So you made all the pieces into a quilt.'

'Yes... I hate waste!' Rose sighs. 'I think I was more upset about what I'd done to the clothes than what I'd done to myself...'

Calum stops chewing and swallows. 'Was that when you...?'

'Yes. With my shears. I'm still alive because I'm a lazy cow and I don't keep my shears as sharp as I should, so they didn't cut very deep. And I cut *across* my arms instead of along them, so the damage was superficial. But it was very messy.'

'Somebody found you?'

'My daughter, Megan.'

'Christ...'

'When I was in hospital – that's *mental* hospital, they had to section me, I was still raving – I decided I would make this quilt. I think that's how I put myself back together again. I sat weeping and sewing... for months.' Rose smoothes the quilt, stroking it repeatedly.

Calum is silent for a few moments and then says softly, *'And tears shed there shall be my recreation.'*

Rose looks up. 'What's that?'

'It's from *The Winter's Tale*. Leontes, after he's driven his wife into an early grave. It's one of Shakespeare's serious puns. Recreation... Re-creation.'

'I like that. That's good.'

They sit in silence. Eventually Rose says, 'The design is known as *A Thousand Pyramids*. I sewed it all by hand after I'd managed to convince my psychiatrist that I could be trusted with needles and pins. But they wouldn't let me have scissors. I had to bite the thread with my teeth, which was tedious. And humiliating.'

Calum lays a reverent hand on the quilt. 'So much pain... yet it's beautiful.'

'Thank you.'

After a while he asks softly, 'D'you think you're still a suicide risk, Rose?'

'No, I don't think so... Not now. Oh, I don't know...' She says wearily, 'I suffer from bi-polar affective disorder – that's the label.'

'Manic depression?'

'Do you know much about it?'

'Some. The teaching profession has its share of manic-depressives. They're one of its strengths.'

She smiles at him gratefully and continues. 'I've been on medication for many years now and that has stabilised me, but I can't work properly while I'm on it. My feelings become blunted, I don't *see* things, there's just no joy, it's a kind of living death. I've tried reducing the dose – I've even stopped taking it once or twice – strictly against doctor's orders – but then I get ill, sometimes with dire consequences. I'm being a good girl again and taking the damn stuff, but probably not enough. So, mood-wise, I'm a bit unstable... I've been learning about self-management techniques and I'm trying to take control of my illness myself. I think if I live quietly and simply and monitor my moods, I may be able to keep on an even keel on a reduced dosage. But it's risky... Coming here is an attempt to simplify my life, focus on work. I *have* to be able to take care of myself as there's nobody else to do it.'

'I think we demonstrated this morning that you don't have to go it alone. The emergency services round here are pretty efficient,' he says, indicating the bottle of whisky on the bedside table.

'You've been wonderful.'

'It's nothing special, we do this for anyone – even folk we can't stand!' Calum shakes his head in mock dismay. 'Indiscriminate generosity – it's terrible!' He takes another bite of his sandwich and frowns. 'But do you no' have any family – apart from Megan, I mean?'

'No. I threw Gavin out. Megan's grown up now and lives in Carlisle. I don't see her very often. We're not particularly close... In fact we have a rather stormy history.'

'What about her father?'

'He left us when she was a baby.'

Calum chokes on his mouthful. 'Your life's been one long party, hasn't it, Rose?'

'I've no idea where he is now and no desire to know. My parents are dead... I'm an only child... I had some good friends in Fort William but we lost touch while I was ill, in and out of various hospitals... Some people just can't deal with mental illness, they don't know what to say... Then when Gavin and I split up – well, some of my friends belonged to the climbing world and they tended to side with Gavin, naturally. Some moved away... So I'm pretty much alone. But I'm used to it now. It means I can keep to my little routines. Life springs no surprises and I can be utterly selfish about work. It probably sounds a pretty dull life to you.'

'I don't think you could ever describe the struggle to survive as *dull*. I think you deserve a bloody medal. And a lot more besides.'

'Oh, I've got everything I want – a new start, new friends, a new identity almost. And I have peace and quiet... You've no idea how noisy mental hospitals are! *Awful* places... The TV's always on *and* the radio... There are Hoovers going and trolleys rattling... People moaning and weeping in corridors, shouting, hallucinating...'

'Aye, and that's just the staff... Look, Rose, I've got to go. I'll drop by later. I've got a planning meeting after school and I can't really cut it.'

'I wouldn't hear of it. Don't worry about me, I'll probably sleep now. I feel exhausted!'

'All the talking, I expect. I'll bring some food in for you this evening. You might have got your appetite back.'

'I don't want to be any trouble.'

'It's no trouble, it's a pleasure, so will you quit spoiling my fun?' He stands up and strokes a tendril of damp hair away from her cheek.

Rose looks up at him. 'Shona says you used to like playing Doctors and Nurses when you were little.'

'Did she now, the cheeky wee besom... Rose, you have no idea how lucky you are to be an only child.'

Pink.

Pink little girl, pink dress with pink ribbons, pale pink skin, clean and scrubbed, like sugared almonds, like coconut ice, powdery soft, pink and white.

Inside my pink skin: a mess, a mass of slugs and snails and puppy-dogs' tails. (No, that's what little boys are made of...)

I watch the boys, bright-eyed boys, moody and mean, with their long brown limbs and blood-stained knees, their white wolf teeth, muscle and bone, climbing, falling, shouting, laughing, pointing at the pink girls.

I am not one of them.

I am not pink.

I am *orange*.

When Calum returns with a carrier bag of groceries he finds Rose sitting on the floor of the workroom, still in her nightdress, surrounded by heaps of fabric and empty shoe-boxes. She doesn't look up.

'Rose! You shouldn't be out of bed! What is it that you want? Will you let me help?'

'I can't find the green I want... I know it's here somewhere. I remember saving it. It's a particularly nasty green... acidic, like that seaweed, you know, the stuff on the beach I was looking at the other day. It's that sort of green, a lime green with a sulphurous tint to it. *Chartreuse.* But I just can't seem to find it... Sit down and help me look.'

Calum is aware of a cold churning in his stomach. He kneels down beside her. She dazzles him with a playful smile, her eyes shining, but unfocused.

'I've had a brilliant idea, you see – *another* brilliant idea! I've been lying in bed thinking and I've decided I'm going to make a map of my mind. A mind map! Don't you think it's a wonderful idea? Then perhaps I won't lose it any more. My mind I mean, not the map... And if I have a map, I can't get lost, can I? But the colours...' She starts to rummage through the fabric again. 'They have to be exactly right... They must be here somewhere! I need a *diseased* sort of green... but not putrid.' She laughs. 'I don't think I'm *that* bad, do you? Not yet, anyway...' She picks up a fragment of russet silk and examines it. 'I remember when I was *this* colour... but that was years and years ago...'

Calum's heart is thudding. He lays his hands gently on her shoulders.

'Rose, look at me... When did you last take your medication?'

'What?' She frowns. 'Oh... after lunch, I suppose. I always take it after meals.'

'You didn't take anything while I was here. You didn't eat any lunch. You said you weren't hungry.'

'Of course I ate lunch! We sat together in the café...' She looks confused. 'Didn't we?'

'That was yesterday, Rose. Have you taken any since then?'

'I don't remember. I don't think so... Oops...' She screws up her face. 'I don't think I took it yesterday either... Well, I did but then I was sick.'

'What do you need to do, Rose? Will you let me ring Dr. Kerr?'

'No, no, I'll be fine!' She bows her head and starts to examine fabric scraps again.

'Rose –'

'Just get me my tablets, Calum, will you? They're in my handbag – on the sofa probably. There're two types. Bring them both – and a glass of water.'

Calum calls out from the sitting room. 'You're still running a temperature. Away up the stair to your bed – I'll bring everything up.'

'But I want to find that green –'

Calum reappears at the door with the handbag, 'Rose, do you want me to carry you?'

'Ooh, my very own Rhett Butler! But the handbag spoils the macho image a bit.' Calum takes a threatening step towards her. 'All right, all right, I'll come quietly.' She looks down at the scraps of fabric and pats them. 'Don't touch anything – I know that green is here *somewhere*...'

'Look – another nice autumn day, Rose!'

They assail me, assault me with their cheerful lies.

I look through their glass...

A garden. A formal garden. Neat, well-kept, like a park.
Dead.

Look closer...

Daisies lounge presumptuous on the lawn. Petals have dared to fall from the rose bushes.

Rebellion.

Birds have crapped on the wrought-iron benches, livid, magenta shit, stained with the juice of elderberries. Leaves are beginning to fall and not in tidy piles. Life is dying. Messily. Gloriously.

Look closer still...

Leaves, the colour of disease. Blistered arteries craze a jaundiced parchment of decay, withering, crackling, recoiling from my gaze...

Beautiful death.

'Your illness is a terrible gift, Rose...'

Happy Deathday to you
Happy Deathday to you
Happy Deathday, dear Rosie
Happy Deathday to you.

Rose swallows tablets watched anxiously by Calum. 'I think it's you who need the tranquilliser, Calum. Don't look so alarmed – I know what I'm doing! I'm just a bit high, that's all. These will soon bring me down to earth... This one will probably send me to sleep – which is a shame because I was having such fun.'

'Get into bed, Rose.'

'Oh, I thought you'd never ask... Are you joining me?' She hooks her fingers over Calum's belt and pulls him towards her, reaching for his mouth with hers.

'*Rose!*'

'All right, all right – I'll be good.' She scowls and climbs into bed.

'Are you sure we shouldn't get Dr. Kerr?'

'God, no! I couldn't face another lecture from him about the folly of living alone and trying to reduce my meds!' She giggles. 'That would be a fate worse than death.'

Calum takes off his jacket, pulls up a chair and sits beside the bed. She registers his neatly pressed cords, crisp white collarless shirt and waistcoat. 'Gosh, you look nice! Are you going somewhere special?'

'The Burns Night Supper. At least, I was. I'm not sure you should be left alone.'

'Oh, stop fussing, I'll be fine. It's not the getting high that is so very dangerous anyway. That can be great, a lot of laughs. It's the coming down afterwards. After all the flashing coloured lights comes the darkness... And by the time the darkness descends you can't really see the point of taking the tablets – that's if you haven't already thrown them away while you were looping the mental loop.'

'I think I'll stay.'

'But they're expecting you.'

'Och, I've two left feet and one fiddle more or less won't make any difference.'

'You play the fiddle?'

'Aye. Very badly.'

'I bet you don't. Do you have it with you? Would you play for me now? I'd love to hear you.'

'Maybe later.'

'It might calm me down,' she wheedles. 'A bedside serenade – how lovely! I shall feel like Cosima Wagner on her birthday, being woken by the *Siegfried Idyll*.'

'Should you eat something, Rose? All those tablets on an empty stomach... I brought you some tinned soup.'

'Yuk!'

Calum persists. 'Look, I'll do a deal – you eat some soup while I play to you.'

She wrinkles her nose. 'It's not oxtail is it?'

'Scotch Broth.'

'But of course!' Rose claps her hands. 'Music, Maestro, please!'

Calum stands at the foot of my bed, rolls up his sleeves and tunes his violin. I lean back against my freshly plumped pillows and feast my wandering eyes. The soup and drug cocktail is beginning to hit me. The sharp edges are gone, the harsh lights dimmed. Fog begins to descend.

Calum looks up grimly from under his dark fringe of curls.

'You're going to regret this.'

'Can't wait.'

'Well, don't say I didn't warn you. Shona's the musical one in the family.'

'Really?'

'Voice of an angel. Especially when she's drunk. Aye, you've missed a rare treat tonight at the supper.'

'Never mind – I'm in for a treat now.'

'Did you finish that soup yet?'

'Yes, and it was a truly horrible experience.'

'Well, here's another...'

And Calum begins to play a slow, mournful air, a look of fierce concentration on his face. His hands and bowing arm are fluid and relaxed, his wrist flexes elegantly, holding the bow poised above the strings. I am hypnotised by the way the lamplight catches the pale protruding bones of his wrist, the play of shifting muscles in his forearms. I see rather than hear him play.

He lowers the violin.

'That was *beautiful*, Calum. What was it?'

'A traditional tune called *My Laggan Love*.'

'Thank you. It made me want to cry.'

'Aye, it used to have that effect on my violin teacher, but for a different reason... Are you feeling sleepy yet?'

'A bit. If I do fall asleep – '

'I'm staying, whether or no'. It's that or I fetch the doctor, Rose.'

I find I am flooded with relief, have to fight back tears of gratitude. 'But – won't Shona be worried about you?'

'I'm over twenty-one... And she knows where I'll be. I said I'd look in on you this evening. She'll know I've been... waylaid.'

***

Gavin
falling
somersaulting
like a string-cut marionette
limbs flailing
ropes flying
a dance of death
accompanied by jingling karabiners at your waist
till
you
hit the rocks
and bounce
then hit some more
and split
your helmet open
like an egg
and your blood spills out
sticky and red
mixed with sharp white fragments of bone
grey gobbets of brain
oozing on sun-warmed rock.

You lie broken at the foot of the mountain
your limbs pointing to the four corners of the earth
your lips drawn back in a perpetual grin.

What a blast
what a way to go
the ultimate, Gavin

the highest high
the biggest turn-on
the hardest hard-on

Death, Gavin.

Yours.

Rose wakes with a loud cry and sits up. The room is dark but for a small pool of light. Calum has been reading by torchlight. He switches on the bedside lamp. Rose is shaking violently.

'A nightmare?'
'Yes.'
'A bad one from the sound of it.'
'Yes... What time is it?'
'A little after midnight.'
'Have you been sitting there all evening?'
'No. I made myself something to eat a while back. I've been reading and drinking Donald's whisky. Can I get you anything?'
'I'm thirsty.'

He hands her a glass of water. She swallows greedily. 'You really don't have to stay.'
'I know.'
'Are you going to sit in that chair all night?'
'Probably not. When I get tired I'll go down and sleep on your sofa.'
'You'll freeze.'

'No, the stove is burning nicely down there. I've been feeding it.'

'You think of everything...' Rose looks distractedly around the room, then puts her hands over her eyes and starts to cry.

'What is it, Rose? The dream?'

'Gavin... He's here... now...'

Calum sits on the edge of the bed and takes her in his arms, a chaste, almost brotherly embrace, yet Rose flinches. He releases her. She utters a sound, something between a laugh and a cry. 'I don't remember the last time anyone *touched* me!' She shakes her head. 'I don't remember... what it *feels* like.'

'It feels like this.' He takes her carefully in his arms again.

Rose sags against him and cries. 'I have such terrible dreams!'

'I know, I was watching while you slept. I didn't know whether to wake you or not. D'you want to talk about it?'

'No... But will you please keep holding me?'

'Aye.'

'I've soaked your nice shirt.'

'No problem.'

Her head against Calum's damp chest, Rose listens to the sound of his steady breathing, counter-pointed by the distant rumble of breakers on the shore outside her house. She begins to feel drowsy again.

'Calum?' she whispers.

'Aye?'

'Would you think it absolutely appalling if I asked you to sleep with me... but not make love?'

'No. I wouldn't.'

113

'I mean, I don't even want to try. I just want to... *sleep* with you. Wake up and not be alone.'

'Aye... That would be nice.' He releases her and stares into her eyes. 'You're sure now?' She nods. He stands awkwardly at the side of the bed. 'I expect you'd prefer me to keep my clothes on?'

'Well, not all of them. Hang on a minute.' Rose leans over to the far side of the bed and pulls open a drawer. 'There are some men's pyjamas in here somewhere.' She looks up at him quickly. 'Oh, they're not Gavin's! I bought them for the fabric – 1930s silk – but really they're too good to cut up and they're much too big for me to wear. They'll probably fit you. Here, try them on.' Calum takes the bundle of paisley silk. 'There's some spare toothbrushes in the bathroom cabinet.'

'Thanks.'

After a few minutes he returns from the bathroom clad in pyjamas, his clothes folded neatly in a pile. Rose smiles at him. 'You look nervous.'

'I am.'

'Don't be. I know what I'm asking is bloody impossible.'

'Not impossible – but hard.' He smiles. 'Och, maybe *difficult*'s a better word under the circumstances...'

She pulls back the bedclothes. 'Shut up and get into bed.'

They lie on their sides, facing each other, not touching.

Calum speaks first. 'How are you feeling now?'

'Better... Safe. Yes, I think what I feel is *safe*... Would you turn out the light?'

As he turns over she slips an arm around his waist and presses herself against his back, her face nestling between his shoulder blades. He freezes.

'Rose?'

'Mmm?'

'I promise I won't try anything in the night, but... I can't promise I won't get an erection.'

'That's okay – I'll take it as a compliment.'

They listen to each other's breathing for several moments, not daring to move.

'Rose?'

'Mmm?'

'Will you still respect me in the morning?'

Sleeping with the sea
on the sea
rising and falling with the waves
I'm carried far out into the darkness
sheltered in the broad hollow of his back.

I am wrecked
ship-wrecked, shattered
clinging, battered
to a spar
floating, drifting
clasping the hull of his ribs as they rise and fall
with the surge of the sea
the swell of his breath.

The sea snarls hungry at my door.
Beyond the slap and spatter of wind-flung spray

a gale groans at my window

The sea rolls him over, belly-up
an arm flails
heavy, like a piece of timber
pinning me against the mattress.
I surface
take his bony hand
dead-weight heavy
touch rough fingertips scoured by mountainsides
pillow my aching head
on the indolent, undulating muscle of his arm.
Silk slides and rasps against my cheek.

A sigh
a susurration of seething foam as the waves retreat.
A muffled, rhythmic thud
My blood?
His heart?
Both perhaps, in unison.

I am safe.
For one night at least.
Safe, moored to this man.

When Rose wakes she finds Calum sitting on the edge of the
bed, dressed, looking down at her.

'Good morning,' he says softly. 'I've got to go, I'm afraid. I've brought you some tea. It's by your tablets. And there's a letter for you. It came yesterday but I forgot to give it to you.'

'Thanks. Did you sleep all right?'

'Aye.' He grins. 'Eventually. And you?'

'Yes, I did.'

'Any nightmares?'

'No... I slept really well.'

'Obviously we should do this more often!'

Rose picks up the envelope and examines the handwriting. Her breath catches. 'It's from Megan.'

'I'll leave you in peace to read it, then. I'll maybe drop by later... Rose?'

'What? Oh, yes – sorry, Calum. I was thinking... about Megan.'

'It's not likely to be bad news, is it? Do you want me to stay while you read it?'

'No, I'll be fine. You mustn't be late for work.'

He bends and kisses her cheek. 'Take it easy, now.'

When he has gone Rose stares at the envelope again, trying to dismiss a sense of foreboding. She tears it open.

22nd Jan

Dear Mum,

Thanks for your recent letter. It was good to hear you're settling down and making some new friends.

I have a favour to ask and no, it's not money! I've chucked my job here and I've decided to take a bit of a break. Working at the travel agent's didn't really work out – I was just sitting on my arse all day

117

behind a VDU and the money wasn't that good. But don't panic – I've got the promise of a summer job at an outdoor centre in Snowdonia. There's also the possibility of a similar job on Raasay, that little island off Skye.

So I'm trying to make up my mind what to do next. If it's all right with you I'd like to come and stay for a week or two. I know January is hardly the best time of year to come but as I'm between jobs I thought I might as well. I need to do a bit of thinking and there are just too many distractions here in Carlisle. I thought I could maybe check out the place on Raasay on the way home.

I decided to write rather than phone so as not to spring things on you. I remember how the phone used to make you jump and I know you might not want me around, complicating your new life, so do say if it's not convenient. If you don't have a spare bed I'm happy with the sofa. I can bring my sleeping bag. I'll cook while you work!

It seems ages since I saw you and I'm looking forward to catching up. You sound fine in your letters but I wonder if you're actually giving me the whole story? Please look after yourself.

Love,
Megan.

When she has finished reading Rose folds the letter carefully and replaces it in the envelope. As she reaches across the bed for her tea she notices the dent in the pillow where Calum's head lay. She smoothes the sheet on his side of the bed, hoping to feel some residual warmth from his body, but it is cold. So is the tea.

Rose tosses the letter on to the floor and addresses the ceiling. 'Bloody hell, Megan! Your timing could have been better!'

CHAPTER SIX

A BLINDING, BRIGHT JANUARY MORNING. A sign that winter, if not over, at least no longer holds us fast. The wind has dropped to a stiff, very chilly breeze. If you were mad enough to visit the Hebrides in winter, today would be a good day to do it.

My daughter is mad enough.

I have tidied the house and cleaned the bathroom and kitchen. I have made up a camp-bed in the work room and donated my electric blanket to the worthy cause of keeping Megan warm. I have bought red and white wine, fruit juice and a half bottle of whisky. The fridge is stocked with patés and cheese, a wooden bowl overflows with fruit and there are tinned soups in the larder.

There were no fatted calves to be had at the Co-op.

I am ready too early. Even if I get stuck behind a flock of sheep it will not take me an hour to get to the airport. I refuse to be early. I will not stand and wait, not any more. I would rather be late.

I have done too much waiting in airports.

We are the camp followers. A motley crowd of women and children waiting for our men folk to return from battle, bloody but, we hope, unbowed.

Maggie is waiting for Dave.

Birgit is waiting for Simon.

Jude is waiting for Andy.

And I am waiting, with Megan, for Gavin.

The flight from Nepal has been delayed five hours and conversation dried up some time ago. Our silence is punctuated by cups of coffee and Maggie's frequent visits to the loo. No one complains. Our men are all alive. *All* of them. They've suffered nothing worse than weight-loss and frostbite. How could we – *dare* we – complain?

Maggie is pregnant. When Dave left they didn't know. Now she shows. She's been sick for weeks and nobody knows if it's the pregnancy or the fact that her doctor husband is climbing Mount Everest. Maggie hopes that the baby will stop Dave climbing. We know it won't. So does Maggie, in all probability.

Birgit tried to persuade the men that she was fit enough to go, that she was good enough, but failed to penetrate their boys' club outing mentality. I suspect they didn't want a woman to see them fail. Well, not a woman climber, certainly not a *German* woman climber. The final decision was Dave's and he told Maggie (who told Jude when she thought I was out of earshot) that they all thought Gavin might be distracted by having a woman on the expedition.

So Birgit, eaten up with anxiety and jealousy in equal measure, has become thin. As Maggie waxed, so Birgit waned. Always svelte and sexy despite her muscle, Birgit has become skeletal. I note with furtive satisfaction that it doesn't suit her.

Jude is asleep. She knows Andy is alive, or at least he was when he boarded the plane and so she sleeps, dreaming no doubt of the expedition's Hard Man, the glum, Aberdonian ex-alcoholic who has neatly replaced one expensive and dangerous addiction with another. Jude actually preferred him alcoholic because, she said, it was cheaper and his life expectancy was slightly longer.

Birgit is shaking Jude. The plane has landed. They are in England. At Gatwick. *Alive*. Maggie has started to cry already – hormones or relief, it's hard to say. I squeeze Megan's hand and we set off for Arrivals.

When Gavin eventually appears he is smaller than I remember him. Shorter. Thinner. *Older*. Can anyone change so much in four months? He is walking with a stick, bowed under a rucksack that seems almost as big as him.

When he sees us the smile is the same. He lifts a hand in salute. The conquering hero. Two bandaged fingertips, but – I count quickly, fearfully, like a newly delivered mother presented with her newborn – he still has the full complement of fingers and thumb.

Gavin limps over to us and Megan charges, flings her arms round his waist, buries her head in his chest. She catches him off-balance and he nearly falls. I wonder just how weak he is. He puts an arm round her and they walk towards me, both grinning.

Tears of relief, of joy, tears of fierce anger that he has put me through this torture, will do so again and I will let him. I wanted to be composed, serene, not let him see the agony of waiting that I have endured, the bitter resentment I feel, but the hot tears flow and I bow my head unable to look at him any more.

He folds me in his arms. I cannot hold his body because of the rucksack. I press myself against him, reassuring myself that he is real, he is whole. I hold his face in my hands and kiss his peeling mouth, laughing, crying. His head feels smaller, bonier, just a skull; his nose is skinned and scabbed, his eyes bloodshot. He is beautiful.

Megan is tugging at my arm. 'Gavin says he's brought me a present from Everest!'

'Wow! You lucky, lucky girl!'

Gavin is reaching into a side pocket of his rucksack. Megan holds her breath. I am expecting some Nepalese beads, a prayer flag maybe, or a tiny Buddha. He produces a piece of undistinguished rock, about the size of Megan's fist. It looks like limestone. For a moment she doesn't understand. She thinks it is one of Gavin's practical jokes and her lip begins to wobble. The bastard savours the moment.

'Gavin – tell her!'

'This, Megan, is a piece of rock from Everest Base Camp.'

She squeals, snatches the rock and kisses Gavin. I don't recall her ever kissing him before, not once in the two years he has lived with us. I am absurdly pleased.

'And what, Mr. Mountaineering Hero, did you bring for *me*?'

He smiles and says simply, 'Me.'

***

122

I don't spot Megan immediately because she is taller than I remember her. Megan stopped growing five years ago – when she fitted neatly under Gavin's chin – but she is always taller than I remember her. Not tall, just taller than the girl I remember.

I am easy to spot amongst the small group of locals meeting the Glasgow flight, a parakeet amongst the crows. Megan waves, heaves a rucksack up onto her shoulder and strides towards me. I wave back and feel foolish, tearful. It must be six months since I last saw her. She has cut her lovely long hair. It's now short and spiky. She is wearing ethnic dangly earrings that draw attention to her pretty ears and neck. I decide the new hairstyle suits her. It is uncompromising, almost brutal, yet still alluringly feminine, a combination characteristic of my dear daughter.

She stands before me, hesitant, smiling so hard I know she must be close to tears. My eyes prick too. I put my arms round her and squeeze.

'Hello, darling!'

'Hello, Mum...'

'Oh, let me *look* at you! You look so different! I hardly recognised you. You've lost weight...'

'No, not much. It's the hair...' She pulls at tufts self-consciously. 'What do you think?'

'I think it's wonderful! Your ears will freeze off here, but don't worry, I've got plenty of hats.'

'Oh, Mum...' The tears gather on her long, dark lashes. Megan never needed mascara.

'Darling, what is it? What's wrong?'

'Nothing...' She laughs and rubs her eyes. 'I'm just so pleased to see you! And you look... so happy!'

'I *am*, Megan, I truly am! You know that saying – I died and went to Heaven? Well, I did and this is it. Welcome to Heaven!'

In the absence of flowers Rose has arranged a collection of shells and pebbles in a dish on Megan's bedside table – an up-ended plastic toy-box disguised with an Indian scarf. There is a small pile of books about the Hebrides and an OS map, 'in case you fancy going off exploring on your own. There's a bird book too and a pair of binoculars. I remember how you used to like watching birds... And there're some trashy novels... Not mine – Shona lent them to me. They look gruesome.'

Megan laughs. 'You've thought of everything, Mum.'

'Don't suppose so for one minute... Look, this is the control for the electric blanket... and here are some coat-hangers...' Rose looks around the workroom and sighs. She is beginning to feel tired and edgy. 'I'm sorry you're so cramped in here, but it's no use sleeping in the sitting room – people tend to walk right in.'

'Without knocking?'

'Oh no, they knock or call out, *then* walk right in. At least you'll have a bit of privacy in here. I'm afraid there's no proper curtain. I didn't need a curtain for a workroom and I wasn't really expecting any guests until the summer... I've tacked up that sari – you can just tie it to one side when you want more light. Oh – I know what I've forgotten...'

Rose disappears. Megan hears footsteps going up and then down the stairs. Rose re-appears with a carved wooden mirror. 'This is the only mirror I possess. I'll use the bathroom cabinet. There! I think that *is* everything!'

'Thanks, Mum. I really didn't want you to go to all this trouble... I'm sorry, I didn't really think – '

'Don't be silly! The only trouble was having to tidy up the workroom, but that was long overdue so your visit gave me a good excuse.'

'Have you done much work since you've been here?'

'Quite a bit. I've finished a private commission and I've started on some pieces which I shall probably exhibit in the summer.'

'You're planning an exhibition already?'

'Well, yes... Not on my own.'

'Who with?'

'A neighbour. Calum Morrison.'

'I thought you said he was a poet?'

'He is. We're planning an exhibition of words and textiles – textiles inspired by poems, poems inspired by textiles. We're going to display work by local schoolchildren too. We think it might appeal to the tourists in the summer.'

'Sounds great. Where will you hold it?'

'At the Arts Centre in Lochmaddy. It's not a very big space – we'll easily fill it.'

'Is there a theme?'

'Our working title is *The Encumbrance of Words*. It was something Calum said when we were talking about the differences between visual and verbal art. I was trying to explain what one of my textiles meant.'

'Have you got anything to show me yet?'

'Well, nothing that's finished. I'm still playing around.'

'Is the black piece on the wall for the exhibition?' Megan points to an irregular-shaped patchwork of many different black fabrics embroidered and embellished with black silks and beads.

'Well, yes, if I ever get to the stage that I'm happy with it. It's called *Basalt* 2. It's a response – a reply in a way – to a poem of Calum's called *Basalt*.'

'What's it about?'

'Calum's poem? I wouldn't dream of asking... He'd never tell you anyway. He says, "I just write the stuff".'

'Isn't basalt a rock you find on Skye?'

'Yes, it's a black volcanic rock formed from cooled lava. The Cuillin are what's left of huge volcanoes. I've put a book about geology on your bedside table if you're interested. It's fascinating! I'm really getting into it.'

'So, let me get this straight... Your piece – called *Basalt* 2?'

'Yes.'

'...is a response to Calum's poem called *Basalt* and you're going to exhibit them together, as a sort of pair.'

'Yes. But we're not going to explain either of them. *The Encumbrance of Words*, remember?'

Megan looks for a few moments at the forbidding black piece on the wall. 'It's quite disturbing...'

'You should read the poem!'

'Sinister almost.'

'Oh, good! I must have got something right.'

Megan approaches and examines the piece more closely. 'What's the shiny black stuff that you've pleated?'

'A bin liner.'

'Really? You'd never know! And the torn gauzy bits?'

'Old black tights.'

'These knotted cords look like bootlaces.'

'They are. And I made the distorted grid effect by stretching a pair of fishnets. It's all very female and domestic.'

'And you won't tell me what it's meant to be about?'

'Calum's poem,' Rose says simply.

'And what do *you* think Calum's poem is about?'

'Well, I can only say what it's about for *me*.'

'Which is?'

'Suicidal despair.'

'Oh... Do I get to meet this guy? He sounds a bundle of laughs.'

'Actually, in a rather dour, Highland way, he *is*.'

Megan pours red wine while Rose serves two bowls of French onion soup.

'My favourite! You remembered!'

'Of course! Not homemade, I'm afraid, but it came out of a classy tin...' Rose raises her glass. 'Cheers! Or *slàinte*, as we say round here. Welcome to North Uist, Megan.'

'Thanks. Cheers!'

They eat and the ensuing silence is slightly too long for either woman to feel comfortable.

'Why did you choose this place?' Megan asks abruptly.

'This house? It was cheap, simple, near the sea – '

'No, I meant this island. Did you really need to come this far... to get away?'

'Yes, I think so... I wanted absolute peace and quiet – no traffic, no double-glazing salesmen, no lawnmowers! I decided that if I was going to try to manage my condition without being drugged insensible then I needed to give myself the best possible environment, which for me meant a very controlled environment, controlled by *me*.'

'So you could avoid triggering mood swings?'

'That's right. I can keep my life very simple here. Predictable. *You'd* call it boring. I can withdraw or get involved as much as I want to and people don't mind. They think I'm odd, I'm sure, but I probably don't seem *that* odd because they accept that you'd have to be a bit crazy to choose to come and live here in the first place.'

'So they see you as an English eccentric?'

'Very probably. But that seems a small price to pay for what I get in return. More soup?'

'Yes, please.'

'You really don't need to worry about me, you know. People respect each other's privacy, but if you're in trouble – like when I had 'flu recently – neighbours turn up with food parcels and offers of help. And it's not like they're doing you a big favour, Good Samaritan style, it just comes naturally to them. Calum calls it "indiscriminate generosity". Caring for others, keeping an eye open for people, is bred in the bone here.'

'Something to do with the isolation, I suppose.'

'Plus the island character. People have a different set of values here. Life isn't about getting and spending because nobody gets much and there's nowhere to spend it anyway. It's a hard life in many ways, but people don't lock their doors – they feel safe. Do you know, there's no crime to speak of – just a bit of drunken driving and the odd brawl after one too many drams. So you see, it's possible for me to live alone here and yet feel perfectly safe.'

'I think I understand... But it still sounds terribly lonely to me.'

Rose shrugs her shoulders. 'Well, it's all relative, isn't it? Lonely to me was living in Fort William on my own... Afterwards.'

Megan is silent.

Rose stands and gathers up the soup bowls. 'Shall we have some coffee?'

My coffee is cold. On the next table a child excavates the sugar bowl; another blows bubbles into her lemonade. Their mother sits eyeing the rain anxiously, eking out her cup of coffee, postponing the gathering up of her bags and brood.

I remember another café. Gavin sitting opposite, tea unattended, laughter about nothing, nothing at all. I remember how I threw back my head and he touched my long hair, marvelling.

In a mirror opposite I search for the face Gavin saw but I see only pale, sagging flesh, eyes puffy with unshed tears, lips pressed tight together.

He'd said I was beautiful. With him I was. I had seen it for myself, looking over his shoulder in the bathroom mirror, eyes alight, hair tousled from bed, skin glowing.

The lemonade is finished and the children begin to fight over the sugar bowl. Their mother remonstrates half-heartedly, then smiles at me. She can tell I, too, am a mother. I smile briefly, bow my head. I study my newspaper, unseeing.

Megan is nursing a cup of coffee by the wood-burning stove when there is a tap at the front door. Before she has got to her feet Calum appears at the sitting-room door.

'Oh, hello... I was looking for Rose.'

'She's just popped out to the Co-op. She forgot to buy milk. She'll be back soon.'

'You must be Megan.'

'Yes.'

He steps forward and shakes her hand firmly. 'I'm Calum Morrison, one of Rose's neighbours.'

'Oh... Yes, she's mentioned you in her letters.'

'Has she?' Calum looks surprised. 'Did she tell you about her school visit?'

'Yes, she said you'd invited her to show her work. Did it go all right? Mum doesn't usually cope very well with crowds of people. I was surprised when she said she'd agreed to do it.'

'Aye, she coped brilliantly! She was a big hit with the kids. That's why I'm here really.' He holds out a sheaf of papers. 'Can I leave these for her? They're poems my pupils wrote inspired by her visit. I think she might be interested to read them.'

'I'll tell her when she gets in. Or would you like to wait and tell her yourself? I've just made a pot of coffee. Oh – there's no milk though, not till she gets back.'

'Thanks, you're very kind, but I've got a stack of marking a mile high. I'll be getting back... Tell Rose those are photo-copies. She can keep them.'

'Right.'

'I'll no doubt be seeing you again.' Calum heads towards the door, then turns. 'I hope you enjoy your stay on Uist... *Ceud Mìle Fàilte.*'

'Sorry?'

'The traditional Gaelic greeting. It means a hundred thousand welcomes. We don't believe in doing things by halves.'

Megan smiles and follows him to the door. As she opens it and looks outside she narrows her eyes against the dazzle of pale sunlight and the vast expanse of steely sea. She laughs, shaking her head. 'I just can't get over that view! The Atlantic just outside your front door! I grew up with a view of Ben Nevis from my bedroom window but I think this beats even that.'

'Aye, and it's only January. You should come back in May or June. There aren't words to describe it.'

'But I thought you were a poet?'

'Aye... but not a good one. Are you staying long?'

'A week or so maybe. I'm not sure. It depends how long Mum and I can stand each other's company!'

'Do you no' get on?'

131

'I suppose we get on as well as can be expected. Mother and daughter relationships can be fraught, can't they? I think Mum and I have driven each other to Hell and back several times.'

'It can't have been easy growing up with your Mum's illness... and no dad.'

Megan looks at him uneasily. 'She's told you the family history, then?'

'No, not much. Just why she's here. On her own.'

'She hates talking about the past. We never, *ever* discuss it. You must be good at getting people to open up.'

'Aye, well, if you're no' used to it, half a bottle of whisky can break the habits of a lifetime.'

Megan laughs. 'She never drinks either!'

'Aye, I know. We've had a terrible corrupting influence on her. Watch out if you're here for more than a few days – it's good clean air, but it's no' exactly good clean living.'

'It will do her good!'

'The air or the corruption? Och, I'm blethering... I'd best be going.'

'Calum... Did she tell you about Gavin?'

He hesitates. 'Aye, she did... That was a bad business.'

'What did she tell you?'

'Not much. Just that he went off with another woman... and then she cracked up.'

'She's still not over it. Over *him*.'

'I know. But I think she may be making some progress.'

'Really? I hope you're right. I suppose the fact that she's talking about it has to be a good sign.'

'Maybe so.' Calum is silent for a while. Eventually curiosity overrides his better judgement. 'What was he like, this Gavin?'

'Hard to describe really... ' Megan shivers in the doorway and folds her arms across her chest. 'Glamorous, in a scruffy, disreputable sort of way. A magnet for women.'

'Aye, I gathered that much.'

'I can't really say how Gavin seemed to outsiders – I grew up with him. I resented him to begin with, gave him a really hard time. But in the end I could see why Mum loved him the way she did. And he was brilliant when she was ill... Gavin was a total hero to me. A kind of father-figure, but more of a friend than a father. He could be a complete pain in the arse of course, but then so could I. Mum used to accuse us of ganging up on her.' She smiles. 'I suppose we did sometimes...'

'*Please* can I go with him?'

'No, it's far too dangerous.'

'Not really, Rose... She'd be safe as houses on grit-stone. With me, anyway.'

Rose snaps at him. 'Gavin, please don't encourage her.' She turns back to her daughter. 'You're far too young to go climbing, Megan. Maybe next year.'

'Gavin started when he was twelve!'

Rose sighs. 'Yes, well, Gavin's parents must have been out of their minds.'

'They didn't know, actually.'

'Gavin!'

'Sorry!'

'Mum, I'm nearly fifteen, I'm not a little kid! I'm more likely to be killed crossing the road than climbing in the Peak District in the middle of summer.'

'It's true, Rose.'

'Shut *up*, Gavin! She's not your daughter!'

'As you never cease to remind me...'

'It's bad enough having to worry about *you* coming home on crutches without having to worry about what might happen to her.'

'I just think it's a shame. For Megan... and for me. I would really like to teach her. But if you don't trust me enough – '

'Of course I trust you, but she's my only child, she's only fourteen and climbing is a very dangerous sport.'

'Now that's where you're wrong! It's *perceived* to be dangerous because deaths and injuries and dramatic rescues make the headlines, but when you consider the number of people who climb, the number of accidents is minute! And there's always a reason for those accidents – crap equipment, poor judgement, inexperience, freak weather conditions... None of that would apply if I take Megan to the Peaks. She'll be a lot safer with me than if she goes to some tin-pot outdoor centre with the school and gets sent up the Ben in a blizzard with some inexperienced PE graduate who can't use a compass.'

'He's right, Mum.' Megan is clearly impressed with Gavin's arguments. Rose is not.

'No, Gavin.'

'*Mum!*'

'I'm sorry, Megan. I just can't bear the thought... It's bad enough worrying about Gavin. Please – let's drop it.'

Megan turns to Gavin, mute appeal in her brimming eyes. He puts an arm round her shoulders. 'Maybe another time, eh, Meg? There'll be other opportunities, I promise.'

'Will there? Not all the time *she's* running my life.'

'Megan, that's not fair! I just don't want you to get hurt, that's all.'

'You just don't want me to have fun! You don't want me to grow up! You want me to be your little girl, staying at home, looking after you!'

'That's nonsense!'

'Then let me go with Gavin!'

'No, and that's the end of the discussion. I don't want to hear another word about it. Gavin had no business discussing this with you without clearing it with me first.'

'I didn't think you would object.'

'You *don't* think – that's your trouble.'

'And you think far too bloody much, that's yours! For God's sake, Rose – girls of Megan's age are out there drinking, doing drugs – '

'Having sex!' Megan says, with relish. A pained look from Gavin indicates that she may have overstepped the mark.

'Yes... having sex... All of it illegal and all of it *far* more dangerous than climbing.'

'Maybe so – but I can't *stop* her drinking or having sex if that's what she chooses to do. I *can* stop her climbing.'

Another pained look from Gavin indicates that Rose has now overstepped the mark. Megan walks up to her mother and shouts in her face, 'I hate you!' She rushes from the room

135

and stumbles up the stairs. The muffled sound of crying can be heard coming from the room above.

'*Shit*...' Gavin says with emphasis. 'I think you just made a big mistake there, Rose...'

'Don't *you* start – this is all your fault!'

'Yeah, I know... Sorry.'

'I'm back.' Rose appears at the door with a bag of groceries. 'Sorry I was gone so long. I bumped into several people I knew and you have to stop and chat.'

'That's okay. I had a visitor. Calum Morrison called while you were out.'

Rose arranges her face to suggest no more than polite interest. 'Oh? What did he want?'

'He left you some poems written by his pupils. He said you could keep them.'

Rose falls on the sheets of paper, leafing through them. 'Oh, how wonderful! Look, there's loads of them... Oh, little *Kenny's* written a poem! Calum said I could keep these?'

'Yes, he said they were photocopies.'

'Oh, *bless* him...' She looks up from the poems to see Megan gazing at her. Rose endeavours to sound matter-of-fact. 'You see what I mean? People are so thoughtful round here. Always doing each other favours.'

Rose retreats to the kitchen and starts to unpack groceries. After a few moments she calls out to Megan. 'So – you had a bit of a chat, did you? With Calum?'

'Yes, he stayed for a few minutes. I love the accent...'

'What did you talk about?'

'Your visit to the school... the poems... How you've taken up drinking whisky.'

Rose appears in the doorway looking aghast. 'It was just the once – and I was only drinking to be polite! It's considered very rude here to refuse people's hospitality. Did he say anything else about me?'

Megan laughs. 'What is this – the Spanish Inquisition? He was only here for a few minutes. Unfortunately.'

'What's that supposed to mean?'

'Well, he's a bit of a hunk, isn't he? You made him sound a dry old stick in your letter – teaching English and Gaelic. I thought he must be at least fifty.'

'No, he's thirty-nine... His sister told me,' Rose adds hurriedly.

'He looks younger than that.'

'Yes, I suppose he does.'

'Is he married?'

'Divorced.'

'Girlfriend?'

Rose hesitates. 'I don't think so.'

'*Really*?'

'Well, how would I know? It's not the sort of thing that would crop up in conversation. I think maybe there *is* someone...' Rose says, avoiding Megan's eyes.

'Can you think of an excuse to invite him round?'

'Oh, Megan, don't be daft! You're only here for a couple of weeks!'

'I know! All the more reason I should be given opportunities to absorb local colour and meet the natives –

especially the six-foot, blue-eyed variety. Is he interested in anything other than Gaelic and poetry?'

'He climbs,' Rose replies gloomily.

'Oh, Jesus...'

I'm sitting at the foot of the climbing wall in Fort William watching climbers: Gavin, Dave, Andy, Simon and Birgit. Actually I'm really only watching Gavin who in sport climbing now outclasses even Dave, something of a local legend, but now past his best. He doesn't have Gavin's panache, his flexibility.

Birgit does, however, and her legs are as long as Gavin's. The pair of them are showing off to each other while Simon and Andy discuss a bouldering problem. Simon is belaying Birgit rather absent-mindedly. Dave, tall and solid as an obelisk of rock, belays Gavin, for all the world as if he is fly-fishing – calm, contemplative, as if belaying weren't the most boring sport activity in the world, which it is.

Dave isn't bored, but God knows I am. Bored and tired of listening to Gavin show off. As a result of an international climbing career, Gavin can swear, fuck and order a pint in most European languages, including Glaswegian. He is now talking to Birgit in German, quite unnecessarily since her English, though pedestrian, is excellent.

Birgit's throaty laugh and my worm's-eye view of her neat little arse are really beginning to piss me off. This wall is boring, my coffee is boring, climbers are boring, especially when they are climbing. The only thing more boring than a bunch of climbers climbing is a bunch of climbers *talking* about climbing.

Gavin must be about to do something flash. Everybody seems to be watching him – even Birgit has stopped the Teutonic chatter. His circus trick performed, Gavin drops neatly and intentionally to the ground, a feline acrobat. Dave nods. Andy grunts, 'Nice one,' the climber's equivalent of a round of applause.

Simon lowers Birgit to the ground where she makes a song and dance of mopping her armpits and between her breasts with a little towel, watched by all the men except Dave who is coiling rope with Zen-like attention to detail.

Gavin finally catches sight of me. He looks surprised, almost uncomfortable. He approaches, drinking from a bottle of water.

'Hi... What are you doing here?'

'Waiting for Megan. She went swimming with Katie. I said I'd meet them here and take them home. I didn't know you were climbing... I thought you were supposed to be at Dave's?'

'We were, then we thought we'd get in a bit of practice.'

'Oh... Will you be much longer?'

'We were going for a pint afterwards. Why don't you come?'

'I'm taking Megan and Katie home, I told you.'

'So join us later.'

'Maybe...'

'Why not?'

'You'll all talk climbing. It's so boring for me, Gavin. I can't really join in.'

'Course you can! We won't talk climbing all evening anyway.'

'Yes you will.'

'Well, I won't be late.'

'Yes you will.'

'Rose...' He's beginning to sound annoyed.

Birgit limps over to us and stands next to Gavin rubbing her shoulder. 'Hello, Rose! And how are you today?' She is as tall as him, as tanned and as blonde. They make a good-looking pair.

'Fine, thanks, Birgit'.

Gavin looks at her, his head cocked on one side. *'Was ist los?'*

She wrinkles her pretty little nose. *'Mein Rücken tut weh...'*

'Wo?'

'Hier...' Birgit raises her arms and tries to rub her shoulder blades, an action which thrusts her breasts in the general direction of Gavin's face. He moves behind her and gently but firmly starts to knead the muscles in her shoulders. 'Simon!' he calls raucously, 'Your woman needs some attention!'

'It looks to me as if she's getting plenty of that,' I say in an undertone. 'See you later, Gavin. Enjoy your evening... *Auf wiedersehen*, Birgit.' Birgit beams at me and waves; Gavin scowls.

CHAPTER SEVEN

THE SILENCE IS NOT THE SAME. The house is silent but not empty. Megan is downstairs, sleeping, dreaming. I cannot hear or see her but I know she is there and so the silence is not the same.

I stare into the darkness until my eyeballs smart, frightened to fall asleep. In my dreams Gavin returns and I cannot bear the cold daylight pain of waking, realising he is not here, will never be here again.

I think of Calum lying in Gavin's place.

Dark. Thin. So much hair. The back of his neck, pale, almost white, where the sun never penetrates.

Do you *know*, Gavin? Do you somehow know that I slept with Calum? Are you with me always, *in* me? Is my skin still the skin you touched, or have those cells all been shed and replaced? Is there any part of me that still bears the imprint of your touch?

My hair. My long hair, longer now, knew your hands.

If I cut it off you will be gone from my body, Gavin, finally. Expunged. Exorcised. The connection will be cut.

Cut...

'Don't.' Calum said 'Don't.' Whisky words mumbled in the rain as he lifted a hand to touch my hair, then didn't. A connection between us, even though nothing happened. Nothing at all.

***

'Why don't you, Rose?'

'Cut my hair?'

'No. Fuck the poet – what's his name? Calum?'

'Yes.'

'Why not? He obviously fancies you. Don't you fancy him?'

'I find him attractive, yes.'

'So?'

'I can't. I mean, I don't want to.'

'Bullshit! You get wet between the legs just thinking about him.'

'Damn you, Gavin! How do you know that?'

'I know *you*, Rose. Inside out. It never took much to get you going... Bed was fucking marvellous, wasn't it? You must miss all that.'

'If it was so marvellous why did you – '

'Don't let's go into all that again. I told you – it meant nothing to me.'

'And everything to me.'

'Only because you *let* it, Rose. You don't fuck with your brain, you do it with your body, for Christ's sake.'

'How very convenient! How utterly *male* to be able to compartmentalise like that. If only I could have done that!'

'So fuck the Scot, Rose. Go on – you deserve a good time. You've bloody earned it. He climbs, doesn't he? So he'll be fit... Can you even remember what it feels like, Rose, all that hard muscle? You used to like all that.'

'Shut up, Gavin.'

'Fuck him, Rose. Then tell me all about it.'

'I won't need to tell you, Gavin – you'll *be* there, watching, you sick bastard!'

'Yeah, that's right, I suppose I will... But I won't know what it's like for you, Rose, what it's like *inside* you. You'll have to tell me that.'

'Get *out*, Gavin! Get out of my mind!'

I sit bolt upright in the bed, drenched with sweat and tears, tears of anger and shame. I weep quietly so as not to wake Megan.

Rose sits on the floor of the library in the community school surrounded by books on geology, geography, land formation. Engrossed in note-taking, she doesn't register a large pair of scruffy trainers as they approach, then come to a halt beside her.

'Some light bedtime reading?'

She looks up, startled. The effort to focus, to re-adjust to her surroundings is palpable. 'Oh, Calum... Hello! Shouldn't you be at work?'

'It's Saturday.'

'Oh... Yes, I suppose it is. Sorry. One day is much like another to me.' She notices that he isn't smiling and says nervously, 'I'm reading up on geology.'

'So I see.'

'There's a good range of books here. Better than I was expecting.'

'Aye, it's a popular topic.'

During the silence that follows Rose feels at a disadvantage as Calum towers over her. Looking up at him she can see the long white scar under his jaw partially masked by the shadow of weekend stubble. She makes another lame attempt at conversation. 'Are you here choosing books?'

'Not exactly. I've brought the twins. You'll have noticed an unacceptable rise in the noise level... That's Duncan and Eilidh engaged in heated literary debate. They were driving Shona mad and Aly was trying to do his homework for once, so I said I'd take them out. Then it started to rain... So we fetched up here. I'm supposed to be reading to them in a moment. *Hairy Maclary from Donaldson's Dairy*, I believe. You're welcome to join us,' he adds grimly.

They do not speak for a while. Rose stares at his trainers, notes that the muddy denim hems of his jeans are frayed. Shouts and giggles from the twins punctuate the soft, constant hum of computers. Calum crouches down beside her and opens a book at random, flicking the pages, unseeing.

'I've missed you, Rose.' She says nothing. 'I dropped by the other day but you weren't in. I met Megan.'

'Yes, I know.'

He looks round the library. 'Is she here?'

'No, she's at home. Probably still in bed. She's not exactly a morning person... I had a bad night and felt like getting out of the house so I left her a note. I thought I'd do some research.'

There is another long silence. Calum sighs. 'Is this how you want to play it, Rose?'

'What do you mean?'

He lowers his voice. 'Maybe you've forgotten, but the last time I saw you we'd just spent the night together. Since then – nothing. I'm... *confused*, to say the least.'

'I did ring – after you left the poems – but there was no answer.'

'That was days ago.'

'Yes, I know. I'm sorry. Things have been... difficult since then.'

'Because of Megan?'

'Yes, I suppose so. The house is in chaos... She's camping in my work-room and... I'm not sleeping much at nights.'

'Aye, you look jiggered.'

'Yes, I am... I'm sorry Calum, but I think I can only deal with one thing at a time. Megan used to call me a bear of very little brain – and that isn't even wired up properly. I don't really know how to deal with... all this. *Us*. And I don't really want Megan to know how things are between us.'

'And how *are* things between us?'

'On hold, I suppose. Can you put up with that for a couple of weeks?'

'Oh, aye... I'd just like to know, that's all. I wondered if you'd had second thoughts. Or if maybe that night had meant nothing to you... It meant something to me.'

'And to *me*! I'm sorry I haven't told you. I somehow thought you would know. You seem pretty good at reading my mind.'

The floor vibrates as two pairs of small sturdy feet pound across the library. The twins, seven years old, dark and bright-eyed like their uncle, cannon into Calum who cries out in mock-pain. Duncan climbs onto his back and Eilidh closes the book in Calum's hands with a snap.

'Time for our story!'

'You promised.'

Calum pulls both children down into his lap. 'Are you forgetting your manners now? Say hello to Rose.'

The children look up shyly. 'Hello, Rose.'

'Hello! You've got a lot of nice books there, Duncan.'

'Aye, we're going to have a story!'

Calum's face brightens. 'Jings! Are you reading to me then, Duncan?'

'No! You're reading to us!'

The children giggle and Calum groans. 'Not Hairy Maclary?'

'From Donaldson's Dairy!' they chant in unison.

'Okay, go and sit yourselves down on the cushions – I'll be over in a wee while. I just want to finish talking to Rose.'

'Five minutes,' Eilidh says firmly, holding up the fingers of one hand and thrusting them in Calum's face. The twins run back to the children's section and flop onto large floor cushions. Rose watches them and smiles.

'I wish I enjoyed my family as much as you appear to enjoy yours.'

'Being an uncle is a hell of a lot easier than being a parent, you know that. Are you no' enjoying Megan's visit then?'

'It's that obvious is it?'

'Not to her, I'm sure.'

Rose sighs. 'I don't cope well with changes in routine. With *people* really. And things have never been... comfortable between Megan and me.'

'Aye, she said something to that effect.'

'What did she say?'

'Nothing much, just implied that you rub each other up the wrong way. She seems well aware of the difficulties.'

'You didn't tell her about us, did you?'

'Of course not.' He shrugs. 'What's to tell, anyway?'

'Ouch.'

He smiles. 'Am I sounding bitter?'

'A little.'

'Put it down to terminal sexual frustration. '

'Megan asked if you had a girlfriend.'

'Did she now?'

'You made quite an impression, I think. Another reason it was difficult for me to come clean about our relationship.'

'Aren't I a bit old for her?'

'Aren't I a bit old for you?'

'You're not starting on *that* tack again!'

'Why don't you have a girlfriend, Calum? A man as kind and clever and as attractive as you – it doesn't add up.'

'I'm a closet gay. I'm just using you as a smokescreen.'

'Bollocks. Why, Calum? Why has there been no one since Alison?'

'Who says there hasn't?'

'You've never talked about anybody.'

'That's because I don't like talking about the past.'

'Why not?'

'You know,' he says, getting to his feet, 'Reading *Hairy Maclary* to the twins is beginning to seem like a really attractive proposition.'

Rose grabs his arm and pulls him back down. 'Why, Calum? What aren't you telling me?'

'What aren't *you* telling *me*, Rose?'

'You don't trust me, do you?'

He stares at her. 'No, I don't believe I do.'

She releases his arm and leans back, blinking. 'Well... That told me.'

'I don't trust you, Rose. Not yet. I like you a lot and I fancy you like hell but no, I don't think I trust you. I don't trust you not to hurt me and despite the capable, all-things-to-all-people, pillar-of-the-community exterior I am in fact as complete a fucking *mess* as the next man. So for now, if you don't mind, I'll keep my own counsel. What you see is what you get... I'm straight, single, solvent and sound of wind and limb. There are no mad women in my attic and, believe it or not, I don't have to fight off an army of females intent on beating a path to my bedside. I'm flattered that Megan is puzzled by my single status but if she's thinking of remedying that tell her she'd be wasting her time – for the moment my attentions are fixed elsewhere.' He puts a hand behind Rose's head, pulls her towards him and kisses her hard on her gaping mouth. 'If you want to see me, give me a call. Otherwise I won't trouble you again.'

He stands up and wheels round, calling sharply to the twins. 'Duncan! Eilidh! Choose your books now. We're going home.'

A wail goes up. 'Aw, but you *promised*!'

'You said you'd read us a story!'

'Aye, I will. *Two* stories. At home. Now take your books up to the counter and get them stamped.' The children run off, mollified.

'Come to supper, Calum.'

He turns back and looks down at Rose. '*What?*'

'Come to supper.'

'When?'

'Tonight.'

He opens and closes his mouth, trying to frame words, then drags a hand backwards through his hair and says softly, 'Okay.'

'But I don't want Megan to know about us... yet. So you can't stay over.'

'I wouldn't expect to. Especially not after the way I've behaved this morning. What time?'

'Seven o'clock?'

'Okay.'

'Calum... I'm making this up as I go along.'

'Aye, that's fairly obvious.'

'You won't say anything to Megan?'

'No, I won't.'

'Thanks. And thank you for the kiss.'

'I expected you to slap my face.'

'No. I was just very surprised.'

'Pleasantly surprised?'

'Oh, yes. Very... I think about your mouth all the time.'

'Do you?' She nods and smiles. 'Aye, well my thoughts are a wee bit more wide-ranging... but we won't go into that now. I promise to behave myself this evening. See you at seven, then.'

***

At the Co-op Rose bumps into Shona who seems more than usually pleased to see her.

'Och, it's yourself, Rose! Just the lady I was wanting to speak to!' Shona draws Rose aside to a chilly alcove beside the frozen foods. 'I was wanting to ask you – are you completely recovered from the influenza?'

'Yes thanks, Shona. It was a three-day wonder.'

'That's good! Only I remember last year poor wee Effie – Angus' wife, you know – was laid very low for some weeks afterwards.' Shona lowers her voice to a piercing whisper. 'She was never herself again after that... Then in the summer of course she passed on, poor soul.'

'I don't think I'm in any immediate danger, Shona. And I understood from Angus that Effie was a good age when she died.'

'Oh, aye – sixty-five – but that's no age at all for these parts!'

'I know – *Tir nan Og.*'

Shona beams. 'Are you learning the Gaelic now?'

'Calum's taught me the odd word or two. I really must sign up for a proper class.'

Shona waxes confidential again. 'Did you know it's my wee brother's fortieth birthday next week?'

'No, I didn't.'

'Aye! We're planning a surprise party for him! You're invited, of course. Megan too, if she'd like to come.'

'Thank you. What a lovely idea.'

'Och, no doubt he'll hate all the fuss, but Donald and I thought everyone could do with a good party. February is a terrible month, the worst of the winter. In December you've Christmas and Hogmanay to liven things up and in January you've Burns Night, but *February*...' Shona pulls a disgusted face. 'Ach, I'd just as soon sleep through it and wake up on the first of March! So – you'll come to our wee celebration?'

'Of course! When's it to be?'

'Saturday night. Get there before eight. I've invited Calum over for supper. He thinks it's pizza and birthday cake with the bairns, so you're not to breathe a word, mind.'

'No, of course not. Can I help out with the food? I'm not much of a cook but I can make a decent lasagne.'

'That'd be grand, Rose! Calum loves Italian food. Could I leave that sitting in the bottom of the Rayburn?'

'Yes, it'll come to no harm. Can I do anything else to help?'

'Well, I was wanting to ask you a favour...' Shona hesitates and looks embarrassed.

'Oh, for goodness sake, Shona – give me a chance to repay some of the kindness you've shown me! How can I help?'

'Well, I was wondering, as you're our nearest neighbour, do you have anywhere we could hide some food and drink? If I have crisps and nibbles lying around the house they'll get eaten by the bairns, and as for the drink – well, that never seems to last long with Donald, especially when Calum's around. Those two do enjoy a dram! So I was wondering... '

'Yes, of course! You can hide the booze in my shed and I can easily make room for extra food in my workroom. I've got some space in the freezer too if you want.'

'Thanks, Rose, that's a weight off my mind. My only worry now is if Calum turns up to watch football with Aly on Saturday afternoon and we don't get a chance to set up for the party... I don't want him there before eight.'

'Oh, I might be able to sort that.' Rose detects a flicker of surprise, then keen interest on Shona's part. With her head on one side and a look of mischievous amusement in her eyes, the resemblance between brother and sister is marked. Avoiding Shona's gaze, Rose continues. 'You know Calum and I are planning an exhibition?'

Shona nods. 'Aye, he was telling us about it the other night. He said it was one of your brainwaves.'

'Well, that remains to be seen, but the thing is, I can easily ask him over for a meeting about it. There's a lot we need to discuss and Saturday would be a good day to do it. If you send Donald for the stuff in the morning I'll invite Calum over for tea and try and keep him there for a couple of hours. Does that sound okay?'

'Rose, you're a wonder! Are you used to all this cloak and dagger stuff then?'

'I'm a double agent on the run from MI5, Shona. We call this deep cover.'

Shona laughs uproariously at the modest witticism and claps a hand on Rose's back. 'D'you know what we say, Rose? "A man may do without a brother – but not without a neighbour"! '

***

Rose staggers through the front door with her library books and shopping and announces, 'Spaghetti Bolognese tonight. Calum's coming for supper.'

Megan looks up from her magazine. 'Yummy!'

'Is that referring to Calum or my Spag Bol?'

'Both, I suppose. You didn't invite him round on my account, did you?'

'No, of course not! But I think you'll enjoy an evening of his company. You can talk to him about the outdoor centre on Raasay. He might have some contacts there. And I'm afraid I need to talk to him about the exhibition. You have my permission to doze off when we start talking poetry... Or better still, go and do the dishes.'

'Is Calum bringing anyone?'

'No. It'll just be the three of us. Although I suppose I could give Angus the Post a ring... He'd no doubt appreciate a bit of home cooking.'

'Angus the Post? Is he *thick* or something?'

'No, that's his job. He delivers the post in a little red van. Drives like a maniac.'

'Is Angus another one of your handsome Hebrideans?'

'Well, I'm sure his wife Effie thought so before she passed away.'

'Mum, how *old* is Angus?'

'Well, now,' Rose says confidentially, 'Nobody actually knows, but the general opinion is somewhere between sixty and death.'

***

As they prepare for the evening Rose and Megan are in high spirits. After a long bath Megan emerges, fragrant and flamboyant in tight-fitting black trousers and white shirt. She would look boyish were it not for her pendulous earrings and a quantity of eye make-up.

'How do I look?'

Rose looks up from her chopping board and is speechless for a moment. Megan wrinkles her nose. 'Too dressy? I haven't brought anything else apart from jeans and sweaters.'

'No, you look... gorgeous. I was just surprised... It's silly but I always forget how beautiful you are.'

'Well, thanks, but everyone always said I take after you. Aren't you dressing up?'

Rose laughs self-consciously. 'No, I'm not bothering. It's only Calum. And I haven't really got time now – he'll be here soon.'

'Can I help?'

'Well, you could wash that lettuce – no, that's a dirty job, you'll spoil your blouse... You could chop some tomatoes for the salad and maybe that green pepper. There's a sharp knife by the chopping board.'

Megan switches on the radio. 'Do you mind?'

'No, go ahead.'

Rose does mind. She would have liked to talk, to be companionable over the food preparation, the pair of them, as it was once, before Gavin.

***

154

Megan is rolling out pastry for jam tarts and singing.

'*The Queen of Hearts*
She made some tarts
All on a summer's day...'

Rose leans across and sprinkles flour over the rolling pin. 'Don't press too hard, Megan. You need a light touch with pastry. We won't be able to peel it off the worktop if you flatten it too much.'

'I'm going to be a cook when I grow up.'

'Oh, good. You can cook me lots of lovely dinners.'

'And I'll make you a cake *every* day.'

'Ooh, delicious! I shall get very fat.'

'Fiona Fraser's mummy is very fat.'

'She's not fat, darling, she's pregnant. That means she's going to have a baby. Fiona will soon have a baby brother or sister.'

'Which?'

'I don't know. No one will know till the baby's born.'

'I'd like to have a baby brother.'

Rose says nothing.

'Can I, Mummy?'

'What, darling?'

'Can I have a baby brother?'

'No, Megan.'

'A sister?'

'No, darling, I'm not going to have any more children.'

'Why not?'

'Because... I don't have a daddy for them. You need a daddy to make babies.'

'Can't you *get* one?'

'I don't want one! And I don't want any more babies. I've got you and you've got me and that suits me just fine.' Rose puts her arm round her daughter and kisses the top of her head.

Megan rolls out her pastry, thinner and thinner, until it creeps off the end of the worktop and hangs, suspended in the air.

'But *I'd* like a baby brother... *Or* a daddy... Daddies throw you up in the air and catch you!'

Megan re-tunes the radio until she finds some pop music then turns up the volume. She sings and moves her body in time to the music. As she stirs the meat sauce Rose watches her daughter and smiles. 'Shall we have a drink?'

'Yeah, great.'

Megan resumes her singing and begins to gesticulate with the knife to the beat of the music. Rose pours two large glasses of red wine and raises one to Megan. '*Slàinte!*'

'Cheers!' Megan grins at her over the rim of her glass and drinks deeply.

An old Supremes number starts up and Rose closes her eyes. 'Ah, now *this* is what I call rock music! They don't make them like this any more!' Rose starts to sing *Stop in the name of love* and Megan joins in, dancing round the kitchen, glass in one hand, knife in the other, holding it like a microphone. Rose starts to giggle.

Afterwards, Rose realises that she heard the knock, heard a voice call out, so she wasn't as startled as Megan when Calum suddenly pushed open the kitchen door.

As Megan spins round, the contents of her glass fly though the air and splash onto her shirt. Her hand, holding the knife, swings round towards Calum, inches from his chest. Before Rose can even register what is happening, Calum has grabbed Megan's wrist and yanked her arm up in the air. With his other hand he has pushed her against the wall and holds her there, pinioned with his forearm across her chest. The knife clatters to the floor. Megan is screaming. Rose has to shout to make herself heard.

'Calum, let her go! *Calum*! Look at me!'

He swivels his head round, still holding Megan pinned to the wall. He looks frightened and confused. Suddenly his body sags and he releases Megan who runs from the kitchen, sobbing. Grey-faced, Calum stares at the knife on the floor. 'Jesus Christ *almighty*...' Rose stoops to pick it up, then drops it quickly into the sink. Calum is still staring at the floor. 'Did I hurt her?'

'No, I don't think so. You just scared her half to death.'

His voice is barely a whisper. 'I just saw the knife... coming towards me. She looked like Davy from behind... the short hair... and the knife... *Jesus*, I'm sorry, Rose! You must think I'm a bloody maniac! Are you sure I didn't hurt her?'

'I'll go and check in a moment but I don't think so. You pinned her up against the wall with your body weight. You didn't grab her throat or anything.'

'Thank Christ for that...' There is an awkward silence, then Calum starts to speak rapidly. 'They taught us self-defence at school. In Glasgow, I mean... How to protect ourselves without damaging the kids. There are ways. "Reasonable restraint" they call it. Anything more than that and you can be done for assault – ' Rose lays a hand on his arm and he stops talking. 'Oh, Christ, Rose – should I go and apologise, or should I just leave?'

'You're going nowhere. You're going to sit down and have a drink while I go and explain to Megan. Do you mind if I tell her – about your being attacked?'

'No, not if you think it will help.'

'Did you bring a bottle of whisky?'

'Aye.' He produces a half bottle from inside his jacket. Rose takes three glasses out of the cupboard and pours a generous measure into each. She hands one to Calum.

'Start drinking.' She picks up the other two glasses. 'I'll be back in a little while. Don't you dare go away. And if you could manage to stir the contents of that saucepan now and again I think there's a good chance we might salvage the evening.'

She kisses him on the cheek and leaves him standing in the middle of the kitchen, staring at his glass.

When, some time later, the two women emerge from Rose's bedroom, Megan has changed her wine-soaked shirt and re-touched her eye make-up. As they walk into the sitting room Calum gets up quickly from the sofa.

'Megan, I'm so sorry. I offered to leave but Rose said I'd to stay and in any case I wanted to apologise... Did I hurt you?'

'No, you didn't actually. I was screaming blue murder because you frightened me, that's all. I didn't even hear you come into the kitchen. The first thing I knew, I was up against the wall. I didn't even realise it was you – I thought it was some mad axe-man.'

'Aye, well, you would... I'm really sorry.'

'It's okay, Mum's explained. About what happened to you. It must have been awful.'

'Aye, I suppose it was. It didn't feel like it at the time.' He shrugs. 'You cope. You even laugh about it afterwards. Life goes on. But it seems these things don't go away...' He shakes his head, as if in disbelief. 'It happened five years ago! But when I walked into the kitchen and saw that knife coming at me, honest to God, I was *there*... You were Davy! All I could think was, I had to get the knife off you before someone got hurt... I'm so sorry, Megan.'

'Stop apologising – I'm fine. It's my own stupid fault anyway for dancing round the kitchen wielding a knife!' Megan is horrified to see that Calum's eyes are wet and vacant and that he has started to shake. 'Mum – get him another whisky.'

Rose goes to retrieve the whisky bottle from the kitchen. When she returns Megan has an arm round Calum and is repeating softly, 'It's okay... *really*... it's okay!'

CHAPTER EIGHT

S UPPER IS PAINFUL. Calum drinks steadily, first whisky, then wine. There is brittle laughter, the tinkle of our bright, tight female voices, too high-pitched, undercut by Calum's dry, deadpan one-liners.

But Megan is captivated. And captivating.

Drunk, unreasonable, I hate her, hate myself and pour us all another drink.

Megan announces that she will wash up. Calum offers to help, not quite making it out of his armchair. I rouse myself and insist he remain seated. Megan doesn't actually scowl at me but I'm sure she wants to. Hearing her hum and clatter in the kitchen I fear for the china.

Calum is silent. Sprawled and sunk into his chair, his long legs extended across the hearth rug towards the wood-burner, he appears to doze, then murmurs, 'I'm neither as drunk nor as merry as I'm pretending to be, Rose.'

'No. I know.'

The stove hisses and splutters. Calum sighs.

'I ought to go. But I don't want to...'

'So stay.'

'It's very pleasant sitting here... Peaceful. Domestic.' He swivels his head, looks at me and smiles. 'You should be sewing.'

'I can if you like – I hate sitting with my hands idle.'

'Go on, fetch your sewing, woman. Pander to my dark fantasies.'

'It will have to be some hand-quilting. I draw the line at darning socks.'

As I stitch I remember...

The door ajar. Distant blue hills and the white sparkle of a cottage clinging to the curve of the road. Megan's daisies in a jug by the window, stark simplicity, white against the deep dark of the loch. The wind-blown sky changing constantly, like the sea. The first raindrops begin to fall on hills now purple. Wind whips washing on a line.

Joy.

Joy.

My chair creaks. You stir. I look up from my sewing and gaze at your dozing profile, your beauty still a visceral blow.

I shake my head in habitual disbelief, that you should be here, with *me*, that you should be *you*.

What is it that moves me so? Your eyes are closed, your body clothed, your hands, frosted with golden hairs, lie limp, sculpted in your lap, but my breath comes unevenly. I think it impossible to withstand the assault, if it comes, of your open eyes. I will not be able to contain the intensity, the immensity of what I feel for you. Not simple love, nor simpler lust, but an overwhelming need for you that I fear will annihilate me, or at least unfit me for my normal existence of making tea, cooking supper, feeding cats.

Your eyes open slowly, reluctantly and you breathe deeply. Your chest rises and falls and I note, with tender irrelevance, a loose button suspended on a wisp of thread.

If you do not touch me, hold me, now Gavin, I shall surely die...

I remember the banality of love.

Calum shifts in his chair. 'You're thinking of Gavin.'

Rose looks up from her sewing, startled. 'Yes, I was. How did you know?'

'A look in your eye. And your breathing changed. I'm getting to know the signs.'

'I was thinking of Gavin, yes,' Rose examines her stitching closely. 'But I wasn't *wanting* him.' She looks up, into Calum's eyes, a darker, brighter blue than Gavin's. 'I was remembering... Remembering a time when I did want him. Very badly.'

'And what put that in your head?'

Rose arches her brows. 'I can't imagine,' she says primly, but the corners of her mouth are twitching. Calum sinks down into his armchair, smiling. She gives him a beady look. 'I suppose you're going to sit there now looking insufferably smug.'

He laughs and shakes his head. 'Never underestimate the size of the Highlander's inferiority complex. No, I was just thinking of the old hippy excuse for sexual promiscuity.'

Rose frowns. 'Remind this old hippy.'

'If you can't be with the one you love, then love the one you're with.'

Megan puts her head round the door and calls, 'Who's for coffee?'

Calum has gone. The two women sit either side of his empty chair. Megan yawns.

'Tired?'

'Mmm... It's very late.'

'Yes. I tend to be a bit of a night owl. You don't need to keep me company, you know.'

'I don't think I can be bothered to move... You know, I've been trying to figure out what it is that's odd about this house.'

'Odd? In what way?'

'Well, there's something I can't quite put my finger on... It's full of all the old familiar things – the kitchen table, this armchair, the quilts...'

'There are lots of new things too. Well, new to you. They're actually second-hand.'

'Yes, but they're your *style*. They go with all the old stuff. *Our* old stuff. They blend in, so everything seems very familiar...'

'So what's odd? Have you worked it out yet?'

Megan looks around the room, puzzled. Rose remembers games of I-spy and a cross little face. She realises then what Megan means about the room, knows what she is about to say, but it is too late to change the subject.

'There are no photographs!' Megan says triumphantly.

'No. There aren't.'

'There isn't a single one anywhere! Our house used to be full of photos, do you remember? My baby photos and school photos – I hated them but you always bought them. And there were holiday photos with Penny and John at Whitby... and we had photos of you winning prizes and cups for your quilts. You used to hide them behind the letter-rack on the mantelpiece. And there were loads of photos of Gavin on his expedit – '

The words die on Megan's lips and she puts her hand over her mouth. Neither woman speaks for several moments.

'I'm sorry, Mum... Oh, God, how could I be so *stupid*!'

'It's okay, Megan. I could see where this conversation was going to end up – I just couldn't divert it in time.'

'I wasn't thinking! I was just making conversation, remembering how things used to be, before...'

'Yes, I know.' Rose puts her sewing down and takes a deep breath. 'There are no photos. I destroyed every photo of Gavin I could lay my hands on, even the expedition team shots – all those hopeful, shining faces, smiling for posterity. Some of them were my friends and some of them never returned...' Her voice catches. 'I can't believe I did that. I must have been mad. But then, as I recall, I was.'

'Mum – '

Rose ignores her. 'I destroyed all the holiday photos I took of you and Gavin. Afterwards I realised I hadn't actually *had* many photos that didn't include Gavin.' She smiles. 'Do you remember how he'd always hog the camera? He was so bloody photogenic – and didn't he know it! After I'd destroyed all the evidence, all I could see was gaps, blank spaces where my life had been. So I took down all the rest of the photos, the ones that *weren't* of Gavin – there weren't that many – and put them away in a box. They're in my bedroom somewhere. It was a great relief really, not to have my past staring back at me, not ever having to look at the great gaping hole where Gavin had been.' She pauses. 'I suppose you still have some photos of him?'

'Yes. A few.'

'Don't ever show them to me.'

'No. No, I won't.'

Rose picks up her sewing again and peers at her stitches. She lays the work aside and rubs her eyes. 'I can't see. I'm going to bed.'

'Mum...'

'I don't want to talk about it any more, Megan. It's been a hell of an evening, what with one thing and another. I've had enough. I'll leave you to turn out the lights. Goodnight.'

At 4.00am Rose abandons the struggle to sleep and sits up in bed, her head throbbing, throat parched. Shivering, she gets out of bed, pulls on a dressing-gown and opens the wardrobe door. Taking a battered buff envelope from a box she returns to bed.

The envelope contains photographs of various sizes, some of them dog-eared, some mounted in card folders. She skims through them quickly. She pauses at a creased black and white photo of a little girl in an elaborately tiered and be-ribboned party dress. The girl wears shiny black shoes and drooping long white socks. She stands proudly beside a new bicycle.

Rose's tenth birthday. She remembers that the bicycle was blue and silver. The dress was pink, as were the ribbons at the end of her auburn plaits from which her frizzy corkscrew curls were already beginning to escape. She had hated the dress, loved the bicycle. To her child's mind the bicycle had seemed like a reward for having to wear the pink dress.

Rose continues her search. When she reaches the last photograph she repeats the process, slowly this time, examining each photo carefully. Eventually she is satisfied.

There are no photos of Gavin.

She knows there are no photos of Gavin because she destroyed them all, deliberately, systematically and without exception. But Rose hoped she might have missed one, that two photos might have stuck together, that Gavin might appear, faint, out of focus, uncharacteristically self-effacing in a wedding group perhaps. But Rose was thorough. Gavin is conspicuous by his absence.

On top of the pile is a photo of Megan in hill-walking gear, striking a triumphant 'Hillary pose' on the summit of Ben Nevis, having completed her first ascent, aged fourteen. Gavin had taken the photo of Megan smiling into the sun, her eyes screwed up against the bright light.

Rose leans forward and holds the photo closer to the bedside lamp. On the ground in front of Megan is a shadow. A man's shadow. The photographer's shadow thrown by the sunlight into the foreground of the picture. It could be anybody but Rose knows it is Gavin. She can in any case just discern the serrated shadow of his hair; she recognises the angle of his tilted hips.

It is Gavin.

She thought she had destroyed every last trace. She had meant to. Rose stares at the photo for a long time, her stomach churning. She presses the shadow briefly to her lips. Fighting waves of nausea and self-disgust she shuffles the photo back into the middle of the pile then pushes them into the envelope. She drops it onto the floor and turns out the light.

Staring into the darkness, she waits for sleep.

The following morning Megan wakes early after a fitful night's sleep. She lies in bed listening out for the noise of traffic, dogs barking, children playing. There is nothing. A wall of silence except for the hush of the sea.

Irritated, she gets up and makes herself a cup of coffee. There is no sound yet from Rose's room. Megan pulls on her trainers and heads for the beach where there will at least be gulls for company.

Chilled and miserable, Megan is considering turning back for the consolations of a cooked breakfast when she sees a familiar figure running along the beach. She waves. Calum waves back and jogs towards her.

'Good morning, Megan! You're up early.' He stands panting, hands on hips.

'Couldn't sleep. Too much booze I expect.'

'Is there such a thing now? I'll take your word for it.'

'Are you in training?'

'No, I just like to run. It helps me think. Energises me. And it's a great morning for it. Will you just look at that sky...'

'Yes, it's very beautiful,' Megan says, without much enthusiasm. 'But I don't know how you stand the *quiet*.'

Calum grins. 'Is the lack of nightclubs beginning to get to you? If you're wanting a bit of excitement, have a word with my sister... She could take you along to her ceilidh-robics class – if you think you're up to it.'

'Ceilidh *what*?'

'Ceilidh-robics. It's the next big thing. Well, on Uist anyway.'

'You have to be kidding.'

'Honest to God. Ask Shona. Fridays at eight. Don't be late.'

'I think you're having me on. I may be gone by Friday anyway.'

'Where are you off to?'

'I'm going to Skye to see a guy about a job at the outdoor centre on Raasay. Mum said you might know something about it.'

'Aye, I worked there for a while. I used to live on Skye and I did a season teaching at the centre.'

'Climbing?'

'Aye, and water sports – kayaking, windsurfing. It's a grand way to spend a summer. What's the job?'

'Climbing instructor. Just beginners. Kids mostly, on single pitch routes. Hill safety, rope management, just basics. They're looking for more female instructors.'

'I didn't realise you climbed.'

'Gavin taught me. Much to Mum's disgust. Then I got bitten by the bug, as you do. I got bored doing Highers,

168

dropped out of school and bummed around a bit doing dead-end jobs for money. Now I'm wondering if I can make a career out of my hobby. I can't decide whether to go back to college and try and get some qualifications or to get work experience somewhere like Raasay.' She pauses and looks up at him.

Calum looks surprised. 'Are you asking my advice?'

'Yes, I suppose I am.'

'Well, now – that's a tough one. Raasay would be very good experience and I'm sure you'd love it, but...' He shrugs. 'Och, I'm a teacher and you know what I'm going to say.'

Megan pulls a face. 'Go back to college.'

'Raasay will always be there! The jobs will always be there. Outdoor education is a real growth industry. You'll not enjoy college if you're the oldest student on the course and the longer you stay out of full-time education the harder it will be to return.' He shakes his head and sighs. 'Tragic, isn't it? The way dynamic, young teachers degenerate so rapidly into boring old farts.'

Megan laughs. 'You certainly haven't! I wish you'd been teaching me English – I probably wouldn't have quit.'

'Don't be deceived – I make my pupils' lives a misery with my relentless enthusiasm.'

'That's not what Mum says. She says they adore you.'

'Unlikely, but if they do it's probably because I explain the smutty bits in Shakespeare. You're shivering. Shall we jog for a wee while? The going's good on the wet sand.'

'Yeah, great.'

***

169

When Rose finally draws her bedroom curtains and faces the morning she is surprised to see two figures running side by side along the fringe of the sea. She is about to pick up the binoculars she keeps on the windowsill, then realises she doesn't need them. She knows the figures are Calum and Megan.

Calum is skimming stones.

Megan sits on a rock, counting the bounces. 'Four... Best score so far.'

'I'm just warming up. The next one will make it to St. Kilda.'

'Who's she?'

'"She" is a group of islands. Out there, forty-five miles to the west. At the edge of the world. You can just about see them on the horizon today.' He points.

'Does anybody live there?'

'Not any more.' Calum skims another stone. 'But there were folk living there until 1930.'

'Really?'

'Aye. They used to come here for the night life...' Megan lobs a shell at him. Calum ducks. 'Ah, the bright lights of Lochmaddy... Except that in 1930 they weren't that bright because we didn't get electricity until the '60s.'

'How on earth did people survive out there?'

'On St. Kilda? Bird-hunting. The men-folk used to climb the cliffs in their bare feet to rob nests of eggs and young birds.'

'Why bare feet?'

'Better grip. But many died in the attempt. The community survived until they aroused the interest of Victorian missionaries and tourists. The islanders started to barter for goods and they lost their economic independence. Then their number was reduced by imported diseases – they had no resistance to mainland bugs. Eventually the population got so small that living there was no longer viable. The last few islanders were evacuated in 1930 at their own request.'

'Have you ever been there?'

'Aye, once, when I was a boy. Angus the Post – have you met Angus yet? – his mother was born there. He took her back for a visit. She wanted to see the old place again before she died. Angus took my parents and me along for the ride. He had his own boat. I was that excited, I was sick before we even put to sea... And I was plenty sick while we were at sea. It's a hell of a journey.'

'What was it like when you got there?'

'Beautiful. Eerie. And the noisiest place on earth.'

'How come?'

'The bird colonies. There's two hundred and fifty thousand pairs out there. Gannets, puffins, fulmars... That's half a million birds. You can't hear yourself think.' Calum skims another stone out towards St. Kilda. 'Och, maybe that's no bad thing...'

***

Calum and Megan walk along the shoreline side by side, hands plunged in coat pockets, collars turned up against the wind.

'Did you tell Rose where you were going?'

'No. I thought I'd just be out for a few minutes. She was still in bed.'

'Should you be heading back, maybe? She might be worried about you.'

'Yes, I suppose so. Though I must say she does seem a lot more relaxed here than she did back in Fort William. She thinks this place is Heaven. She feels she's finally got away from Gavin, I suppose.'

Calum is silent for a moment. 'That's not my impression.'

'No?'

'No. She may be physically distant from him and distant in time – she hasn't seen him for five years, right?' Megan nods. 'But she's still living with him. He's in her thoughts, inside her head... I wouldn't be surprised if she actually talks to him. No, I don't believe Rose has escaped.' He mutters to himself. *'The mind is its own place and in itself can make a heaven of Hell, a hell of Heaven.'*

'What's that?'

'Some lines by Milton. From the appropriately titled *Paradise Lost*.' Megan looks baffled. 'It seems to me,' Calum explains, 'that Rose carries her own hell around with her in her head, with Gavin starring as the Prince of Darkness.'

'He really wasn't that bad, you know,' Megan says sharply.

'No, I don't suppose he was. I was just telling you how I think Rose sees things. I'm sorry if I spoke out of turn.'

'That's okay – it's not as if Gavin was my dad. But my loyalties were always divided. She was hell to live with at times. I don't know how he put up with it.'

'He loved her, I suppose.'

'He must have... He did try to explain to her about the climbing, the expeditions. She was always so miserable and worried when he was away, convinced he was going to come home in a body bag.'

'Aye, well, that's understandable – there's a good chance of that when you're engaged in the kind of high-risk stuff Gavin was into.'

'He always said he would know when his time was up, would know when to quit.'

Calum laughs softly. 'Aye, we all say that.'

'Gavin was so confident... He never even thought he might fall, let alone die. He said you could tell, you got a feeling who was not going to make it, who wouldn't be coming back. Sometimes it was obvious – some guys became obsessed, you know? Really out there on the edge. Gavin said that type was "too committed to survive", it was only a matter of time... He laughed at men like that. He laughed at the whole bloody thing. Nothing seemed to touch him – cold, pain, exhaustion, injury, even the death of his friends.'

'It's a survival mechanism. You tell yourself you're invincible.'

'Gavin thought he was. But he was wrong.' Megan turns away from Calum and looks out towards St. Kilda. 'He couldn't handle the split with Mum... and what happened to her afterwards. He couldn't laugh about that. He couldn't put it behind him and move on. I think it broke his heart. Which came as a terrible shock to Gavin Duffy, climber, athlete and super-stud,' Megan says harshly. 'Because up till then he hadn't realised he *had* a heart.'

'Gavin Duffy?'

Megan looks back, surprised. 'Yes. Did you know him?'

'No... I think I may have met him once. Well, I met a guy called Gavin Duffy. Maybe it wasn't Rose's Gavin.'

'White-blond hair, blue eyes. Very good-looking. Shorter than you. He was covered in freckles in summer.' Calum is nodding his head slowly. 'Where did you meet him?'

'I don't remember... Climbing on Skye most probably. Megan, you won't mention this to Rose? I think it might upset her.'

'You must be joking! I would never mention Gavin in Mum's presence.' Remembering her blunder of the previous evening, Megan says hurriedly, 'I think I'd better be heading back. She'll be wondering where I've got to. Do you want to come and have some coffee?'

'No, thanks. I'm supposed to be playing football later with my nephew who will undoubtedly thrash me. Shona's giving me lunch as a consolation prize.'

'Maybe see you later then?'

'Aye. Will you thank Rose for me, for the supper last night?'

'I think you already did that. Several times.'

***

They are walking back along the beach together. If they look up now they'll see me at the window and think I've been spying on them.

Have I?

Megan is turning off towards the house, she's trudging up though the dry sand above the high-tide line. But Calum is standing at the water's edge, facing out to sea. The wind lifts his hair and fills his billowing jacket like a sail. It must be a trick of the light, a distortion of perspective that makes him look so small, so dark against the white sand. He stands hunched, still, like a cormorant, black, waiting on a rock.

CHAPTER NINE

ON SUNDAY THE WEATHER IS TOO BAD to consider even the shortest of walks. Rose offers to drive Megan around the island, but her daughter shows little interest in sightseeing and settles down on the sofa with one of Shona's paperback thrillers. Sitting with her sewing by the wood-burner, Rose breaks a long silence.

'Megan, I don't know how to ask this without sounding like I'm trying to get rid of you, but have you decided yet when you're going home?'

Megan looks up from her book. 'No, not really. Am I getting in the way then?'

'No, not at *all*,' Rose lies, 'It's just that there's a party on Saturday night. It's Calum's fortieth birthday and Shona's throwing a surprise party for him. I wondered... if you'll still be here?'

'Well, I had been thinking about going at the end of the week,' Megan says vaguely, 'But I suppose I could stay for the party. Sounds fun.'

'Oh, I don't know about that... There'll be all sorts of people there – neighbours, elderly folk and Shona's children of course... There won't be many young people. You might find it all a bit... dull,' Rose says hopefully.

Megan is not discouraged. 'No, I'd like to go. It'll be worth it to see Calum's face when he shows up. You never know – maybe some of his climbing mates will come.'

'Shona's certainly invited them. The ones on Skye might come over on the ferry. I don't really know who's coming, I'm just hiding the booze. And I said I'd make a big lasagne as a contribution to the food... What's wrong?'

Megan is chewing her lip and looking worried. 'I've got a problem.'

'Oh, don't worry if you can't spare the time – I'm sure Shona doesn't really expect you to come. You'd probably be very bored anyway.'

'No, it's not that, it's just that I don't have anything to wear. I wasn't expecting to have to socialise. Could I have a look through your wardrobe? You might have something I could borrow.'

'My clothes will all be much too big for you.'

'I could wear one of your shapeless, hippy things with a big belt.'

Ignoring the slur, Rose replies tartly, 'I don't think I have any big belts.'

'Well, a scarf or something?'

'I'm much taller than you, Megan – my clothes will be too long.'

'I could borrow some high heels. We take the same size.'

'I don't have any! I gave them all to Oxfam knowing I wouldn't need them here. Uist isn't exactly the last word in trend-setting fashion, you know. But by all means, ransack my wardrobe. Be my guest! I'm flattered you think I possess anything that you're prepared to be seen dead in.'

'Thanks, Mum.' Megan fails to notice Rose's air of patient martyrdom and returns to her book.

After an uneventful day spent reading, dozing and eating the food that is put in front of her, Megan claims she needs an early night and retires to her bed in the workroom. Sitting up late with her sewing, Rose wonders – not for the first time – what has brought Megan to Uist.

On Monday morning Shona appears at the back door and beams at Rose, her eyebrows mobile. 'Rose,' she hisses, 'Could I have a wee word?' She looks anxiously over her shoulder.

'Come in, Shona. Would you like a coffee?'

'In a while maybe. I was wanting to ask you – is it okay if I bring over some contraband?' Rose looks puzzled. 'Some of the party food and drink,' Shona whispers.

Rose wonders who Shona thinks might overhear their conversation, then realises with a smile that the party conspiracy is simply the latest form of home-made entertainment in what must be a hard and monotonous life.

'Yes, of course, Shona. Shall I come over and give you a hand?'

'Och, no – I'll load up the car and drive over. You're sure it's no bother now?'

'I'm honoured to be part of the plot. Does Calum really have no idea?'

'No – even the bairns don't know! They think I'm just batch-baking for the freezer. Put the kettle on, Rose – I'll away and fetch The Goods,' Shona says with upper case emphasis and a wink.

***

Shona clearly intends to go one better than Our Lord and feed the five thousand not with loaves and fishes, but sausage rolls, mini-pizzas, pâté and quiche. Rose's freezer is soon filled to capacity. Cardboard boxes full of beer and whisky are unloaded and concealed in the workroom. Megan, making coffee in the kitchen, laughs out loud as Shona appears at the back door stooping under her final load – a full black bin-liner carried over her shoulder.

'Shona, you look like Father Christmas! What on *earth* have you got in there?'

'Och, it's just a few wee bags of crisps.'

Later the weather improves and Rose insists on taking Megan out for a drive to see the island. They set off heading south on the road that circles North Uist with Rose pointing out sites – and sights – of interest as they drive.

'On the other side of those dunes is the Atlantic.' She winds down the window. 'Hear that roar? You should see those breakers... There's nothing between us and Canada. It can be pretty wild at this time of year, but glorious in the summer. Mile after mile of clean, empty beaches. A man and a dog constitute a crowd. You feel as if you've been shipwrecked on a desert island... On your right now we have the RSPB reserve, Balranald. A lot of the tourists come here for the birds... It's a lovely walk in the spring and summer. You've come at the wrong time of year really...' Rose looks sideways at Megan who is staring out of the window, refusing to be drawn on the purpose of her visit.

'What are those piles of bricks outside people's houses?'

'Bricks?'

'Well, they look a bit like bricks – black blocks of something.'

'Oh, the peat stacks! It's fuel – peat cut into brickettes. They make a lovely fire when they're dry. That's the distinctive smell in the air here – peat burning on open fires. Of course not many people have fires nowadays – they've gone over to central heating like everyone else. The attraction of free fuel can't compete with the convenience of flicking a switch for instant warmth. But some people still stick to the old ways and cut the peats in the summer, then bring them home and stack them carefully to dry out. It's quite a knack. Some of the stacks are so carefully built they're almost works of art. I've photographed some of them.'

They drive on through the drizzle, meeting few cars on the single-track road. Rose swerves to avoid a suicidal black-faced ewe that suddenly decides the grass is greener on the other side of the road. Surveying the low-lying, boggy and largely uninhabited terrain, Megan says, 'There are more sheep than people!'

'Oh, almost certainly,' Rose answers.

'It's kind of... *bleak*, isn't it?'

'Do you think so? I think it's rather beautiful, but I admit it's an acquired taste. I love all the subtle shades of green and brown, the moss and lichen and the heather – it's like a glorious tapestry... And you have such vast expanses of sky here. A bit like Norfolk, but the light is quite different here – it's a northern light, much brighter, *cleaner*. A lot of artists live and work here because they like the light.'

'But it's all so flat. So exposed.'

'Well, yes, if you compare it to Skye or the Highlands, it's flat. But we've got some decent hills – Ben Lee and Eaval. Eaval's the wedge-shaped hill that gives Uist its distinctive outline... It feels flat here because you can see so far. There are no big buildings in the way to block the view, so when you look what you see is mostly sky.'

'Skye?'

'Not Skye, the island – the blue stuff,' Rose says, pointing upwards. She falls silent, disappointed that her island has been found wanting in topographical interest.

They drive southwards over the causeway to Grimsay, the tiny stepping-stone island between Uist and Benbecula and Rose stops the car at the short causeway leading to Benbecula. The walls at the side of the road are low and the wind is whipping waves into a frenzy right across the road.

'I wouldn't fancy walking across there now,' Megan says.

'Even driving can be a bit hairy. But people used to walk across before the causeway – they waded across or went on horseback at low tide. Benbecula comes from the Gaelic *Beinn a' bh-fhaodhla* which means Mountain of the Fords – although I think calling Rueval a mountain is pushing it a bit... The high school where Calum teaches is on Benbecula. It's the only one so all the older kids go there. There's another causeway on the other side of Benbecula taking you on to South Uist. Soon there'll be yet another to take you over to Eriskay, which is a really tiny little island. Would you like to continue south? Or we can turn back and circle North Uist. We could have tea at the Arts Centre in Lochmaddy.'

'Is that where you're holding your exhibition?'

'Yes. And they do jolly good home baking.'

'Well, I didn't really fancy crossing that causeway in this wind.'

'Where's your spirit of adventure, child? Lochmaddy it is, then.'

Rose suddenly stops the car in what appears to be the middle of nowhere and turns to Megan. 'Fancy taking in a stone circle as the rain's stopped?'

'Yes – is it spooky?'

'No, not really. Utterly benign in fact. But I think there's a certain energy there... Well, I can feel it. See what you think.'

They tramp a little way across the heathery moorland, ascending Ben Langass, a low hill, until they come upon a modest collection of lichen-covered stones, the largest not much bigger than a man. Megan doesn't conceal her disappointment. 'Oh... It's not exactly Stonehenge, is it?'

'I didn't say it was. But look at the view – isn't it fantastic?' From their elevated position the women can see as much water as land. 'If you view North Uist from the air it looks like lace – there are so many small lochs. It's a fisherman's paradise. About a third of it is water and the sea is clawing back more land all the time. We'll be the first to disappear when the icecaps melt.'

'What's the big land mass on the horizon?'

'Skye.'

'It looks huge!'

'It is huge, compared to Uist.'

'So what's this stone circle called?'

'It's known as *Pobull Fhinn*.'

'Which means?'

'Finn's People. Because of the scale of the stones I suppose. They aren't very big.'

'And you say you can feel an energy here?'

'Can't you? Inside the actual circle?'

Megan takes a step further into the circle and looks around. 'No... I don't think so.'

'Oh, I expect I imagine it.'

'Shall I test you?'

'How?'

'Shut your eyes and I'll walk you round and you tell me when you think you're inside the circle.'

'Gosh, how very scientific! Okay... Don't walk me into a bog will you?'

Megan takes Rose's arm and leads her, giggling at first, on a meandering route. 'Shut up and concentrate, mother! This is a scientific experiment into the paranormal. And no peeping!' Rose stumbles forward, led by Megan who eventually comes to an abrupt standstill. 'Right – keep your eyes shut. Where are we now?'

'Wait a minute, I have to feel... No... no, we're not inside it. Am I right?'

'I'm not saying. Come on, we're off again.'

After a few moments Megan brings Rose to a halt again and waits.

'Oh yes... I think we are... We *are* inside the circle now.' Without a word Megan drags Rose back and forth and then halts again. Rose says tentatively, 'Yes, I *think* we're still inside... I'm pretty certain...'

'Open your eyes.'

Rose looks about her, blinking. 'We are!'

'Yes. And you were right the other two times as well.'

'*Was* I?'

'How do you do it?'

'Can't *you* feel it? I get a sort of humming feeling... I don't know how to describe it really... It's just a kind of energy that I pick up.' Rose shrugs. 'It sounds really silly – but when I'm inside the circle my *teeth* vibrate...'

The women stop for tea at *Taigh Chearsabhagh* in Lochmaddy, the capital of North Uist, a quiet coastal village enlivened by the comings and goings of the ferry to Skye. Rose shows Megan the exhibition space and the heritage museum and they settle down in the cheerful café with a pot of tea and cakes.

Megan tucks in happily. 'So what is this place exactly?'

'An arts centre... a meeting place... a café... They run workshops here and sell souvenirs to tourists and they make lovely cakes. It's actually a very old building and it stands on the site of an even older one – *Taigh an t-Salainn* – which means The Salt House. It was built in the early seventeenth century to provide salt for the herring industry. King Charles I set up a herring fishery here, hoping to make a fast buck out of the fishing grounds of the Minches. Hard to imagine this sleepy little village as a hive of industry, isn't it? And before that it was a rendezvous for pirates. But now it's quite respectable, unfortunately. More tea?'

'No, I'm fine, thanks.'

'Well, come outside and I'll show you where I was sitting when I decided I was going to come and live here.'

Rose leads Megan away from *Taigh Chearsabhagh* to a little roadside promontory overlooking a small bay where a bench is placed to take advantage of the view eastwards, a view of the sea littered with countless little islands and skerries through which the Skye ferry is obliged to weave its way to berth at Lochmaddy.

'This is one of my favourite spots. Isn't it gorgeous? With the bay and all those little islands... And it's always so calm here, positively balmy. Listen – you can't hear anything but seabirds and waves lapping... I was sitting here waiting for the ferry to Skye. I thought Skye was where I was going to live. I'd stayed there with Gavin, it was familiar and handy for the mainland... Then while I was sitting on this bench – I think it was May, I can remember there were wild flowers scenting the air – Uist just grabbed hold of me by the lapels and said, "Come and live here!" So I did. And I love it, I absolutely *love* it. And I love that Gavin was never here, that you've never been here. It's *my* place, I can re-invent myself here. Begin all over again without being encumbered by my past. Does that make sense?'

'Yes, it does. But it sounds so... *hard*. I wish you had more support, Mum. More friends, more of a social life.'

'Oh, my life wouldn't suit you – wouldn't suit most people, I suppose. But I didn't want excitement or commitments, or any kind of... *complications*. And people, relationships bring all those things, don't they? Friends, lovers, husbands, children – they all make life complicated. I'd had enough of all that. I wanted to simplify...' Rose laughs. 'You're looking very sceptical, Megan!'

'Am I? I suppose it's because I don't really buy it. I don't really believe anyone can survive all on their own – or should have to. You least of all, Mum. What's that quotation about islands? *No man is an island,* or something...'

'*No man is an island, entire of itself; every man is a piece of the continent, a part of the main...*'

Megan nods. 'Yes, that's the one.'

'*If a clod be washed away by the sea, Europe is the less...* Well I hardly think Europe is the less for this particular clod having been washed away, do you? Come on – let's go home.'

CHAPTER TEN

THE FOLLOWING SATURDAY MORNING Rose makes a huge lasagne while Megan washes up after her. After lunch they both sign a birthday card for Calum. Rose resents having to share the card's blank space with Megan's signature, especially as she made the card herself. It depicts in fragments of collaged fabric the outline of a mountain range against a bruised purple sky. She thinks the mountain ridge looks a little like the Cuillin and hopes Calum will notice the similarity. Her gift, which she has not mentioned to Megan, is wrapped and waiting by the front door.

Rose looks at her watch, then telephones Calum.

'Hi, it's Rose. Are you busy?'

'No, not really. Planning next week's lessons, pretty much on auto-pilot. What can I do for you?'

'You can come and have tea with us. I've got something I want to show you. Something I've made for the exhibition.'

'I'll be right over. By the way, Rose – '

'Yes?'

'I'm over to Shona's for supper later – she didn't invite you and Megan by any chance, did she?'

'No...' Rose tries to sound nonchalant.

'Oh.' Calum is audibly disappointed. 'I'll see you in a few minutes, then.'

Rose telephones Shona to give her the all-clear.

***

Calum is greeted at the door with a ragged chorus of *Happy Birthday*. Megan holds a plate of four chocolate cupcakes, each decorated with a lighted candle.

'I got them in the Co-op. One for each decade,' Rose explains.

Calum stares open-mouthed and then starts to laugh. 'How on earth did you know?'

'Shona. Isn't that why you're invited to supper tonight?'

'Aye, that's right.'

'Is it actually your birthday today?' Megan asks.

'Aye. Do you not see I'm dressed in black? I'm in mourning for my misspent youth.'

'Talking of black, come and look at this. Megan, would you put the kettle on?' Rose takes Calum's arm and leads him to the door of the workroom. 'Close your eyes.' She positions him in front of the completed *Basalt* wallhanging. 'All right – you can open them now.'

Calum blinks several times and is silent.

'Well? What do you think?' Rose asks nervously.

'Is this for the exhibition?'

'Yes.'

'Is it one of my poems?' he asks, awestruck.

'Yes.'

'*Basalt*?'

'Yes!' Rose claps her hands, excited. 'You recognised it! What do you think?'

'I... it's...' He shakes his head slowly from side to side, staring at the hanging. 'I don't know what to say. I was about to say it's beautiful but that seems... inadequate. In any case

188

it's too *disturbing* to be called beautiful. It's... astonishing! And you've done it just using black. Black and more black...'

'Yes. Different blacks. You probably didn't realise that blacks are different, the way whites are different. Working in monochrome is where textiles really score over paint – you can achieve so much by playing around with different textures.'

'Aye, I really feel I want to touch it.'

'Go ahead. You know I don't make untouchable things.'

Calum approaches the wallhanging reverently and lays his fingertips gently on the surface of the cloth. 'It has a kind of crust... It's... *crustacean*... Surprisingly solid, isn't it?' he says, taking hold of the edge of the fabric. He lifts it, feels the weight, then peers closely at the stitching, fascinated. 'So thick and... *dense*. There are so many layers...'

'Like your poem.'

He looks up at Rose, surprised. 'Aye, I suppose so.'

Calum runs his fingers through the tangled curling fragments of black muslin hanging from the bottom edge of the cloth, a gesture that reminds Rose of the way he drags his fingers through his hair when thinking. 'I like the dangly pieces. They look kind of fragile compared with the rest of it. Ephemeral...' He points at a crater towards the centre of the work. 'Is this meant to be a mouth?'

'It means whatever you want it to mean.'

He grins at her. 'Now where have I heard *that* before?' He takes a step back from the wall. 'All this stitching, this swirling pattern here... I'm wondering if it's meant to be a face?'

'Can you see a face?'

'Aye, I can.'

'Then there's a face.'

He nods. 'An agonised face. Twisted. Tortured. I think that's what's so unsettling about the piece. Underneath these abstract layers there's a face – buried almost.' He points. 'These slits – they look like eyes to me... and this big circle, this hole could be a mouth. Or is it maybe... a wound? The hanging pieces, the shreds of cloth, they're coming out of the mouth... like words. Or a cry.' He shakes his head, suddenly excited, emphatic, as if realisation has dawned. 'No – it's a wound and this is blood. It's weeping black blood. Haemorrhaging grief.'

'Ugh – how *horrible*!' Megan is standing in the doorway, her arms folded across her chest, shoulders hunched. Rose turns to look at her, startled. She had forgotten her presence. Megan shrugs. 'I thought it was just an abstract thing... You know – *patterns*.'

'It is, Megan if that's what you see. There are no right answers. I'm just interested to hear Calum's response, especially as he wrote the original poem.'

Calum turns to Rose and asks gravely. 'Is my poem as unsettling as this?'

'I think "gut-wrenching" might be a better description.'

'Is that so? Well then, Rose, you've shown me my poem. I think you've improved upon it!'

'No. It's just different. Different medium, same message. More or less.'

'What are you going to call it?'

'*Basalt 2*, of course.'

'Thank you,' he says solemnly. 'I'm flattered.'

'So you should be,' Rose says briskly, suddenly embarrassed. 'Imitation being the sincerest form of flattery. Let's have some cake! Did you make some tea, Megan?'

'Yes. Where do you want it?'

'In the sitting room, please.' Rose moves towards the door then looks back at Calum who seems reluctant to leave the hanging. She walks back and they stand side by side, surveying her work.

'I'm so glad it speaks to you.'

'Aye, it does. Volumes. It makes me feel – och, quite emotional. I feel like a proud new father!' Rose laughs. 'No, I *do*! That's our wee bairn. I sowed the seed. And you've given birth.' He shoots Rose a sidelong glance. 'But I've thought of a better title.'

'What's that?'

'*Immaculate Conception.*'

Calum opens his birthday card ('It looks like the Cuillin ridge – was that intentional?') and eats a second cupcake. He declares turning forty has not been as traumatic as he feared.

'Are you doing anything tonight to celebrate?' Megan asks with an innocent smile. Rose glares at her in mute warning.

'No, not particularly. My sister's making pizza and we're having a big family meal. It's her birthday too next week.'

'Is it indeed?' Rose exclaims. 'Well, she kept that quiet!'

'Aye, that's why I've told you. Shona doesn't know yet, but I'm taking her and Donald out to dinner at The Dark Island Hotel on Friday – if I can get a sitter for the bairns that is.'

'I'll do it. Why didn't you ask me?'

'I wasn't hinting, Rose.' He looks at her doubtfully. 'They can be a bit of a handful, the four of them. Are you sure you wouldn't mind?'

'Not at all. I'd be delighted to do something for Shona. I'll teach them to sew. Or they can play with my button box – children always love that.'

'That'd be grand. I'll go ahead and book the table if you're sure you'll manage?'

'Of course I will.'

Calum grins. 'I can't wait to see Shona's face. She'll be so surprised...' Rose and Megan smile and exchange glances of smug complicity.

While Megan clears away the tea things Rose sees Calum to the door. She hands him her wrapped present. Calum looks surprised.

'For me?'

'Just a little something. I thought you might like to have it.'

'What is it?'

'Open it and see!'

He tears away the tissue paper to reveal a roll of fabric, about the size of a tea towel. He unrolls the cloth and stares open-mouthed.

'It's the sample for *Dunes, Luskentyre*', Rose explains hurriedly. 'The maquette I made before I tackled the real thing... I came across it in a box the other day and since I really have no use for it I thought you might like to have it.' Calum is still silent so Rose prattles on. 'It's not quite the same as the full-size one. I think I managed to improve on this a bit. The reclining figure is a bit too obvious in this version, don't you think?' She grinds to a halt.

Calum looks up at last. 'You're *giving* me this?'

'Yes. I'd like you to have it. I know you'll appreciate it, even though it's only a practice piece.'

'It's a bloody work of art, woman! Rose, I am more pleased than I can say – thank you!' He ducks his head and kisses her swiftly on the mouth.

'Happy Birthday, ' she replies faintly.

Later, while Megan occupies the bathroom for what seems like a very long time, Rose opens her wardrobe doors and rifles through the few clothes she now owns. These consist of a strange mix of the eminently practical and the wildly romantic. Thick woollen jumpers, jeans, tweed skirts and a black suit co-exist alongside ruffled gypsy blouses, tiered velvet skirts and dresses ranging from a beaded 1920s number to a 1960s Indian kaftan. Rose could bear to part with none of these even though she knew she would almost certainly never have opportunities to wear them. She strokes the dresses on their hangers, then selects a calf-length black woollen skirt and a red chenille jumper and lays them on the bed.

Megan appears at the bedroom door, pink and tousled, wrapped in a towel. 'Bathroom's free! Can I come and get dressed in here?'

'Yes, of course. Come and see if you can find anything to wear.'

'What are you wearing?'

'Oh, just a jumper and skirt.' Rose indicates her outfit with a wave of her hand.

Megan pulls a face. 'Mum – it's a *party*. Aren't you going to dress up a bit?'

'People don't dress up very much here...'

'I'm sure Shona will,' Megan says, suppressing a shudder.

'Anyway, it's quite a nice jumper... And it's red,' Rose adds uncertainly.

Megan ignores her and starts to rattle coat-hangers. 'You've got so many lovely things! Why on earth don't you wear them?'

'I didn't keep them to wear, I kept them because I couldn't bear to part with them. I've kept them as textiles really.'

Megan pulls a black and white polka-dot dress from the wardrobe. 'Oh, I used to love this... Wear this!'

'It's a 1950s *sun-dress*, Megan.'

'Yes, but it's got the bolero jacket to match. You can wear that on top.'

'It's too low-cut.'

'Rubbish. If you've got it, flaunt it. You look terrific in this – I remember.'

'Do you?'

'Yes. You wore it on that holiday in Crete.'

'And I haven't worn it since... I don't suppose it still fits me anyway.'

'Try it on.'

Rose looks longingly at the dress and then at her skirt and jumper lying on the bed. 'I suppose I *might* be too hot in a jumper...'

'Of course you will. There'll be loads of people there so it's bound to be warm.'

'Well, I'll try it on – but if I look ridiculous, you will say, won't you? I'd hate to look like mutton dressed as lamb.'

'No chance. But if you do, I'll tell you.'

An hour later the two women are dressed, be-jewelled and made-up. Megan has chosen a tie-dyed flame silk tunic to wear over her own black trousers with a string of Rose's jet beads. Rose has been prevailed upon to wear the '50s dress and jacket. She regards her image in the mirror doubtfully. 'I still think it's too low-cut – for a woman of my age, I mean.'

'It isn't, Mum – it's just that your boobs haven't seen the light of day for years. Honestly, you look great! Gavin used to love you in that outfit...' There is a tense silence that Megan rushes to fill. 'Shall we have a drink before we go? There's the remains of a bottle in the fridge.'

Without waiting for an answer Megan heads for the kitchen. Rose fiddles with her hair, removes her earrings, then puts them back on again. She plucks at the bodice of the dress in an attempt to reveal less cleavage but gains only a millimetre or two of extra coverage. She makes a mental note not to lean forward in the course of the evening.

Megan reappears with two glasses of wine. 'Here's to us! Aren't we a gorgeous pair? The men of North Uist won't know what's hit them.' Rose, unconvinced, smiles dutifully and raises the glass to her lips. Her expression changes suddenly and she lowers her glass. Megan frowns. 'What's the matter, Mum? Are you all right?'

'It's nothing... I just – I think I'll just sit down for a bit.'

'What is it? Are you ill?'

'No, really, I'm all right... Sorry, I just suddenly had a horrible thought.'

'What?'

'I was just thinking about Calum and his climbing mates... Then I thought – wouldn't it be dreadful if *Gavin* turned up?'

'Oh, Mum,' Megan squeezes her mother's hand. 'He *won't* be there.' Her eyes flood. 'You really mustn't worry – I promise you, Gavin won't be there...'

A T A QUARTER TO EIGHT SHONA is orchestrating the lighting of our candles. Light bulbs have been removed from the kitchen and sitting room so Calum cannot turn on lights when he arrives. There must be fifty people crowded into the torch-lit sitting room and hallway. Children and some of the women are sitting on laps; the bulkiest men have been banished to sit on the stairs and Shona's brood have been herded together at the entrance to the room. Four-year-old Fergus is asleep in Donald's arms, oblivious.

Shona hands out white candles to most of the assembly. 'Stand by with your lighters and matches everybody and light your candles as quick as you can when I start to sing. Murdo, have you got that bucket of water handy?'

'Aye-aye, Captain.' A sharp salute from young Murdo McLean, our part-time policeman, teased unmercifully for his movie-star good looks and devotion to body-building. Megan has clocked him already.

'I doubt we'll be needing the water, Murdo, but just in case... Now, remember, nobody is to move while the candles are lit – and you'll know right enough when to blow them out. Rob and Uilleam, will you have the light-bulbs at the ready...' Rob MacDonald and Uilleam Campbell, the tallest of Calum's old school friends, are positioned under lampshades. 'Get those bulbs back in *before* the candles go out, boys... Aly, when the lights go on, *that's* the signal for you and the weans to throw those streamers, okay? Try and throw them over Calum if you can...' Shona pats her chest nervously, breathless with excitement and anticipation. 'Now all we have to do is wait for himself...'

'Supposing he's late?' Aly asks anxiously.

Shona whoops with laughter and pats Aly's head. 'My wee brother has never been late for food in his life! Wheesht! I think I can hear him. Hush, everyone. Candles at the ready...'

We hear the back door open. Calum calls out in Gaelic. Silence. There are several clicks as he tries the kitchen light switch. In the darkness I hear stifled giggles. Calum calls out again. Footsteps approach and the door handle rattles. I think the children are going to lose it but they stand firm.

'Shona?' Calum's voice in the darkness and the frantic flicking of a switch. A beautiful clear soprano voice starts to sing *Happy Birthday*. One by one forty candles light up till the room looks like a giant birthday cake. Calum emerges gradually from the darkness, his eyes wide, jaw dropped. As the last note sounds, the children shriek, 'Make a wish! Make a wish!'

Calum shuts his eyes, then, pantomime-style, blows towards the forty candles. We each blow out our candle, electric light returns and Aly yells 'Now!' The children pelt Calum with streamers as a contingent from the Skye Mountain Rescue Team launch into a rousing chorus of *For he's a jolly good fellow*, accompanied by Shona on kazoo.

Calum is speechless.

The Mountain Rescue Team present Calum with a magnum of champagne and an obscene greetings card that he refuses to show to any female guest. In the kitchen there is much ribald laughter when Calum grasps the bottle and starts to open it. Shona, removing a tray of sausage rolls from the oven, says archly, 'If you're intending to do what they do at the end of the Grand Prix, Calum, I'll thank you to take the bottle outside. I expected to have to wash the floor but I'll no' be washing the *ceiling*...'

Calum's handling of the bottle is a model of circumspection but as the wine starts to erupt a roar goes up from his audience. He lifts the giant bottle with both hands and drinks. Foam trickles out of the corners of his mouth, down over his chin and soaks the front of his jumper.

Shona 'tuts' half-heartedly.

The sitting-room is thick with cigarette smoke and the reek of beer and whisky, living – rather than healthy living – being the Hebrideans' priority. Donald circulates with a bottle repeating like a mantra his personal philosophy: 'It's no health if the glass is not emptied!'

Shona, resplendent in a Caribbean cocktail of bright colours, surveys the scene with evident satisfaction until she spies some dirty plates on the laden table. She swoops down on them and retreats to the kitchen, shaking her head and announcing to nobody in particular, 'Och, beauty won't boil the pot...'

***

Rose picks a streamer out of Calum's hair.

'I suppose you knew about all this, Rose?'

'Of course. You're eating my lasagne.'

'You made this? It's delicious.'

'Thank you.'

A slight, awkward pause filled by Abba's *Dancing Queen*.

'You look beautiful.'

'Thank you.' She looks down at her dress, smoothing it nervously over her thighs. 'It was Megan's choice actually.'

Another awkward silence. Calum sets down his empty plate. 'Do you want to know what I wished for, Rose?'

'No, I don't think so. In any case, I think I can probably guess...'

Little Kenny MacNeill saunters over to Rose nursing a can of Coke.

'Hello, Miss.'

'Hello, Kenny! How nice to see you.'

'Great party!'

'Yes, it is. Are you enjoying yourself?'

'Aye, Miss.'

'Call me Rose, Kenny.'

'Thanks, Miss. Sorry – *Rose*.'

'I enjoyed your poem, Kenny. Mr. Morrison let me have a copy. Did he tell you we'd like to feature it in the exhibition?'

Kenny looks puzzled and faintly suspicious. 'Why, Miss?'

'Because we like it! And we like it because it's good! It's an excellent poem, Kenny.'

'Thanks, Miss...' Kenny is silent as he tries to assimilate this new and astonishing piece of information.

'Miss?'

'*Rose*.'

'Rose – do you know of any footballers that write poetry?'

Rose treads carefully. 'No, Ken, I don't believe I do... But lots of poets play football. Mr Morrison for one.'

'But he's *crap*, Miss.'

'As a poet or a footballer?'

'Footballer, Miss.' Kenny drains his can with a flourish and says 'His poetry's no' so bad...'

'I've been having a discussion with one of your critics.'

'Oh?'

'Kenny.'

'Oh.'

'He says you're a crap footballer.'

'Aye, true enough.'

'But you'll be pleased to hear he thinks your poetry is no' so bad.'

'He said that?'

'Yes.'

'*Kenny MacNeill* said that?'

'Yes.'

Calum beams. 'I've arrived!'

***

Abba have given way to Gloria Gaynor who is assuring us *fortissimo* that she will survive. I speculate as to whose record collection we are listening to and decide it must be Shona's.

Dr. Kerr is drinking lemonade alongside Angus the Post who looks as if he'd prefer to be drinking in more congenial company. As I pass they both nod and, switching to English, enquire after my health. Hot Chocolate launch into *You Sexy Thing* and I suspect the Mountain Rescue team of importing seditious CDs. Angus taps his foot discreetly.

Dr. Kerr inclines his tall, unbending frame towards me. 'I was just remarking to Angus, Rose, on the detrimental effects of the causeways that now link the Uists.'

'Oh? I thought everyone was pleased you no longer had to wade across at low tide. That used to be pretty dangerous didn't it?'

'Indeed, but now there are dangers of a different kind.'

'The traffic you mean?'

'I was referring to dangers of a less temporal nature, Rose,' Dr. Kerr says loftily.

Angus catches my eye. His are twinkling. 'Dr. Kerr was alluding, Rose, to the peril of spiritual decline.'

'Eternal damnation, Angus – no less!'

'I'm sorry? I'm afraid I don't quite understand...'

'From North Uist, Rose, it is now but a short step to Benbecula,' Dr. Kerr explains, referring to the neighbouring island, 'and from Benbecula another short step to the Catholic shores of South Uist where one may *shop* on the Sabbath.' Dr. Kerr pauses to allow the full horror to sink in. He continues. 'One may – so I am *told* – even rent videotapes on the Sabbath, so it goes without saying that there will be washing hung out to dry, crofts being worked, business transactions and the like, all taking place on the Lord's Day. We always knew such things went on,' says Dr. Kerr in a tone that hints at institutionalised Devil worship, 'but now with the causeways it is all too easy for the rot to *spread*, for folk to travel and observe the free and easy ways of the south. It can only weaken the moral fibre of the islands – is that not so, Angus?'

'Aye, these are terrible godless times we live in...' Angus rubs his nose in a vain attempt to disguise a smile. 'So you be careful now, Rose, when you go gadding about in your automobile, lest you be drawn into sin by the fleshpots of South Uist.'

'Oh, I will, Angus, I'll definitely bear that in mind. Would you two gentlemen excuse me? I think Shona needs some help in the kitchen...'

Calum is deep in Gaelic conversation with Murdo McLean. Megan is eyeing them both from across the room whilst jiving with Eilidh. Murdo gesticulates with his whisky glass; Calum nods, says something barely audible out of the corner of his mouth. Murdo laughs uproariously and punches Calum on the upper arm. He staggers slightly, nods again, unsmiling, then empties his glass.

The more Calum drinks, the more judicially sober he appears.

***

I have tucked myself away in a dark corner. The room has begun to spin and I close my eyes.

'Enjoying yourself, Rose?'

I'm startled by a familiar voice, but I cannot see who is speaking.

'Why aren't you dancing?'

'*Gavin*?'

'God, you *are* pissed.'

'Not as pissed as you from the sound of it.'

'What else is there to do but drink? No one will talk to me.'

'You weren't invited.'

'A detail... I see you wore my favourite dress.'

'I didn't wear it for you.'

'You going home with the teacher?'

'No, of course not.'

'You two still haven't got it together then?'

'With Megan here?'

'Yeah, I can see that might cramp your style a bit... But from the looks of things you want to get a move on, Rosie old girl, or you might just miss the boat...'

Megan is looking predatory. She sidles over to Calum and Murdo, glass in hand. Calum is talking and ignores her. She slips her arm round his waist and rests her delicate hand on his hip. I watch her fingers flex. When he finally turns towards her, her hand grazes the back pocket of his jeans, lingers, then flutters up to tweak her hair. As Calum speaks to her she tilts her head upwards, arching her neck, inviting. Her teeth flash in the subdued light, a white gleam, like the snarl of an animal.

Calum is standing in front of me. One of us must be reeling because the room appears to sway.

'Will you no' dance with me, Rose?'

'I don't. I mean, I can't.'

Calum splutters. 'Everyone can dance! You just haven't drunk enough, woman.' He raises a half bottle of whisky and aims it in the general direction of my glass.

'No, I've got plenty – ' He pours anyway as I quickly retract my glass. The whisky from the bottle spills over my hand. The whisky in my glass slops over and trickles down inside my dress, gathering between my breasts. Calum watches it travel. I watch him watching.

'So you won't dance then?'

'No... Thanks.'

He sighs, then lifts my wet hand to his lips. I think he is about to kiss it but instead he licks off the spilt whisky, looking at me, not my hand.

'Why didn't you dance with him?'

'It's none of your business, Gavin.'

'My, we're touchy!'

205

'Leave me alone! You're just a figment of my imagination anyway.'

'You say the sweetest things... Why don't you dance with him, just to spite me?'

'It's very tempting, but I'm afraid I don't trust myself.'

'You don't trust yourself? Now, *that's* the kind of excuse a guy could live with! What are you afraid you might do, Rose? Come on, you can tell me of all people – and you'll have the added satisfaction of knowing that every word will hurt.'

'Will it?'

'Like a knife.'

'Well, in that case...'

'Go on.'

'If I *did* dance with Calum – I have no intention of doing so, you understand – If I did, I don't think I would be able to refrain from threading my fingers through his hair and cradling his head in my hands.'

'Nice... For starters. Go on. You can do better than that, Rose – I hardly felt a thing.'

'If I danced with Calum I don't think I could cope with the feel of his chest against my breasts... Especially since he's doused himself in champagne. All that damp wool...'

'Now you're talking...'

'And if he were to exert the slightest pressure in the small of my back while we danced I know my hips would gravitate towards his until I was grinding my pubic bone against his – hopefully – hard cock – '

'Ouch...'

'And if I allowed that to happen then no power on earth would be likely to stop me grabbing his arse and – '

'Okay, I get the picture... You *are* pissed, Rose.'

'As a newt. Which is why I won't be dancing with Calum. This party's a family affair, Gavin. *Pas devant les enfants...* Especially not mine.'

Calum dances instead with Eilidh. She stands as high as his elbow, gaudy in pink and silver lycra, like a diminutive pop star. At climactic moments in the music Calum lifts her effortlessly, high into the air, swinging her round. Her face is ecstatic. She gazes at Calum in frank adoration.

So does Megan.

It's very late. Shona parks herself next to me on the sofa and extends her legs, flexing tired and swollen ankles.

'It's been a great party, Shona. You should feel very proud of yourself.'

'Aye, I think it's only the bairns left now that are sober...' She laughs and points. 'Och, will you *look* at Murdo, now!'

Murdo Maclean, got up in very unconvincing drag, is miming to *Stand by your Man*. Dr. Kerr appears to have left.

Uilleam, Shona and Calum have been prevailed upon to play. Uilleam produces his accordion, Shona her whistle and someone lends Calum a fiddle. Calum claims he's too drunk to play. Shona assures him their audience is too drunk to notice. They start their set with a reel and Duncan and Eilidh make the most of the limited floor-space, swinging each other round and round, whooping and laughing. We all clap in time to the music. I catch Megan's eye across the room. She is propped up between Rob and Murdo, looking very happy. She smiles, then waves at me, a pointless, child-like gesture of affection that brings drunken tears to my eyes.

The party's over. The last few guests congregate in the kitchen. Megan leans her head on Calum's arm, her body sagging against him. Rose is stacking plates.

'Will I see you two ladies home, then?' Calum asks.

'Yes please!' Megan says eagerly. 'My feet are killing me. God, you islanders certainly know how to party.'

Calum looks down at her, frowning. 'You disappoint me, Megan. Murdo says there's a rave on at a bothy not far from here – are you telling me you're no' up for that?'

Megan groans. 'Home! Now!'

'Come on, Rose – we mustn't keep these peely-wally youngsters from their beds.'

Rose picks up an apron and ties it on, fumbling. 'You go on, Calum, I'll stay and help Shona clear up.'

Shona calls out from the sink. 'You'll do no such thing, Rose Leonard!'

'You heard what the lady said,' Calum says briskly. 'Don't worry about clearing up – I'll come back and help after I've seen you home.'

'No, really – I'd like to stay and help. It's a good way to wind down.'

'Look, don't worry about *me*,' Megan says impatiently, 'I can find my own way home, honestly. Can someone lend me a torch?'

'I'd rather Calum took you, Megan. You don't realise how dark it is out there without street lights – and you've had an awful lot to drink.'

'*Mum!*' Megan glowers at Rose.

Calum raises his palms in a peacekeeping gesture. 'No bother. I'll see you home. Save some washing up for me, Shona.' He steers a reeling Megan towards the back door.

Shona plunges her hands into the suds and sighs. 'Wee Calum Iain is *forty*! Och, it makes me feel about a hundred!'

Rose takes a dinner plate from the draining board and wipes it. 'Surely you're not much older than him, Shona?'

'Well, I was at school by the time he was born. I'll leave you to make your own calculations.'

'You still think of him as your kid brother?'

'Aye! To me he was always the bairn – until he was fourteen and suddenly grew taller than me! But I still think of him as wee Calum Iain...'

'He's the youngest?'

'Aye. Our mother was forty-four when he was born. I'd two older sisters and I think I was supposed to be the last of the brood. Then Calum arrived, much to everyone's surprise. A son after three daughters! Our parents were so pleased and proud.' Shona turns to Rose and explains. 'Sons are important in a crofting community. You need a man for the heavy work, whatever these *feminists* might say.' Shona pronounces the word with a curious emphasis that conveys a mixture of scepticism and derision. 'Aye, Calum was a bonny wee bairn, spoiled from the moment he was born, brought up as he was, almost entirely by women... Our father died when I was twelve – I suspect it was the drink that killed him, but mother always said it was a heart attack. Calum would have been just seven. He became the wee man of the family. Mother hoped he'd work the croft like his father, but Calum was clever, we all knew it, and he wanted to try for the university. He wanted to travel, to see the world.'

'When did he start climbing?'

'In his teens. He cut his teeth on the Cuillin and it became a passion with him, an obsession almost. Alison got him to settle down in Glasgow and they were happy for a while. But it was just one thing after another.' Shona shakes her head and scours a pan vigorously. 'That boy's never been what you might call lucky.'

'Calum told me about being attacked by a pupil. He still seems pretty disturbed by what happened.'

'You think so?'

'Yes. I think he possibly suffers from flashbacks. It's a common side effect after traumatic events – accidents and so on.'

'Is that so?'

'Did he have any counselling about what happened?'

Shona scoffs. 'Calum's way of dealing with it was to pretend it *hadn't* happened!'

'Yes, that was my impression.'

'He kept in touch with Davy after he'd been thrown out of school – well, he tried. But it was no use. They never found a way of communicating again – the assault stood between them. And anyway Davy was into these hard drugs, heroin and the like. A year after the attack Calum heard the lad was dead of an overdose.'

'Oh, no!'

'Aye. Calum took it badly. Davy had been a good student, a bright boy apparently, before he got into the drugs. Such a terrible waste. Calum was more upset by Davy's death than the assault.'

'So that's why he tries to make light of what happened to *him*... It's all relative. Relative to death, I mean.'

'Aye... It all came at a bad time for him. Things weren't working out with Alison. He was disillusioned with teaching – not teaching itself, but the educational system. He stopped teaching and started climbing again. Serious, big climbs.'

'Let me guess – Everest?'

'Aye... How did you know?'

'I know the type.'

Shona resumes. 'Alison was *not* happy... They'd been married five years. She was in her thirties and wanted to start a family. Calum didn't. He wanted to climb and write. It was inevitable I suppose that things would break down... A year after Calum was attacked they separated. Calum dealt with *that* by going climbing again. Then... Well, then there were all the tragedies...' Shona looks up from the sink, her eyes troubled. 'Has he told you about those?'

'He mentioned that he'd lost some friends in climbing accidents.'

'Aye, several... He went back to teaching. It was what he knew, what he loved. It provided him with a framework for his life and a secure income, which Heaven knows he needed – he'd run up terrible debts with his climbing expeditions and divorce doesn't come cheap! But as they say, no door ever closed, but another opened... He started to get poems published so he decided to teach part-time and devote more time to his writing.'

'Did he give up climbing?'

'Not altogether. It's in his blood, he'll never give it up, it's a kind of addiction.'

'Yes. I know all about that.'

Shona looks up, intrigued. 'Do you now?'

'Yes. I lived with a climber for five years. He was a fanatic. A real adrenalin junkie.'

Shona nods. 'You'll know then what Alison had to put up with?'

'Yes.'

'Calum gave up the big expeditions after the accidents. He went to live on Skye and volunteered for the Mountain Rescue Team there.'

'Trust Calum to be a hero!'

'He didn't see it like that. He saw it as a way of keeping his hand in, using his skills, climbing without all the expense of expeditions. He said saving lives was just an added bonus!'

'Did you buy that?'

Shona hoists an eyebrow. 'With Davy and all the others dead? No, I did not! In fact I used to worry myself sick that he was just trying to find an honourable way to... to end it all, d'you know what I mean? But I think the team sorted him out, thank the Lord. You met some of them tonight. They're a grand bunch. Calum still goes over to Skye every summer and looks up his old pals. They have a great time.' Shona scrapes plates noisily into the bin. 'Och, I think he's over the worst now... At least, I *hope* so,' she adds uncertainly.

'Yes, I hope so too.'

'He's certainly been a lot more cheerful since you and he became friends, Rose! I think you've done him a lot of good. And this exhibition you're planning, that's given him a real focus for his writing.'

'What do you think of Calum's poems, Shona?'

Shona leans against the sink and stares down into the greasy, grey water, choosing her words carefully. 'Do you no' find his poetry a wee bit *intense*, Rose?'

'How do you mean?'

Shona searches for the words. 'Och, it's like eating a slice of cloutie dumpling – a little goes a long way! It sits inside you and weighs you down. And I find some of his poems depressing... But then I'm no' what you'd call a poetry fan. I don't have much time for reading but when I do I like a good murder mystery!'

'Actually, I don't find Calum's poems depressing. But then I first read them when I was very depressed. A long time ago, when I was ill. I found them... exhilarating. So alive. So vivid. They *are* dense, I know what you mean, and I'm not sure I always understand what he's trying to say, but then I've never subscribed to the idea that you have to understand poetry to enjoy it, any more than you need to understand music to enjoy it.'

'Have you told him what you think of his poems, Rose?'

'I've tried to. He doesn't make it easy.'

'Aye, I know.'

'I suppose I found – I find – his poetry a comfort. A comfort because he seems to have made something beautiful out of all the pain, salvaged something from those wasted lives. I really admire that... I really admire *him*.'

Shona gives Rose a long look. 'A friend's eye is a good looking-glass,' she says with a warm smile. Rose is about to reply when the back door opens and Calum walks in. Shona thrusts a tea towel under his nose. 'It's yourself, Calum. We were wondering what had happened to you.'

He pours a shot of whisky into a dirty glass and sits down on a kitchen chair. 'That was a great party, Shona. Thanks a lot.' He raises his glass to her, then downs the whisky.

'Aye, well, I'll expect the same from you next week when *I'm* twenty-one.'

'It's all in hand, Shona. I've booked the Scotland Rugby Team for a strip-o-gram.'

'Och, well, *that'll* be something to look forward to,' Shona says mildly. 'But it's back to auld claes and porridge for you now, Calum,' she says as she removes the empty glass from his hand and deposits it in the sink. 'Will you not make yourself useful for once and see Rose home? Donald can finish the washing up. We've already done most of it, you were gone so long.'

'Aye, sorry – Megan lost one of her shoes. Come on, Rose, I'll see you home.'

Rose ignores him, covering dishes with tinfoil. 'What about these leftovers, Shona? Your fridge is full – shall I take some back and put them in mine?'

'No, don't worry – Donald and the bairns will likely finish them up for breakfast. Away with you now. Do you know what time it is?'

Rose nods and smiles. 'Yes, I turned into a pumpkin hours ago.'

CHAPTER TWELVE

CALUM AND ROSE WEAVE THEIR WAY UNSTEADILY along the road. Rose looks across to her house, just discernible in the moonlight.

'Megan's light is out already.'

'She was pretty tired.'

'She might have left a light on for me. Young people can be so selfish.'

'She was pretty drunk as well.'

'Well, she'd better not puke over any of my work or there'll be trouble.'

'Why wouldn't you dance with me, Rose?'

'I didn't dance with anybody, Calum.'

'I know, I was watching. Not even Murdo McLean, Uist's answer to Tom Cruise. Can you not just smell the testosterone coming off that guy? Or is it his aftershave, maybe? Heady stuff – but wasted on you, obviously... Why wouldn't you dance with me?'

'Was it really that important to you?'

'Aye. You were the only woman I wanted to dance with. And the only woman I didn't dance with.'

'I'm sorry. I wanted to...'

'So?'

'I didn't trust myself to. I thought everyone would guess what was going on... And I couldn't face a ragging from Megan.'

'What do you mean?'

'When she's not being totally inconsiderate she treats me with the deference one usually reserves for the elderly or the terminally ill. It's very annoying and hardly conducive to letting your hair down... Calum, we're going the wrong way.'

'No, we're not.'

'You're supposed to be taking me home.'

'I didn't say whose.'

'No, it's too late, I'm too tired, I don't want to get into all that now – '

'Just a coffee! And maybe one little dance? I won't tie you to the bed, I promise.'

'Calum – '

'Please, Rose – I haven't seen you alone for days and God knows when Megan's going home. Can't we just *talk* a wee while? I've put away so much whisky I'd be good for nothing more.'

Rose sighs. 'Oh, all right. One coffee then.'

Calum puts the kettle on, selects a tape and drops it into his cassette-player.

Rose laughs. 'You weren't serious about dancing were you?'

'Deadly. Do you like Sting?'

'Yes. I do actually. Such intelligent lyrics.'

'Used to be a teacher. Had the sense to get out. My hero.'

'I love this track. I forget what it's called...'

'*Fragile*. Shall we dance?'

He holds out his arms.

***

'The kettle boiled.'

'Aye.'

'Shall I make the coffee?'

'Would you have to let go of me to do that?'

'Yes.'

'I'll pass on coffee then.'

'The music did actually finish.'

'Aye, you noticed that? Shall I turn the tape over?'

'Would you have to let go of me to do that?

'Only with one arm. Watch...'

Rose sighs. 'I really ought to go, Calum. Megan might be listening out for me. I don't want to worry her.' He is silent. 'She might ring Shona and wake her.'

'Megan won't stir till lunchtime tomorrow. I mean today. Please stay, Rose.' She says nothing. He releases her and looks into her eyes. 'D'you really no' want to?'

'A part of me wants to stay. But another part wants to run away and hide.'

'Because you're scared? Of me?'

'No, of course not.'

'But you are scared, aren't you?'

'Yes... Oh, just back off, Calum – you really don't want to get involved. I'm such a *mess*... and it's all too complicated.' She picks up her coat from the sofa but Calum takes it from her and tosses it back down again.

'But I *do* want to get involved. And I don't think you're any more or less complicated than anyone else, Rose, it's just that your illness has made you self-aware, self-consciously so. That and your paint-stripper honesty, that's what makes things difficult for you. You feel things, you see things and you say them. That's the artist in you. In *me.*'

'You're just trying to talk me into bed.'

'How hard are you having to fight to stay out?'

'You arrogant sod!'

'Aye, I know, but it's the truth, isn't it? I think you've wanted me since the first evening we spent together at Shona's, when I saw you home... You wanted me then but you sent me away. Tell me that's not true.'

'My body wanted you, my *mind* rejected you – and I can't trust either of them, Calum! My drugged and sensible mind said you were too young, too nice, far too deliciously fuckable – and I wasn't going down that road again – I'd come here to avoid all that. I wasn't going to be hurt and... *humiliated* again.'

Calum sighs. 'I'm not Gavin.'

'No, you're not.'

'But you wish I were,' he says irritably.

'No, of course not! If you were anything like Gavin I wouldn't be here now, don't you understand that?'

'I'm trying to... Tell me, Rose, if we make love now, what in Christ's name do you think can happen that is so very terrible?'

She says nothing for a long while, then: 'If we make love, Calum, I will start to live with the fear of losing you.'

'You didn't lose Gavin – you never had him! You had an understanding, a shared life together, a history. From all that you've told me about him, you came third in his life anyway – after himself and climbing. All that kept you together was trust, Rose, and that's a fragile thread. You can't bind someone to you with that. It doesn't make much of a leash either. Gavin was just a guy whose eye wandered after five years. I'm not saying it was an okay thing to do, but it happens. Folk forgive... Or they break up and get on with their lives, begin again. But you've let him take everything. Why shouldn't you have another chance?'

'You don't understand.'

'Too bloody right, I don't! I think you owe me an explanation, Rose. You grab me by the balls – literally! – you invite me into your bed, you cry on my shoulder and tell me all about your earth-moving ex-lover – but I'm not allowed to touch you without written permission!'

Rose sinks onto the sofa, leans forward, head in hands. Her hair falls forward and hides her face. 'If I have nothing, it can't be taken away,' she says quietly.

'It's a living *death*, Rose, that's what you've chosen! You've walled yourself up so no one can get at you – but haven't you noticed? You can't get out.'

Rose sits upright. She lifts her head slowly and gazes up at Calum standing in front of her.

'I hadn't looked at another man until I met you. Not in five years... I suppose I finally felt safe enough to put my head up above the parapet. And I thought it was nothing serious.' She smiles and shakes her head. 'You were younger than me – I thought a lot younger. That somehow disqualified you, made you "safe". I thought I could just lust from afar, which God knows, Calum, I did. I have lusted for England!'

He kneels, takes her face in his hands and kisses her. She recoils for barely a second and then her hands are on him, pressing and sliding, searching for his flesh. Calum fumbles at her breasts, undoing the buttons of her dress. Suddenly, she puts her hands on his chest and pushes him away.

'No!' She covers herself up and sits hunched over.

'What?' Calum sits back on his heels, dazed. 'What did I do? What's the matter?'

'I can't.'

'Why not? Jesus, Rose!' He wipes his wet mouth on the back of his hand. 'You'll never convince me you don't want me now!'

'I'm sorry, Calum. I thought I'd drunk enough... not to care.' She swallows. 'I know it's really silly, but... I can't bear for you to *see* me.'

'We'll put the lights out, I don't mind – whatever you want.'

'No. You see...' Her voice is unsteady. 'I'm covered in scars. It's not just my wrists. My arms... my shoulders... legs... even the soles of my feet. I'm stitched up like a bloody patchwork quilt! Only not half so pretty.'

Calum swallows. 'How...?'

'I walked through a glass door.'

'*Why*?'

'I couldn't find the key.'

Calum's mouth opens and shuts as he tries to find words. 'But surely Gavin...'

'He never saw me like this.'

Calum is silent for several moments, then he stands and starts to pull his jumper over his head.

'Calum, what are you doing?'

'Undressing.' He drops the jumper onto the floor.

'Stop it.'

'No.'

'Are you going to rape me?'

'No, not unless you want me to.'

'So what is this?' Rose laughs nervously. 'A last desperate attempt to drive me wild with desire?'

'Not exactly, as you'll see in a moment.'

Rose stares transfixed as Calum unbuttons his shirt. He stands, kicks off his shoes, shrugs off the shirt and drops it beside the jumper. Standing unsteadily on one leg he removes one sock, then the other, then unzips his jeans.

'Calum, I – '

Ignoring her, he removes his jeans and boxers in one, steps out of them neatly and kicks them aside. He is not smiling and there is an ugly, angry light in his eyes.

'Okay, pay attention now and I'll give you the tour.' He points to his chest, to a mark just below his collarbone, a scar two inches long. 'Glasgow, 1995. This is where wee Davy McAllister's knife went *in*, and this,' he says, tracing the long scar under his chin with a finger, 'is where it went when he pulled it *out*. I suppose I was very lucky he missed my windpipe. And indeed the jugular vein.'

He turns round. His lower back is mottled in shades of pink and plum, patterned with pale, shiny, vertical striations, as if his flesh has been grated. 'This is where I slid down fifty feet of scree in a tee shirt while rock-climbing in the Cuillin, 1985. And if you think *this* looks bad, you should have seen the tee shirt.'

He turns to face Rose again, then looks down at his genitals.

'Oh, aye... This one I call the d-i-y vasectomy.' He points to a scar in his groin, a dark, crater-like hole. 'This is where my ice-axe went in after I'd failed to anchor myself with it during an avalanche. That was Everest, 1995. And finally,' He points down at the floor. 'Note the feet. A strange sort of purplish-grey colour. Not very attractive. You'll have a name no doubt for this particular shade, Rose – would that be puce? You'll note, too, the absence of several toes on my right foot. All the result of severe frostbite, also on Everest. Bonny, aren't I? And *those*,' he hisses, narrowing his eyes, 'Those are just the scars you can *see*, Rose! In here,' he jabs at his temple with a forefinger, 'There are more scars – deeper, uglier scars than any you see on my body!'

He begins to recite, his eyes glittering. 'Al Stevens and Hamish McKenzie – pals of mine since Primary One! – swept to their deaths by an avalanche, Everest, 1995. I was lucky – I got away with the groin puncture... Hugh Davies, a brilliant climber and even more brilliant poet. Died of pulmonary oedema, Mount Aconcagua, 1996. Jim Henderson – och, my mate Jimmy, may he rest in peace! Died of head injuries as the result of a fall, despite the fact that for once the poor wee bastard was wearing a helmet! That would have been the Matterhorn, 1997. Last but *certainly* not least, Chris McIntyre, who also died in 1997 – *Christ*, that was a bad year!' Calum bows his head and fights for control of his voice. He continues, his chest heaving. 'Chris died of exposure and multiple injuries climbing with me in the Alps – another stupid, pointless, accidental death – one which was, incidentally, entirely my fault!'

He shivers violently and looks down at his naked body as if suddenly surprised. He picks up his jeans and drags them on furiously. 'So you see, Rose, if you would just step outside your own fucking head for a few moments you'd see you're not the only one with scars. In any case the worst ones, the most *disfiguring* are never visible to the naked eye.' He zips up his fly. 'I can probably live with yours. Can you live with mine?'

Rose is silent a long while. 'I had no idea...'

'Och, hell – why would you?'

'I've been very selfish.'

He sits down beside her. 'Not selfish, Rose, just self-absorbed. You just want your pain to stop. Believe me, I understand that. I thought I could help you stop it. I thought you could help stop mine.' He picks up his jumper from the floor and pulls it on. 'Will you share the last of the whisky?'

'No, thanks.'

Calum empties the remains of the bottle into his glass. He doesn't drink but stares down into the liquid, swirling it round. 'After the first couple of deaths I carried on climbing, as if nothing had happened. Told myself it's what they would have wanted, Al and Hamish. Did it for them.' He raises his glass. 'For the lads! And up there, there was no past... no future... only the present moment. But things changed slowly... with the other deaths. The past, the deaths took over. I wasn't climbing alone. The corpses, *the ghosts* – Hamish, Al, Hugh, Jim and Chris – they all came with me.' He shakes his head. 'In the end I started to feel like a bloody corpse myself. A walking corpse. Not dead exactly, but not quite alive. Then I realised I didn't really care... if I survived, I mean. That each time I went out on the mountain I was looking to meet death half way. So I stopped climbing. Got back into teaching. Did a lot of writing. Even got some published. It was a life of sorts... I didn't expect to feel anything ever again. Didn't want to. Till I met you. And – to my utter amazement – something came back to life. You, Rose – you *surprised* me... Constantly! I just couldn't figure you out. Just when I thought I'd got you sussed, you'd go and do something wild and unpredictable. You got under my guard. There I was, just trying to be friendly, doing my Mr. Nice Guy stuff – '

'Indiscriminate generosity.'

'Aye... Then I'd see you looking at me, in that scared, kind of defiant way – Megan does it too, you're very alike in some ways – and it's like, my cover's completely blown, I'm looking at *myself*, at how I really am, not how I pretend to be. It sounds really corny, but you brought me back to life. Made me *want* something... Somebody. I thought – hoped – that maybe I'd done the same for you.'

'You have, Calum.'

'I'm glad about that.' He takes her hand. 'I offered you my friendship. I'm offering you – for what it's worth – my body and, for Christ's sake, Rose, I think I'm offering you love. It must be love because I don't think I can cope any more with the meagre amounts of your time and affection that you're prepared to mete out to me as a friend. I want more. I *need* more. And I suppose I'm saying if there's no more to be had, then... I'd rather go back to having nothing.'

Rose nods. 'I understand that.'

'Will you no' give yourself another chance, Rose? You deserve it. And you do feel something for me.'

'Yes, I do. I feel a lot for you, Calum. And I do believe you wouldn't treat me as badly as Gavin did.'

'You know, maybe Gavin was no hero, but he wasn't a complete bastard either, not according to Megan. He saw you through some bad times, she says. So he screwed around...' Calum shrugs. 'There's not many men would say no to sex if it was offered on a plate and they thought they could get away with it.'

'You would say no.'

He laughs ruefully. 'You think so? Aye, maybe... Tonight I said no, but I didn't when I was married to Alison.'

'What do you mean?'

'When Alison and I split up I was in love with another woman. Her best friend. We'd been having an affair for months.'

'No... I meant, what did you mean when you said, "Tonight I said no"?'

He smiles. 'I'm telling tales out of school now. Boasting. See what you've reduced me to?'

Rose is sitting up straight, alert. 'Calum, what did you mean?'

'When I saw her home earlier your daughter offered me a very special birthday present. I was flattered – she's an attractive girl – but I said no. I hope I didn't hurt her feelings too much.'

'Did you tell her why you said no?'

'You mean, "Sorry, hen – I fancy your mother"? No. I thought that would be adding insult to injury.' He drains his glass. 'Odd, isn't it? Must be something genetic.'

'What?'

'You two. You seem to share the same taste in men.'

'Yes.' Rose stares vacantly. 'We do... We did.'

Calum stiffens. He puts his glass down carefully. '*Gavin*?' Rose does not move or reply. 'Gavin and *Megan*?'

'Yes.'

'Jesus Christ Almighty... How old was she?'

'Seventeen.'

'*Shit!*'

'I was going to tell you, Calum... I wanted to. But then Megan sent me that wretched letter inviting herself here. How was I supposed to tell you after that?'

'How could he *do* that to you? How could *Megan*?'

'Oh, I didn't really blame her, not once I'd stopped climbing the walls. She was a child really. I don't suppose she had any idea what the fall-out would be. And once Gavin turned the laser-beam of his charm on you, any woman was lost! Oh, she wasn't the first he'd betrayed me with, but I made sure she was the last.'

'How did you find out?'

'Gavin told me.'

'The gobshite! Why, in God's name?'

'He was drunk. Aggressive.' She closes her eyes. 'Oh, it was all so sordid...'

'Tell me, Rose. If you can bear to.'

'He'd come back from some foreign expedition, conquered another peak, made another bloody first ascent, I don't remember which. He was drunk, naturally. He'd been out with the lads celebrating and – well, he couldn't get it up basically. I hadn't seen him for six weeks and I was tired and fed up. I suppose I wasn't very tactful... I said something about his drinking and he took it very badly, really over-reacted. Gavin liked to think of himself as a bit of a stud and I think he was rattled. I realised afterwards it might have been guilt making him impotent – screwing mother and daughter in the same bed... Anyway it all turned very nasty. He started to abuse me, called me "bloody insatiable" – which I thought was a bit much under the circumstances...' Rose takes a deep breath. 'I got out of bed, completely turned off, but by then Gavin was getting into his stride. Getting it up finally, I suspect... But I'd had enough. I said something stupid, said I wouldn't sleep with him if he was the last man on earth – oh, really original and not the slightest bit true because I loved him and he knew it. He held me – had always held me – in the palm of his hand... But at that moment he wanted to hurt me. So he told me. Made some sick joke of it – "like mother, like daughter". I didn't believe him at first. I laughed. I thought he was just trying to upset me, frighten me. So he went into detail, hideous detail, about what they'd done and where they'd done it. He was way, *way* out of order... Did you leave any whisky?'

'No, I'm sorry. Don't say any more if you – '

'No, I want to tell you.' Rose swallows. 'Gavin said he couldn't resist the temptation to sleep with Megan because it seemed like incest but it actually wasn't, so it was okay.'

'He was one hell of a sick bastard.'

228

'And she had offered apparently. More than once. Or so he said...'

'So it was a double betrayal.'

'Yes. He'd known Megan since she was eleven. She'd grown up with him during her teenage years. She had no memory of her father and Gavin wasn't around often enough to be a real father-figure to her. I always thought he seemed more like an older brother or an uncle. They got on brilliantly. But he was the nearest she ever came to having a dad, the bastard.'

Calum considers. 'I'd have killed him – and smiled while I did it.'

'It did cross my mind. I think if there'd been a gun or a knife on the bedside table, or if I'd thought I was strong enough to strangle him, I'd have done it. But I would have had to go downstairs to the kitchen to get a knife. And I couldn't move. I tried... I tried to walk away from him but I couldn't. I just stood there, weeping, listening to all the poison... And I didn't know if I was crying for her or for me.'

'You threw him out?'

'Didn't have to. He started to pack his things then and there. Then apparently I went and walked through the French windows... I don't really remember much about that... While I was in hospital he cleared all his stuff out. There wasn't much, mostly climbing gear. Books. Cameras. He'd never accumulated possessions. My place had never really been home to him. Just "base camp", I suppose.'

'Have you ever told anyone what happened?'

'Psychiatrists... I didn't tell my friends. I couldn't. That's why we lost touch really. They couldn't understand the break-up and I couldn't explain. They thought I should forgive Gavin. They couldn't see why I was so *angry*. Everyone knew he'd been unfaithful before. They assumed we'd get back together when I came out of hospital.'

She bows her head and is silent. Calum puts an arm round her shoulders and feels her body begin to shudder. Rose sobs silently until her ribcage heaves, then she throws back her head and cries out, 'Make it *stop*, Calum! Please! Please make the pain in my head stop! Oh, dear God – make the *past* stop!'

He cradles her, pulls her head onto his chest, murmurs words, some English, some Gaelic. He peels her tangled hair back from her wet face, holds her and waits. When he thinks there is a chance she might hear him he says softly but firmly. 'Only you can do that, Rose.'

'*How?*'

'Start your future.'

Breathing heavily, she swallows until her voice is almost steady. 'Are you my future, Calum?'

'Perhaps your immediate future... And you would appear to be mine. Which has a kind of reassuring symmetry to it, doesn't it?' He holds her, stroking her head until she gradually relaxes against him.

She mumbles into his chest, 'Calum, I want to sleep.'

'Aye, I think it best. I'll take you home.'

She sits up and turns to look at him, her wet eyes huge, smeared with mascara. 'Can I stay?'

'Of course. Do you want me to ring Megan?'

'No,' she sniffs. 'Megan can go to hell.'

'Okay.'

He stands and offers her a hand to help her up from the sofa. Rose does not rise but looks up at him for a long moment. She lifts both hands and slides them under his jumper, spreading them flat on his smooth muscled stomach. She feels his diaphragm kick involuntarily with a sharp intake of breath. Her hands drop down to the zip of his jeans. Calum does not move. She tugs until his jeans gape open, then lays her fingers gently on the scar made by the ice-axe.

'What was it you said, Calum, about the quilt on my bed? "So much pain... Yet it's beautiful."' She presses her mouth to the scar.

CHAPTER THIRTEEN

WHEN I WAKE THERE IS A STRANGE MAN IN MY BED.
Then I realise I'm not in my bed.

My stomach churns like a washing machine and the room pirouettes. I close my eyes and remember nothing. I open them again and realise that the sleeping man who, with his tangled black curls, black stubble and improbably long black eyelashes lacks only an earring to resemble a pirate, is Calum.

But I remember nothing.

Calum's torso projecting beyond the duvet is naked. I investigate no lower. With a sense of growing dismay I realise that I, too, am naked.

But I remember *nothing*.

He opens his eyes. They shift their focus. His smile is slow, lopsided. 'Good morning, Rose.'

'Good morning.'

He frowns. 'You look like you've just had another of your terrible nightmares.'

'Do I? No... I'm just... *confused*... I don't remember how I got here.'

'How's your head?'

'Pounding. *Awful*. I drank a lot, didn't I?'

'Aye, we all did. It was a great party...'

He doesn't touch me. He is keeping his distance, which surely suggests... 'Calum, I don't know quite how to put this... Did we... did we make love last night?'

His eyebrows disappear beneath his fringe. 'Well now, I don't think of myself as Scotland's answer to Casanova exactly, but I've never had a woman ask me if it *happened* before. '

'Oh God, I'm sorry! All I can remember is you standing in front of me... looking like St Sebastian without the arrows.'

Calum laughs loudly and my head reels at the noise. He props himself up on one elbow and looks down at me, grinning. 'No, Rose, nothing happened. Your virtue is still intact. D'you *really* no' remember?'

'No... I thought I remembered you putting your clothes back *on* again.'

'Aye. After my wee tantrum I offered to see you home, but you said you wanted to stay. Then you started to remove my clothes again... And I returned the compliment. Then we got into bed... I kissed you... and you fell asleep! Kind of Sleeping Beauty in reverse.'

'Oh, Calum, I'm sorry!'

'Don't be. I suspect you saved me from a terrible humiliation. I'd drunk a *hell* of a lot of whisky... I fell asleep too, almost straight away. Would you like some coffee?'

'Yes, please.' He gets out of bed and I see I have indeed spent the night with a naked man. The scars on his back are more noticeable in daylight. I pull the duvet up over my arms, suddenly self-conscious. Shivering, he lifts a dressing-gown from a hook and shrugs it on.

'I need to pee, Calum. Where are my clothes?'

'No idea.' He opens a cupboard and pulls out a corduroy shirt. 'Put this on. It's warm and it'll swamp you.'

He tosses me the shirt and heads towards the kitchenette. I struggle to put the shirt on quickly while his back is turned. 'It smells of you.'

'It shouldn't do – it's clean.'

'Oh... Maybe *I* smell of you.'

His head swivels round suddenly and he looks at me, the mock jocularity gone, his eyes hungry. He swallows and I watch his Adam's apple move behind the black stubble. 'You look beautiful...'

'Thank you.'

'Whatever you wear, you look beautiful... And you were beautiful naked, Rose. I wasn't too drunk to notice... The scars aren't as bad as you think... And they'll fade.'

I get out of bed and pad towards the bathroom. 'I *have* to pee.'

'I'll make some coffee.'

When I return he has lit the stove and made mugs of coffee. I get back into bed and pull the still-warm duvet around me before it occurs to me that Calum might take this as a signal to join me, but he sits circumspectly in a chair, looking chilled and miserable. His dressing gown gapes, framing the scar on his chest, a pale gash against the almost hairless brown of his skin. I look down and my eyes light on his extraordinary feet, the right one two-toed. The skin on both feet is ugly, mottled greyish-mauve. I remember, with the force of a sudden blow, a wound like a mouth in his groin.

'You're cold. Get back into bed, Calum.'

He shakes his head. 'I meant what I said last night, Rose. But you probably don't remember that either.'

'I do. All or nothing.'

234

'Aye. I'm sorry. But it's been a long time for me too.'

'How long?'

'Since I got laid? It must be... nearly two years. Christ, time flies when you're having fun.' He gulps his coffee.

'That's seven years of celibacy between us...'

'Aye.' He's watching me. Waiting.

'We've got a lot of catching up to do... Come to bed, Calum. Let's do it properly this time.'

The weight of him
pressing down
pulling me apart
the shock
filling me
filling the wound
my hands slide over the smooth planes of his body
slopes and dunes of muscle
hard as bone
my fingertips settle into pitted scars on his back
clasp
push
press
wounds like mouths
in his chest
in his groin
his mouth a wound
gaping
his mouth

on mine
in mine
I lay hands on him
mouth on him
I want to heal
heal him
dear God
stop
stop his mouth
stop his mouth with my mouth
stop all the mouths on his body
fill
fill them
with love

Rose lies with her head pillowed on Calum's chest, her body moulded to the side of his. She rests her palm flat on the smooth concavity below his ribcage, feeling his diaphragm rise and fall.

'Are you awake?'

'Aye.'

'I ought to go.' He groans. 'Megan will wonder where I am.'

'The hell with Megan. She'll be asleep.' He pulls Rose closer. She slides her hand down to rest on the hard peak of his hipbone. Calum sighs contentedly.

'Was she very disappointed?'

'Who?'

'Megan.'

'Disappointed? What about?'

'Last night. When you turned her down.'

'Och, I don't know – how would I? We'd both had a fair bucket... She seemed a wee bit *surprised*.'

'Just think – you could have had us both.'

'I'm not greedy.'

'I suppose that's a standard male fantasy, isn't it – a man in bed with two women.'

'Aye, maybe... Not mine. I know my limitations.'

'It must have been Gavin's.'

'Do women no' fantasise about being in bed with two men?'

'I never did. Gavin was as much as I could handle.'

Calum is silent for a while, stroking the hollow in the small of her back. 'Rose... you said if you went to bed with me there might be three people in the bed.'

'Yes.'

'Were there?' His chest rises and falls. Once. Twice.

She wants to lie, but cannot. 'Yes.'

'Oh... How did *I* do?'

Calum stokes her arm gently, following with his fingers the silvery lines of scars, as if he is reading a map. He works his way from wrist to shoulder, then back down again by another route. Rose finds it oddly soothing.

'Your body's... *crazed*.'

'Like my mind.'

'I knew you'd say that... No, I mean, like pottery. There's a pattern of cracks...'

'Like crazy paving you mean?'

'Och, will you stop taking the piss, woman!'

'There are Crazy Quilts too, you know. '

'Aye, I know – that one with the quilted vagina would take some beating.'

'No, it's a particular type of Victorian scrap quilt. Irregular shapes are sewn together any-old-how and the seams are decorated with embroidery in brightly coloured threads. It's like fabric crazy paving. I've got one at home. I'll show it to you. They're chaotic, but beautiful.'

'Like you...'

'I knew you'd say that.'

He resumes his tracing of the patterns on her arms, gently, minutely, as if reading Braille. 'Gavin never saw these?'

'My scars? No. I only ever saw him once after it happened. He came to the hospital... to say goodbye.'

'So no one's ever seen them... touched them before?'

'Apart from the doctor who sewed me up, no.' He is silent. Rose sighs. 'I know what you're thinking, Calum...'

'No, you don't.'

'I bet I do.'

'I bet you don't.'

'You were thinking, "Another first ascent", weren't you?'

'Aye, I was.'

'Bloody climbers! You're all the bloody same!' She elbows him in the ribs. He twists away, then pulls the duvet back. Rose sits up, alarmed, reaching for the cover, but he is too quick for her. He sits astride her so that the only way she can hide herself is to press her body against his.

'Rose...' Calum lays his hands on her shoulders and gently pushes her away, back down on to the mattress. 'You've nothing to be ashamed of... The scars don't matter! I can feel them, but I can hardly *see* them. You're beautiful, woman!' He looks down as his cock begins to stir again. 'You see?' He utters something in Gaelic and smiles down at her.

'What was that?'

'A man's penis never lies!'

'That doesn't sound like one of Shona's.'

'Aye, right enough.'

She runs her hands up over his belly, across the cushion of his chest and grasps the hard curves of his biceps. 'You're beautiful too, Calum, you know that? You may be The Pobble Who Had No Toes, but you are completely and utterly *beautiful.*'

'Aye, I know. But as my big sister says...' He lowers himself and with a deft twist of his hips spreads her willing thighs apart. 'Beauty won't boil the pot!'

As Rose opens her front door Megan leaps to her feet like a startled cat. 'Mum, I've been so worried about you! Where on *earth* have you been?'

'Please don't shout Megan, I've got a splitting headache.'

'Is that all you've got to say? I've been worried to death! I rang Shona but there was no answer.'

'They'll be at church.'

'Where have you *been* all night?'

'In bed with Calum.'

'*What?*'

'You heard.'

'*Calum?*'

'Why so surprised? I thought you rather fancied him.' Megan stares, open-mouthed. 'Oh, perhaps I misunderstood? You aren't surprised that I wanted to bed Calum, rather that *he* wanted to bed *me*.'

'I didn't realise... you and he...' Megan blushes. 'Did he tell you – '

'About you making a pass at him? Yes, he did. Rather reluctantly.'

'Is that why you slept with him?'

'No, of course not! Do you really think I am that petty and vengeful, Megan?'

'I wouldn't blame you if you were.'

'Well, I'm not. Calum and I were an *item*, as you would put it, before you arrived. Your arrival simply delayed things, that's all.'

'I'm sorry.'

'No need to be. You weren't to know and I didn't want to tell you.'

'I hadn't the faintest idea... I would never have – I mean I wouldn't have gone anywhere near him if I'd known.'

Rose stares at her daughter. 'Are you sure about that?'

'Yes, of course! For God's sake, Mum, I was *seventeen*. I was in love! Have I got to suffer for that for the rest of my life?'

'No. I imagine you suffered enough when Gavin dumped you for the next incumbent.'

'Gavin dumped me because he still loved *you*.'

Rose looks away, her breath catching. 'That's not true.'

'It *is* bloody true and I should bloody know! He wanted you back but he was too proud to crawl.'

'Gavin wouldn't crawl because he knew he'd be wasting his time. I would never have taken him back.'

'Oh, Mum, do me a favour – you'd have taken him back like a shot! You'd take him back now! You still love him. You may have fooled Calum, but you don't fool me. Did you sleep with Calum to get back at Gavin?'

'I slept with Calum because the joys of celibacy are much overrated and because I was curious to know how it feels to make love with a man you *like*, as opposed to *worship*. Not that it's any of your damn business, who I sleep with or why.'

Megan, abashed, stammers, 'No, you're right... It isn't... Does Calum know about – me and Gavin?'

'Yes, he does. I had to tell him in the end. He made some feeble joke about you and me having the same taste in men.'

'Oh, God.'

'Yes, it was rather unfortunate. But then you making a pass at Calum was rather unfortunate.'

'Give me a break – I was drunk! He's a nice guy.'

'He's twice your age. But then so was Gavin. What *is* it with you and older men, Megan?'

'Mum, I'm twenty-two. It's no business of yours who I sleep with or why.'

'Touché.' Rose sweeps past her into the kitchen and fills the kettle noisily. Megan follows.

'Please, can we stop this? It's *horrible*. Can we please stop hurting each other? I didn't come here for this.'

Rose ignores the proffered olive branch and puts both hands to her temples and rubs. 'Do you have any paracetamol? Or aspirin? Anything... I don't keep such things in the house. My head is pounding.' She fills a glass with water and drinks it down.

'Yes, in my handbag.' Megan fetches her bag and hands over two foil-covered tablets.

'Thanks...' Rose refills her glass and swallows the tablets. 'Megan, I want you to leave. I'm sorry, but I can't deal with you *and* Calum. I'm not sure I can even deal with Calum. But it would make life easier for me – simpler – if you went home. I'm not really sure why you wanted to come out here anyway. In *February*...'

Megan is silent for a moment, then breathes deeply before saying, 'I came because I had some news for you. I wanted to tell you in person.'

'Oh?' Rose looks up and studies her daughter's face. 'Not good news from the looks of it.'

'No... I've been waiting for a good time to tell you. But I can see there's never going to be a good time. Not now.'

'What is it? Are you ill? Tell me. Is it something serious?'

'No, I'm fine. It's not me... It's Gavin... Mum, Gavin's dead.'

The kettle clicks as it switches off.

'*Dead*?'

'Yes. I'm sorry.'

'*Gavin's* dead?'

'Yes.'

'When?'

'Last summer. July.'

Rose's mouth works for a moment before the word emerges. 'How?'

'A climbing accident... On Skye.'

'Oh... He fell?'

'Yes.'

'I see...' Rose gazes past Megan and whispers, incredulous. 'I always thought I would *know*... I thought maybe my heart would stop beating... How did you find out?'

'I was at Simon's wedding. Gavin wasn't there. So...' She shrugs. 'I knew he must be dead.'

'Yes... Gavin would never miss a chance for a piss-up with the lads.' Rose looks down at the floor, then out of the kitchen window, avoiding Megan's eyes. 'Simon's married, you say?'

'Yes. Last November.'

'We lost touch... I lost touch with all of them. Afterwards. It was a shame. I missed them.'

'Simon asked after you.'

'Did he?'

'Yes. Sent his love.'

'Bless him... And he told you? About Gavin?'

'Yes. He'd had the news from Dave. Dave was with Gavin when the accident happened.'

'Oh... Was Dave all right?'

'He broke both legs.'

'Oh my God... But Gavin – Gavin *died*?'

'Yes... Massive head injuries.'

Rose's hand travels to her mouth, stifling a sound. She swallows. 'Did he – did he die instantly?'

'No, in hospital. In intensive care. He never regained consciousness apparently.'

'I see...' Rose is silent, staring at the plume of steam rising from the kettle.

'He wouldn't have wanted to die any other way, Mum... He was doing what he loved, what he lived for. It's what Gavin would have wanted.'

Rose lifts her head and finally looks at Megan, a strange light in her eye. 'Now that's where you're wrong. Gavin would have wanted to die on Everest, collapse at the foot of the Hillary Step and lie there, frozen and mummified for all time, so that climbers had to step over his body and salute the fallen hero – *that's* what Gavin would have wanted! He would not have wanted to be scraped off the side of the Cuillin and bundled into an ambulance – where's the glory in that? No, Megan, as mountaineering deaths go, Gavin's was definitely second division and he would have *hated* that.'

Megan has started to cry. 'Mum – how can you talk like that? You *loved* him! *We* loved him!'

Rose appears not to hear. 'Was he wearing a helmet?'

'No, I don't think so.'

'Oh, the vanity of that man! *The stupidity!*' Rose opens a cupboard door and takes out cups and saucers, banging them down on the worktop. She yanks open a drawer and rifles noisily through its contents for teaspoons. 'Where was he buried?'

'He was cremated. Gavin left no will... He never said what he would want in the event of – '

Rose laughs, an ugly, staccato sound and rounds on Megan. 'Of course not – Gavin was immortal, didn't you know?'

'Dave thought he'd want his ashes returned to the Cuillin. He couldn't go because of his injuries, so Simon and Andy took them and... scattered them.'

'Where he fell?'

'No. They couldn't face that. They climbed *Sgurr nan Gillean*. Scattered them from there.'

'The Peak of the Young Men.'

'Yes. Simon thought that seemed appropriate.'

'Yes. Gavin would have appreciated that.' Her hands shaking now, Rose puts two teabags into the pot and pours on hot water. She replaces the lid clumsily, chipping it. 'Who did you say Simon married?'

'I didn't. He married his German girlfriend. Birgit.'

'Oh. Good,' Rose says absently, staring into space. 'She was pretty.'

'And pregnant. They've got a little boy now.'

'Simon – a *father*? I don't believe it...' Something fleeting, something like a smile passes across Rose's face, then the blankness descends again. 'What did they call the baby?'

Megan hesitates. 'Gavin.'

With a howl, Rose picks up the teapot with both hands and hurls it through the kitchen window. Megan screams and grabs her mother, dragging her away from the broken glass, sobbing.

'Mummy! No! Please, no! Mummy! Mummy, please... *Please...*'

***

Gavin
falling
somersaulting...
The highest high
The biggest turn-on
The hardest hard-on
Death, Gavin.
Yours.

CHAPTER FOURTEEN

WHEN ROSE HAS CRIED HERSELF INTO EXHAUSTION Megan persuades her to go to bed, then rings Calum.

'Calum, it's Megan... I'm sorry to bother you but could you come over? It's kind of an emergency... Mum isn't well. I'm not sure whether I should ring her doctor. I don't know what to do for the best, frankly and – well, she wants me to leave.'

Calum is at the back door four minutes later, his chest heaving. Megan's heart sinks at the sight, thinking he is having a panic attack, then realises he has run all the way from the caravan.

'What happened? Where is she?' He shoulders his way past Megan. 'Christ, what happened to your window?'

'Mum threw a teapot.'

'At *you*?'

'No.'

'Where is she?'

'In bed. I think she might be asleep now. Leave her for a bit. I want to talk to you.'

'Is she okay?'

'Yes, I think so, but she's very upset. She said she wants to be left alone... but I don't think she should be, Calum.'

'And you say she wants you to leave? Aye, well, Shona and I will keep an eye on her, you've no need to worry.'

'You don't understand... She's in a state of shock.' Calum is very still, his eyes fixed on Megan. 'You see, I came to Uist because I had some news I wanted to break to her... in person.'

'Bad news.'

'The worst for Mum.'

'Gavin.'

'Yes... He's dead, Calum.'

'Aye, I know.'

Calum pushes the door gently and looks into the bedroom. Rose stirs.

He approaches the bed and sits down.

'Rose. It's me. Megan's told me what happened.' He takes her hand and lifts it to his mouth. She opens her eyes but doesn't look at him.

'He's dead, Calum. He's been dead for months, and I didn't know... Isn't that strange?'

'You thought you would?'

'Yes, I did. Foolish of me, but I really thought I would... I was packing up my house in July, in Fort William. Getting ready to move... Maybe that's why I didn't notice. I was very busy...' She smoothes the quilt on the bed and slowly traces the pattern of myriad triangles with a finger. 'I spent years rehearsing Gavin's death, what I would say, what I would do. I even knew what I would wear to his funeral. And in the end I wasn't invited. No one knew where I was, I suppose. Or maybe they were all too scared to tell me... He died on Skye, apparently. Bloody idiot wasn't wearing a helmet.'

'He was.'

Rose turns to look at him, suddenly alert. 'What?'

'Gavin was wearing a helmet. It was smashed in, but he was wearing one.'

'How do you know?'

'I was part of the team that brought him down.'

'So – you've always known?'

'No. It wasn't until Megan mentioned his surname that I realised. Then she described him. I remembered the paper-work. You tend to remember the ones that die... and I always remember names.' He squeezes her hand. 'I remembered yours, didn't I?'

'Tell me what happened.'

'You're sure?'

'Yes.'

'It was pretty bad... Gavin's mate was in a bad way – both legs gone – and it was fairly obvious Gavin wasn't going to make it. They'd been on the hill a good while before we found them. '

'But he wasn't dead... when you found him?'

'No. In and out of consciousness. He spoke once or twice... Asked after his mate.'

'Dave.'

'Aye.'

'Was he in a lot of pain?'

'He was in deep shock, so maybe not... Apart from the head injury, he'd broken an arm. Collarbone too, I suspect. But we made him as comfortable as possible.'

'Did you lower him down on a stretcher?'

'No, he was way too bad for that. The helicopter lifted him off and took him to Inverness.'

'Where he died.'

'Aye... I'm sorry, Rose. There was nothing anyone could do.'

'Once you realised... who Gavin was... why didn't you tell me he was dead?'

'I was going to tell you... when the time was right. But then things got complicated. Between us. And I wasn't sure how you'd cope with the news...' He lets go of her hand suddenly and shakes his head. 'No, that's a bloody lie...' He rakes a hand through his hair, screwing up his eyes. 'I thought if you knew Gavin was dead, you'd fucking *canonise* the man, you'd love him even more! He'd become the complete mountaineering hero – a *dead* hero – the best kind! And I knew I couldn't compete with that, so I didn't tell you... Sad, selfish bastard aren't I?'

Rose is silent for a long time. When she finally speaks her voice is faint but calm. 'Thank you for being honest with me. And thank you for doing what you could for Gavin. I appreciate that... I'm glad you met him, Calum. I think he would have liked you.'

Rose has not moved or spoken for some time. In the bedroom the light is failing and hailstones batter the window. Calum remembers the broken window in the kitchen and wonders if he should go down and help Megan. Peering at Rose he sees her eyes are closed, her breathing is steady. He is about to rise when she suddenly speaks. 'I can't believe he's gone *completely*, that no one is ever going to see him again. I never really thought I would see him again – although I did wonder for one stupid moment whether he would show up at your party. It had crossed my mind that you might know him. Megan thought I was mad and started to cry... Oh – I see now... why she cried. Why she said he wouldn't be there... Poor Megan. I wish I hadn't been so foul to her about you.'

'She'll get over it. Megan's pretty tough. And brave. She didn't have to tell you about Gavin. She certainly didn't have to tell you in person.'

'No.'

'Do you really want to send her away?'

'Yes. I want to be on my own.'

'Rose – '

'I know neither of you thinks I'll be safe, but I'm sure I will. This doesn't really make any difference, does it? All the years I lived with Gavin – and without him – I lived with the idea of his death. It's just become a reality finally. But I need time to think... to think about Megan... about you... and what I'm going to do.'

Calum is silent, watching Rose's hands clutch compulsively at the quilt. 'I think maybe I'm better on my own, Calum... I'm steadier...'

'Rose – '

She doesn't meet his eyes. 'I'm too much for you to take on – too much for *anybody*. And if you – we – later decided... if it ended, I mean, I'm not quite sure what would happen to me. And you climb, so it would be the same old story, it could happen all over again.' Before he can reply she says fiercely,

251

'And don't even *think* about offering to give it up – I wouldn't believe you for one second! I wouldn't ask you to anyway.'

'You asked Gavin.'

'How did you know?'

'Guessed. I was married to a woman whose mission in life was to get me to stop climbing.'

'Yes. I did ask Gavin. I begged him.'

'But you'll not ask me... Why?'

'I wanted Gavin to stop climbing because I couldn't conceive of surviving his death. I knew I wouldn't want to. And I had a young teenage daughter and a history of mental instability – to put it mildly... But things are rather different now.'

'You would survive my death.'

'Yes. I would. I would grieve, but I would survive. I survived before I met you, I survived without Gavin – much to my surprise. I think I actually want to live now. But I don't know what would happen if I got more involved with you, if I... loved you. And I think it would be all too easy to love you, Calum.'

He bows his head and examines his hands, placing his fingertips together carefully, in pairs, reckoning. 'So... This is a gentle and elaborate way of saying it's over?'

'Yes. I'm sorry.'

'You want peace and quiet more than you want to love and be loved?'

'I *need* that, Calum. To survive. To have any quality of life.'

He looks up at her, incredulous. '*What* quality of life, for Christ's sake? Will you no' at least give us a chance? A six month trial?'

'No. I'd fall in love with you probably. I'd get used to you being there and I couldn't bear to have all that happiness again and then... just lose it.'

'Jesus, Rose, this is so bloody calculating – I just can't believe this is the same woman I was in bed with this morning.'

'No, neither can I, but that's the whole point, isn't it? You were in bed with *two* women, Calum – at least! And which of them was *me*?'

'Not the one living half a life.'

'Oh, really? Am I the one who wants to take you to bed? Or the one who wants to run a mile? The one who trusts you, or the one who thinks all men are treacherous, selfish bastards? Tell me, Calum, which of my feelings are real? Because I can't tell, you see, I just don't know! But what I've learned is that if I'm *half*-alive, I stay alive. That's what the medication does to you. I don't want the bloody medication – well, not as much of it as I should take – and so I have to find other ways of diluting myself, slowing myself down, *limiting* what I feel. Can't you see? It *is* calculating because I can't afford reality – not mine anyway. Tell me how a poet could love and live with such a fake?'

He stands abruptly, knocking the chair. He catches it as it falls and sets it upright. 'Okay, Rose, I hear what you're saying. I don't bloody agree, but I see why you think the way you do. The word trust does not feature in your emotional vocabulary, but I can understand that after the way Gavin and Megan treated you. And, who knows, maybe you're right to keep away from me – folk I care for do seem to have a nasty habit of dying on me.' He grasps the door handle, his knuckles white.

'If you or Megan need me for anything – anything at all, day or night – you're to give me a call. And I'll be bloody livid if you don't.'

'Thank you. I'm very grateful.'

'Not grateful enough.'

'Calum, please, that's not fair!'

He hesitates, looking around the room as if he is trying to fix it in his memory. Without looking at Rose he asks, 'Do you still want to do the exhibition?'

She pauses before answering. 'Do you?'

'Aye.'

'Well, then... I don't see why we shouldn't... if you think it will be manageable.'

'Oh aye, we'll manage! We're both brilliant at *managing*...'

'Calum, please try to understand...'

'I am trying.' His voice is low, clotted with emotion. She extends a hand towards him. Calum approaches the bed again, kneels and takes her in his arms. His hair still smells of the toast he burned when he made them breakfast. Rose starts to cry.

'Och, wheesht now...' He kisses her eyelids gently, then her mouth, slowly and at length. When he finally lets her go she stares at his slack, wet mouth, notes his pallor under the day-old stubble and feels her resolution crumble. 'Go. Please, Calum. Go now. I'll be all right.'

He stands again and without speaking walks out of the room. Rose listens to his heavy footfall on the stairs with heavier heart.

***

Just before the shutter comes down
there's a flicker
a final flickering of light
I know that this is it

Just before the shutter comes down
there's a turning of the key
a bolt shoots home
I'm trapped

My mind overflows
vomits up words
I panic
I drown

You say you'll come with me
Would you dare?...
You would dare.
But you cannot come
because I cannot say when or where I am going
or when I will be back

You see I never know
until it's too late
I never know
until just before the shutter comes down
and there's a final flickering of light

***

As Calum descends the stairs Megan is sweeping up glass and pottery shards in the kitchen. She calls out. 'Would you like a bite to eat, Calum? I was just going to make something for Mum...' When he appears in the doorway she is startled by the change in him. 'Are you okay?'

He rubs at his eyes. 'Aye, I'm fine right enough. As well as can be expected.'

'What's happened?'

'Rose will tell you. If she wants you to know.'

'How is she?'

'Calm. Frighteningly calm. But who knows what's going on in her head? I'm away now to get something to block off that window. Donald has some sheets of plywood I think... If you've any trouble with Rose you're to ring me – any time, day or night.'

'Thanks. I appreciate it. If she freaks out I will need you, I'm afraid. Gavin and I sometimes used to have trouble restraining her. It takes two people really. Two *strong* people.'

Calum watches her wrap the pieces of glass and china in newspaper, registers that her fingers are bleeding. 'Jesus, Megan – what kind of a childhood did you have?'

'What childhood? I don't remember any time in my life when I wasn't aware that my mum was different, that she needed looking after and there was only me to do it. Gavin and I were thrown together... Sometimes it was like we were the parents and she was the child. I don't know how I'd have managed without him. I think I was just as scared of losing him as Mum was – for different reasons. Maybe that's why I... did what I did. I was trying to make him *stay*. I thought he was going to leave us... and I couldn't bear it. I wanted someone to look after *me*. And Gavin was the only one who ever did that. Oh, Mum tried! I know she did her best, but Gavin was the only person in the world who ever made me feel safe. And I loved him for it.'

'Rose will maybe understand that one day.'

'Well, at the moment she's insisting I leave.'

'Aye, she said. I can't understand that.'

Megan runs her bleeding fingers under the tap. 'Oh, I suppose she thinks I'll be dragging *you* off to bed given half a chance...' She looks up at him quickly, embarrassed. 'I'd like to apologise, by the way – for last night.'

'No bother. It was a night of indiscretions. Your mother's regretting hers too.'

Megan dries her hands and takes a First Aid kit down from a shelf. 'Oh, take no notice of anything she says, Calum. Especially *now*. She's just dealing with bloody Gavin.' She struggles with a plaster.

'Here – let me...' Calum peels plasters and applies them to her shaking fingers.

Megan blinks back tears, fighting the urge to abdicate all responsibility and lay her head on Calum's chest. She sniffs loudly. 'She'll either go mad or she'll go into shut-down.'

'Let's hope it's the latter.'

'Either way, she wants us both out of the picture.'

'I think in her weird way she's trying to protect you, Megan.'

'About bloody time!' Megan abandons her struggle and starts to whimper. Calum folds another weeping woman in his arms and as Megan hugs him tight, he wonders who is doing the comforting. She reaches for a piece of kitchen towel and blows her nose. 'Oh, God, I'm sorry... Look, let me get you something to eat. It will give me something to do.'

'No, thanks. I'll get that window fixed, then I have a pressing appointment with a whisky bottle.'

'Why didn't you tell me you were dead?'

'I thought you knew.'

'No... I thought I *would* know... if it happened. But I didn't. I didn't feel anything.'

'It doesn't make any difference, Rosie.'

'What do you mean?'

'It doesn't make any difference me being dead. You *knowing* I'm dead. It was over... You never would have seen me again.'

'No, probably not. But I lived with the hope that I might... That somehow things would turn out all right... in the end.'

'It was the end, Rose... *This* is.'

'Is it really, Gavin?'

...

'Gavin?'

...

'Gavin – are you there?'

CHAPTER FIFTEEN

STANDING AT THE FOOT OF THE STAIRS, Megan can hear her mother crying. She recognises in herself a familiar cocktail of anger, shame and helplessness and, in automatic response, asks herself what Gavin would have done. She starts to laugh at the thought of Gavin helping Rose cope with the aftermath of his own death, then realises she isn't laughing, that her cheeks are wet, that she wishes, really *wishes* Gavin were here now to deal with her mother.

She remembers Gavin pouring large gins and climbing into bed with Rose fully clothed, mouthing to Megan over Rose's head to put pizza in the oven. She remembers him talking, talking, non-stop, an endless flow of mental energy channelled towards Rose: Gavin describing the difficulties of a new climbing route; Gavin explaining the byzantine complexities of the plot of *The Usual Suspects*; Gavin singing Springsteen songs in a cod New Jersey accent; Gavin defying Rose to give up, defying her to want to die in the face of his energy, his love of life.

Megan would bring them pizza on a tray and walk away to eat hers in the kitchen, lonely but relieved not to have to deal with Rose, jealous that Gavin would spend the evening upstairs, that when he came down – if he came down – he would be exhausted. Wordless at last, he might bless her with a weary smile, maybe a conspiratorial thumbs-up, but then he'd turn on the TV and fall instantly asleep.

Megan heads for the kitchen, makes toast and tea for Rose and carries it up on a tray. She knocks and waits a moment before entering. Rose sits up in bed, red-eyed, surrounded by crumpled tissues.

'I thought you might like a cup of tea. I've made you some toast and honey. See if you can manage a few mouthfuls.'

'Oh thanks... I'm sorry I'm being such a wimp. What on earth's that banging noise?'

'Calum fixing the window.'

'What window?'

'You threw the teapot through the kitchen window.'

'*Did* I? Oh, God, I'm sorry...' Rose looks at the tray in dismay. She nibbles at a corner of toast, chewing slowly. She swallows then says, 'I don't think I can manage this.'

'That's okay, I thought it was worth a try... Listen, Mum, will you please let me stay?'

'No, honestly, I really think I'll cope better on my own. I'll feel more in control. I can't cope with all the... *memories* with you being here, Megan. Life's been much more difficult for me ever since you got here. I'm sorry, that sounds really unkind... I am trying to break with the past but it's harder with you here.'

'But I don't trust you to be here on your own. I'm worried that you might...'

'Try to kill myself again? Oh, no, why would I do that? It's not as if Gavin and I were still together. I never would have seen him again. I've no reason to kill myself now.'

'There never *was* a reason to kill yourself, Mum, but you tried several times.'

Rose is thoughtful. 'I do see why you're worried. But I can't *think* while you're here, I can't work. And I have to work. It's work that will keep me sane.'

'What about Calum?' Rose is silent. 'He seems pretty upset.'

'I don't want to talk about it now. Please, Megan, I'm so tired. Will you just leave me in peace?'

'If that's really what you want. I'll go tomorrow. Calum says there's a flight to Glasgow. But I'd like to come back for your exhibition, if you'll let me.'

'Of course. I'd love you to.'

'When is it?'

'In the summer. June some time. Ask Calum.'

'You will keep working on that, won't you? You must. The work you've done so far is really good. And you mustn't let Calum down.'

'And don't forget the kids – their poems are going in to the exhibition as well.'

'It'll be great! And it was all your idea.'

'Well, not really. It was a joint thing with Calum. He sparked off the idea.'

'He's a really nice guy.'

'Yes. He is.'

'He said he and Shona will keep an eye on you if I go.'

'Yes, they undoubtedly will unless I make strenuous efforts to prevent them.'

'He would be good for you, Mum. I know he wants to make you happy.'

'Yes... That's what he says.'

'I think it's what he means too.'

'Maybe... Sometimes Calum seems too good to be true. Something doesn't add up, I don't know what it is.'

'You don't trust him because Gavin betrayed you. Because I did. You have good reasons not to trust people – even people who say they love you.'

Rose leans back on her pillows and studies her daughter. Eventually she says, 'You loved Gavin more than you loved me, didn't you?'

Megan looks at her mother and blinks. Her voice when she finally replies is an outraged whisper. 'Mum, do you seriously think I would have done what I did if I hadn't loved him beyond reason? Beyond *everything*?'

'No. I suppose you wouldn't.'

'You loved Gavin more than you loved me.'

'Megan, I loved Gavin more than *life*! I thought I made that pretty clear after he'd gone.'

'And he *is* gone, Mum. Gone for good now. But we're still here. I'd really like us to be friends again, if we can.'

'Yes... So would I... But I need some time. Some space. Come back for the exhibition. We'll talk then. Come back in the summer, darling.'

'Yes, I will.'

'And would you do something for me? When you get home, would you send me one of your photos of Gavin? I don't have any. I'd like to have one... I need one. For work.'

Surprised and relieved that her mother is planning new projects, Megan resists the temptation to ask questions. 'Actually Simon gave me some photos to give you. I brought them with me. I was going to give them to you, after I'd told you what happened. They're photos of you and Gavin together. Nice ones. Simon found them in Gavin's flat when he cleared out his things.'

'Oh...' Rose looks confused.

'Do you want to see them now?' Megan asks gently.

'No... No, thanks. But leave them for me, will you?'

'Yes, of course.' Megan removes the tray from Rose's lap and heads towards the bedroom door.

'Megan?'

'Yes?'

'He *was* wearing a helmet. Calum said.'

'Yes. Dave thought he wasn't. He must have forgotten.'

'I'm glad. About the helmet, I mean. I'm glad Gavin wasn't quite the fool I took him for.'

When Megan returns to the kitchen Calum is packing up his tools. He looks at the barely touched tray.

'How is she?'

'She's talking about work. I think she's planning something.'

'You sound worried.'

'Well, yes... If she starts working now she probably won't eat or sleep or remember to take her tablets. And she wants me on a plane tomorrow.'

'Don't worry, Shona and I will make nuisances of ourselves. I'll call Dr. Kerr out if there's any trouble. And I'll try and find someone to glaze your window tomorrow.'

'Thanks.'

'No bother...' Calum hesitates. 'Megan, can I ask your advice about something?'

'Go ahead.'

'Rose said she'd baby-sit on Friday. It's Shona's birthday and I was going to take her and Donald out for dinner, d'you remember?'

'Yes, I do.'

'D'you think I should hold Rose to that? I mean, it's something in her future, something to keep her grounded in her new life here, in the real world. And I know she feels she owes Shona. I think she probably feels she owes me too. And she enjoys spending time with the bairns... What d'you think? I'm inclined to call in the favour.'

'Yes, I think you probably should. She hates letting people down. But I think she might have forgotten all about it... what with Gavin. You'll need to remind her. Or I can.'

'The other thing I wanted to ask – and this is a hard one for you to answer – d'you think she'd be safe with the bairns?'

'You mean, would they be safe with her?'

'Aye.'

'Yes, I do. I have never known Mum harm a hair of anybody's head but her own. She damages property and she damages herself, but never other people. In fact she used to go to great lengths to avoid me coming to any harm. I remember once when I was quite small coming downstairs in the middle of the night and finding her sitting in the middle of the kitchen floor, calmly smashing her wedding china with a hammer. But all the china was inside a bin-liner... She'd done that because I was always running around barefoot, she'd made sure I wouldn't cut my feet on bits of broken china. When she goes mad it's only mad at one level. At another level she knows exactly what she's doing. It's a kind of *logical* madness.'

'Aye, well, that's the best kind I suppose...' Calum manages a wan smile that doesn't reach his eyes. 'Would you remind her about Friday for me?'

'Yes, of course.'

'If she doesn't want to do it, call me – I can easily ask someone else. I'll be picking Shona and Donald up at seven. Fergus will be in bed by then so Rose will only have three to deal with... And,' he adds grimly, 'They all know how to use the phone in an emergency.'

'Don't worry – if she agrees to do it, she'll be fine. It just depends what happens between now and Friday...'

Megan packs her few belongings into her rucksack then orders a taxi to take her to Benbecula airport in the morning. She takes the photos of Gavin and Rose out of their envelope and examines them. They must have been Gavin's favourites. Simon said he'd found them with Gavin's mountaineering photos. He appeared to possess no family snapshots. Megan had been disappointed to discover that Gavin had kept no photos of her, not even as a child.

All the photos are of Rose, or Gavin and Rose pictured together. In all of them Gavin smiles, his perpetually tanned face creased with laughter lines. Pictured sitting on a wall in Crete, relaxed in tight white jeans and a muscle-revealing white tee shirt, the sun setting picturesquely behind his blond head, Gavin is dazzling, gilded, god-like. Rose ignores the camera – and Megan who was taking the photo – and gazes up at her Apollo.

Megan tries to remember how old she was on that holiday. Fifteen? Jesus, she thinks, was it really any wonder?...

She replaces the photos in their envelope, labels it clearly and puts it in the centre of Rose's worktable. She looks at her watch. It is only 8 o'clock but she feels as if she has aged years in the last twelve hours. She gives up the struggle to stay awake and falls into bed exhausted.

Some time in the night Megan wakes to see a beam of light slashing the darkness. She thinks first of the lighthouse, then realises that it is a torch wielded by her mother who is padding around the workroom in her nightdress. As her eyes adjust to the darkness Megan can see that Rose carries a basket over her arm, that she is collecting items from the table and shelves and dropping them in. As she does so she mutters to herself in a voice too low for Megan to catch.

Megan cannot decide whether her mother is sleepwalking or has taken leave of her senses. She watches for the gleam of sharp objects going in to the basket, but Rose selects paper, pencils, books, pieces of cloth, tiny boxes that rattle. Megan wonders if the boxes contain pills, then remembers the bead and button boxes she played with as a child.

It is 3.00 am and her mother is working.

Rose leaves the room as quietly as she entered and Megan listens to her steady footsteps as they mount the stairs, hears the creak of her iron bedstead as Rose climbs back into bed. Then silence. Megan switches on the light and looks around the room, checks the worktable. The dressmaking shears, scalpel and rotary cutters are still in place.

The envelope of photos is gone.

***

white cream bronze gold
beads buttons pins pearls
silks satins linen scrim

Humpty Dumpty sat on the wall

cut tear slash rip
dazzle sparkle twinkle shine

Humpty Dumpty had a great fall

speckled freckled burnished bleached
crumpled
crushed

All the King's horses

gold lace
gold thread

All the King's men

cutting threading stitching pressing
putting you back together again
golden stitches mend your body

couldn't

pale dead
beads red
blood shed

together again

Fool's Gold *(Iron Pyrites)*
In memoriam
Gavin John Duffy
(1960 – 1999)

***

Rose's week settles into a routine of brief morning visits from Shona and even briefer evening visits from Calum. Shona finds a variety of excuses to call, delivering magazines, home baking, one of Eilidh's old party dresses for re-cycling.

Calum makes no pretence at informality and each evening stands gravely on the doorstep, observing Rose closely. She comes to the door clutching scissors, sometimes a half-eaten sandwich.

Rose doesn't invite Calum in and answers his questions with a distracted air. She appears edgy and pre-occupied, but since she is clearly working hard Calum draws no negative conclusions. Festooned like a Christmas tree with sparkling threads, scraps of gold cloth and the odd sequin here and there, her hair awry and dark smudges under her eyes, Calum thinks Rose has never looked lovelier. He consumes more whisky than usual that week, especially in the small hours when he looks across from the caravan to Rose's house and sees the light at her workroom window. He wonders if she is sleeping at all, hopes she has in fact fallen asleep at her table. He thinks about going to check up on her, pours another whisky instead.

It is Calum who wakes to find his head on a table.

On Friday evening Rose sorts out some sewing to take to Shona's. She packs a torch and Calum's anthology of poems, *Emotional Geology,* now much the worse for wear and littered with post-its. With chemical assistance Rose has slept all day since Shona's morning call, feels rested, but still tense. She has eaten a proper cooked meal, one that even included vegetables and as a precaution she has taken a tranquilliser.

She is heading for the front door when Calum knocks. He is dressed in a dark suit and Mickey Mouse tie in honour of Shona's birthday celebration and is freshly shaven, his hair brushed and shining, although the curls are already beginning to reassert themselves.

'Good evening, Rose. Are you ready?'

'Still checking up on me? Yes, I'm ready.' Rose arranges her mouth into a bright smile. Calum registers her lack-lustre eyes and looks a question. 'You don't miss a thing do you? I've taken a tranquilliser to be on the safe side. I didn't *need* to, but I thought you'd be happier if I did. I'm fine, Calum, I've been fine all week. I'm taking a minimal dose of meds and I am working hard. If I look awful it's because I'm knackered.'

'You don't look awful.'

'No, neither do you. And you smell *wonderful*...' she says, leaning towards his face. 'Oh – we're not supposed to do that sort of stuff any more, are we? Sorry.'

'You wrote the rules, Rose. You can change them, I suppose... Are you walking over to Shona's?'

'Yes.'

'May I walk with you?'

'Of course.'

'Before we go...' He slides a hand inside his jacket, pulls out a folded sheet of paper and hands it to her. 'Your next assignment.'

'Another poem for the exhibition?'

'Aye. Your mission – should you choose to accept it.'

She opens the sheet. There are twenty short handwritten lines. The poem is entitled *Rose Quartz*.

Her hand flies to her throat and she utters a small sound. She presses her lips together hard and shuts her eyes. When she opens them again they are full of tears. 'Oh, *shit!* And I was doing so well! I've slept, I've eaten, I've taken a sodding tranquilliser, then you go and do something like this...'

'I'm sorry... I didn't mean – ' He reaches for the sheet of paper but she snatches it away.

'Oh, take no notice of me, Calum. I'm being an ungrateful cow – as usual. I'm choked and overwhelmed and behaving in an utterly graceless fashion. I'm very sorry. No one has ever written a poem for me or about me before. I presume it's about me?'

'Aye.'

'Thank you. I'm absolutely thrilled.' She sniffs and wipes her eyes. 'And you'd like me to interpret it for the exhibition?'

'Aye. If you can.'

'I can and I will. But I'll read it later, if you don't mind – I daren't read it now... You do understand, don't you?'

He nods. 'I'd rather not be around when you read it anyway.'

Rose looks at her watch, then takes his hand. 'Come in, Calum, I want to show you something.' She leads him into the workroom and positions him in front of her new work-in-progress. Calum stares in silence. Eventually he splutters 'Bloody hell!' in tones of fervent admiration.

Rose stands beside Calum, looking at the new wall-hanging. 'Your mission – should you choose to accept it.'

'What's it called?'

'*Fool's Gold*. Subtitled *Iron Pyrites*.'

Calum studies the white and gold quilt, then shakes his head. 'It's Gavin, isn't it?'

'Yes, I'm afraid it is. But your poem will be a response to the quilt, not Gavin.'

'It's magnificent, Rose. Stunning. You've done him proud. Are you pleased with it?'

'Yes, I suppose so. It didn't turn out quite how I expected – but then they never do.'

They stand side by side looking at Gavin's wallhanging. On the adjacent wall *Basalt* 2 hangs, the negative of *Fool's Gold*, as dark and sinister as the other quilt is light and dazzling.

'Was *Basalt* a memorial poem, Calum?'

'Aye. In a way.'

'So they're a pair.'

'And what a pair...'

Rose looks at *Fool's Gold*, extends a hand to touch it gently and heaves a profound sigh. 'It's finished, Calum.'

He turns and looks at her profile, then back at the quilt. 'Will you not bind the frayed edges? And take out the pins?'

'Oh, I wasn't talking about the *quilt*... Come on – Shona will wonder what's happened to me.'

CHAPTER SIXTEEN

CALUM AND I WALK TO SHONA'S HOUSE, side by side in the darkness, as once we walked before in the opposite direction. Better prepared this time, I shine my flashlight ahead, avoiding the stones and potholes that caused me to stumble and take Calum's proffered arm, an event I now recall with a pang as the first time we touched each other.

This time Calum doesn't offer his arm, doesn't speak. I am aware only of his steady footfall and the faint creak of his leather jacket as he walks beside me. A bitter February wind lifts my hair and tosses it across my face, blinding me. I bow my head and shiver inside my coat. For once I am looking forward to the stifling warmth of Shona's overheated house where Donald – perpetually chilled from fishing or crofting activities – insists on sub-tropical temperatures being maintained at all times.

The distant grumble of the sea fades as we draw near to Shona's. The yellow glow at the windows looks welcoming and I'm relieved that the far from companionable silence between Calum and me is about to end. I quicken my step as I approach the house but faced with the door, I hesitate before entering, turn back and look at him. As Calum draws level he remarks, 'That was the longest silence there's been between us since we met.'

My mind shuffles, plays the card before I'm even aware that I'm responding. 'Apart from when we were both asleep...' It's hard to tell in the dim light of the doorway but I think he flinches minutely.

'No... You talked even in your sleep.' He pushes open the door and, unsmiling, ushers me into Shona's kitchen.

I'm glad I took the tranquilliser.

I should have taken two.

Once through the door Calum goes into comedian kid brother mode, joking with Donald when he hands him a dram, admiring Shona's appalling outfit which does nothing for her other than draw attention to her size. I remark that I have never seen her look lovelier – which is more or less true – and admire the fabric (polyester) and the striking colour scheme (a fuchsia print with citric accents of lemon and lime.) Shona sings the praises of her mail-order catalogue, the source of her astonishing wardrobe and promises to lend it to me. At this point I catch Calum's eye and wish I hadn't. I concentrate firmly on the glass of whisky Donald has slipped into my hand while Shona prattles on, flushed and happy.

'It's so kind of you to baby-sit, Rose – Eilidh has been so excited... But I wish you were coming with us! I said to Calum, he should have invited you – och, it would do you *good* to get out.'

'No, Shona, really – I've been working so hard this week and what with one thing and another...' The sentence hangs in the air, lame, unfinished.

Calum, apparently deaf, is looking out of the kitchen window for the taxi. Shona shoots him a sidelong glance, looks back at me and, barely able to disguise her disappointment, changes tack immediately. 'Fergus is asleep already and he'll not wake, but if he does, give him a drink of milk and he'll soon settle. Duncan and Eilidh go to bed at eight and Aly goes at nine-thirty. Don't let them tell you any different now!'

Shona launches into a list of instructions as to the whereabouts of tea, coffee, biscuits, oatcakes, scones and jam. Eilidh tugs at my hand and drags me off to the sitting room where Donald has banked up the fire in my honour. Aly sits at the table, apparently doing homework, his eyes covertly following *Batman* on the TV. Duncan lies in the middle of the floor, his chin resting in his hands. Both boys mumble, 'Hi, Rose,' without looking up from the TV. Eilidh pulls me down onto the sofa and thrusts an open music-box in front of me and starts to chatter as a tiny ballerina in a pink tutu pirouettes dementedly to *La Vie en Rose*. Aly shouts, "Shut it, Eilidh!" I'm not sure whether he is referring to the music-box or her conversation. Eilidh ignores him and pointedly winds up the clockwork mechanism.

I can see I am in for a long evening.

Shona pops her head round the door. 'Did I tell you where the sugar is, Rose?'

'No, but I'm sure I'll find everything. Don't worry about me.' From the kitchen I hear Calum put on his teacher voice, cutting straight through Shona's wittering, the music box and the Batman soundtrack, to summon his sister to her waiting taxi. Shona kisses her brood goodnight one by one, much to Aly's disgust.

With Eilidh clamped to my side – where I suspect she intends to spend the rest of the evening – I follow Shona to the door and watch as she totters down the path in unaccustomed high heels, like a fastidious ewe picking her way delicately along a stony sheep track. Calum hands her into the taxi, shuts the door, looks back and raises his hand in salute to Eilidh and me, then climbs into the front. As the car pulls away I notice Donald still has a whisky glass in his hand. Empty, no doubt.

I read two stories to Eilidh, quietly, so as not to encroach on *Batman*, then she offers to read to me. I take the opportunity to unpack my sewing bag and begin the tedious task of unpicking one of Megan's old dresses, an emerald velvet party dress that I intend to cannibalise. Eilidh soon tires of her 'reading', which consists of running her finger along a line of text whilst improvising a story based on the illustrations.

She fingers the shiny velvet. 'What are you making, Rose?'

'I'm not making anything. I'm *un*-making. I'm taking this old dress apart so that I can use the fabric to make something else.'

'She's *re-cycling* it,' Aly announces without looking away from the TV.

'What are you going to make, Rose? Another dress?'

'No... I'll probably cut up the fabric into smaller pieces and use it to make a quilt. It's a lovely colour, isn't it?'

'Can you not make it into another dress for Megan?'

'Well, yes, I could – if I had some more of the same fabric. But I can't make *this* into another dress for Megan – it's too small. This was hers when she was young, about the same age Aly is now.' Eilidh eyes the fabric, then looks up at me, a strange mix of excitement and apprehension on her little face.

'Do you like the fabric? Would you like me to make it into something for *you*?'

Eilidh glances across at Aly and Duncan, then takes my hand. She leads me out of the sitting room to the bedroom she shares with Fergus. As she opens the door I whisper, 'Don't disturb Fergus! What is it you want to show me?'

'Wait here,' she hisses and slips silently into the bedroom. I hear the sound of a drawer being opened and closed carefully. Eventually, Eilidh appears, flushed and excited, clutching a carrier bag. 'Come to the kitchen, Rose.' I follow, suppressing a smile at Eilidh's mystery, wondering what her precious parcel contains.

In the kitchen she climbs onto a chair and kneels up at the table. She shakes out the contents of the bag and a swathe of peach satin slithers onto the table, followed by a tiny coronet of battered dried flowers. I lift up a tiny bridesmaid's dress.

'Oh, Eilidh – how pretty! Was this yours?'

'Aye, but it doesn't fit me now. Can you make it bigger?'

'No, darling, I'm afraid I can't – not without some more fabric.' Her face falls and I can see she is close to tears. 'But I might be able to find some fabric in my store that would go with it... Some white satin perhaps. We could probably manage to make something from it – but it wouldn't look exactly like this.' Her lip wobbles and a tear begins to slide out of the corner of her eye. I reach into my pocket for a tissue and dab at her face. 'But now I come to think about it, if we dyed some white fabric the same colour, I'm sure we could come up with something pretty close.' Eilidh brightens and rubs at her eyes with my tissue. She attempts to bundle the dress back into the bag. 'Here, let me fold it for you... Show me what you looked like in your flowers.' She places the coronet carefully on her head and smiles up at me, as if posing for a camera. 'You look lovely! You must have looked very pretty on the day. Are there any photos of you?'

'No.'

'Really? Doesn't Mummy have a photo of the wedding?'

'No. The wedding didn't happen.' Eilidh begins to look uncomfortable. She snatches the bag away from me and hugs it to her chest.

'Oh, that's a shame. Was the wedding called off? I mean, did the couple change their minds about getting married?'

'No... Christina died.'

'Oh... How terribly sad.'

'There was an accident.'

'A car accident?'

'No. In the mountains.'

My innards turn to ice-water. I already know the answer to my next question. I should spare the child, spare myself, but I ask anyway. 'Eilidh... Who was Christina going to marry?'

'Uncle Calum, of course.'

'But... she died?'

'Aye. In an avalanche.' She pronounces the difficult word with an effort. 'So they couldn't get married and I couldn't wear my dress. I cried and cried... *Everybody* cried,' she says, with a shrug of her little shoulders.

'How old were you when this happened – can you remember?'

'I think I was... four.'

'And you're seven now?'

'Aye... It was years and years ago.'

'I've never heard anyone talk about Christina before.'

'Uncle Calum called her Chris, but I liked to call her Auntie Christina. She *would* have been my auntie if she hadn't died,' Eilidh explains. 'But we don't ever talk about her now. After she died Mummy said we must never talk about her in front of Uncle Calum because it made him so sad... Och, don't *you* be sad too, Rose!' She unfolds her used tissue and presses it into my hand. 'Mummy says Christina is asleep in Heaven now and very peaceful and she says Uncle Calum will surely find someone else who will make him just as happy as Christina did! But when he does I'll have to have a *new* bridesmaid's dress, won't I?' She places her little hand on mine and squeezes. 'Will you make it for me, Rose? And can it be the *exact* same colour as this one? Please?'

When all three children are finally settled in bed I sit in an armchair and stare at the blank television screen, trying to piece together the fragments of information that Calum gave me. I try to work out if he has lied, misled me, or simply failed to tell me the whole truth. My exhausted brain stalls at a memory of him standing distraught and naked, reciting names, a litany of death. Al... Hamish... Hugh... Jim... And Chris.

Chris.

I feel as if the ground is giving way beneath me. I sink my fingernails deep into the hideous dralon of Shona's three-piece suite, grip the arms of the chair as if I too might be swept away by an avalanche. The room spins and I'm consumed by the need to see Calum, speak to him, touch him, but I'm uncertain whether I'm more likely to strike him or take him in my arms.

I stare at the clock on the mantelpiece and listen out for the sound of a taxi.

Just before midnight the taxi arrives, having dropped Calum off first. I decline Donald's offer of a nightcap and plead exhaustion. I insist on walking home alone but as soon as Shona has shut the door behind me I set off with my torch along the road to Calum's caravan, walking fast, tripping in my haste over several large stones. As I approach the caravan I can see the lights are still on. I bang loudly on the door and walk straight in. Calum wheels round, spilling the contents of a glass of whisky. He looks startled and dishevelled – barefoot, his Mickey Mouse tie hanging loose round his neck, his shirt unbuttoned. He blinks at me while I catch my breath.

'The poem was no' *that* bad, surely?'

'Why didn't you tell me, Calum?'

'Tell you what?'

'About Chris.'

He stares at me for a moment, then asks quietly. 'Shona?'

'No, of course not! I imagine you've sworn her to secrecy, otherwise she'd have told me long ago. It was Eilidh. She showed me her bridesmaid's dress. Asked me if I could make it into a new dress for her.'

'Ah.' He studies the dregs of whisky in his glass.

'*Why*, Calum?'

He looks up, his face a pale blank. 'Why did Chris die?'

'Why didn't you *tell* me?'

'I did tell you.'

'Don't play games with me!'

'I'm not playing games, Rose. I told you all you needed to know.'

'But you weren't being straight with me, you didn't tell me the whole truth.'

'And what, I wonder, makes you think you're entitled to the whole truth? Shona doesn't know what happened. Christina's parents don't. Nobody knows but me.' He empties his glass and then his eyes scan the room, searching, I know, for the bottle.

'I don't understand... Eilidh made it sound like Chris had died in an avalanche.'

'Aye, she would. That's what she was told. But it isn't true. The truth is worse than that. The stuff of nightmares.' He turns and heads for the kitchen. I follow.

'Will you tell me what happened, Calum. Please.'

'You don't need to know.'

'Maybe I don't – but I think you need to *tell*.'

He bangs his empty glass down on the draining board and stands hunched over the sink, his shoulders tensed. I wonder if he is going to be sick. 'If I tell you, Rose, it's on the understanding that we never mention it again. I don't talk about it. I have never, ever talked about it, except to tell kindly lies to interested parties who had a right to know what happened. They *don't* know what happened, but they think they do... and that brings them a kind of peace.'

He yanks open a cupboard door and takes out a new bottle of whisky. Ignoring me, he walks back to the sofa, sits and pours himself a shot with trembling hands. He raises his glass. *'A' Chairistìona... mo chridhe.'* He drinks, then staring at the floor he begins. 'Christina was my wife's best friend. She and I had a lot in common – we both climbed, both loved the outdoors, we both came from Uist.'

I sit down next to him on the sofa. 'She was a local girl?'

'Oh aye...' He risks a quick look at me. 'We're not just talking personal tragedy here – Chris's death was a loss to the whole community. And it was my fault she died.' He tugs at his tie, removes it and tosses it aside. 'My marriage was a mistake. Things started to go wrong almost immediately... Being married wasn't the same as living together. There were fights over my climbing, there was a lot of stress at work and I took it out on Alison. And after a couple of years of marriage she started the baby blackmail. I knew it was over but I was too tired and busy to deal with it. And too cowardly... To begin with, Chris wanted to try and patch us up but... things changed. Eventually she was wanting me to leave Alison.'

'Did Alison know about you and Chris?'

'Not for quite a while. Chris got a job on Skye and I used to go and climb there and guide during the holidays. Alison didn't realise I was sleeping with Chris while I was there. Sometimes Chris came to Glasgow, when Alison was away... In the end I told Alison I wanted a divorce. And why. She was appalled. I don't know what hurt her most – my betrayal or her best friend's.' He looks at me with a sardonic smile. 'It's a shame you never met her, Rose – you'd have had a lot to talk about.'

He reaches up to a bookshelf and pulls down a photo album, flips it open without looking and hands it to me. A photo taken in what looks like Shona's sitting room shows Calum with a tall young woman, dark, pale and blue-eyed like him. They could pass for brother and sister were it not for the look of mutual adoration. Festooned with coloured streamers, they raise champagne glasses to each other. They look so happy, it hurts. I close the album carefully.

'That was taken in 1997 at our engagement party... People here were ecstatic. I'd come home to teach in the local school and we planned to set up an outdoor activity centre here. We'd bought a big house with a byre we were going to convert into a bunkhouse. We were to be married here and wee Eilidh was to be bridesmaid... As we were already living together we decided we wouldn't have a honeymoon. We wanted to go climbing abroad one last time before ploughing all our earnings into the business. So we did. We went climbing one last time...'

'Where?'

'The Eiger.'

I wince automatically, thinking of the death toll exacted by that particular bastard of a mountain. Calum sees my reaction and nods. 'Aye. Not the wisest of choices... and it was mine. But when the accident happened we were on our way down. It had been a hard climb but the descent should have been relatively easy... We had bad luck with the weather. We were tired... Too tired. And dehydrated. That impairs your judgement and your performance. That's all I can say in my defence... We were descending on a lee slope and it was loaded with windslab. I knew there was a level of avalanche risk but we needed to get down in a hurry. The weather was getting worse and I was worried about Chris who was already showing signs of hypothermia. I led out across the snow, roped up to Chris and it seemed okay. She started to traverse the slope, then there was a sound like a crack... then a great hissing noise... and we were travelling down the mountainside caught up in an avalanche. I used my ice-axes to brake and when I finally came to a standstill I thought I was little worse than winded, but when I tried to move I realised I'd cracked a rib... I'd also broken three fingers on one hand. But I was alive... I didn't know where Chris was but I could feel her whole weight on my harness, so I knew she hadn't been buried in the avalanche, she must be hanging somewhere... I didn't move to begin with, just hung on to the axes and waited for her to take her own weight. But she didn't... I called out but she didn't answer. That was when I started to think there was maybe a dead body on the other end of the rope...

'I was getting very cold waiting so I tried to move to a more secure position, but as soon as I pulled out an axe I was dragged down the slope by Chris' weight. I dug in again and waited some more. The light was fading and we were running out of time. It was hours since we'd eaten or drunk anything – another of my bad judgements. I slithered down the slope, braking with my axes, until I got to the ledge. At some point in my descent Chris started screaming. She'd regained consciousness, I suppose. I remember feeling this great rush of relief that she was alive... That was before I realised just how bad it was.'

Calum puts his head in his hands and threads shaking fingers through his hair, scraping it back from his forehead. 'Rose, I can't do this... Please – don't make me...'

I say nothing, but lay a hand gently on the back of his neck, curving it round the base of his skull. He sits upright suddenly and turns towards me. I am shocked at how tired and gaunt he looks, wonder how long it is since he really slept. He looks at me silently for what feels like a long time, then looks away and continues in a monotone.

'She was suspended in the air at the end of fifty feet of rope. She'd broken both her ankles. She'd have done that when she went over the edge. The rope was too long – another bad judgement. She'd have been flung over the edge during the avalanche. When she got to the end of her rope, she'd have swung back like a pendulum until she slammed into the mountainside. And she'd have taken the impact with her feet – it was that or die – and she'd have broken both her ankles... She'd also lost a glove in the avalanche. She now had a useless frostbitten hand... In other words, she was completely fucked.'

CHAPTER SEVENTEEN

I CANNOT FIND ANY WORDS. Anything other than silence and stillness feels obscenely inappropriate. I watch Calum with my insides aching.

He gives a kind of hopeless shrug and continues. 'She couldn't climb back up... I couldn't haul her up... I tried but I was in a pretty bad way. I was getting weak and sleepy with the cold... I tried to set up a snow anchor using an axe, but I had only one good hand and the snow was soft, just avalanched powder. And snow was falling so fast, I was getting buried. I knew that even if I managed to get her up onto the ledge she wouldn't be able to climb down, I'd have to lower her down the mountain... in the dark... in a blizzard... with a broken hand and a cracked rib. I knew there was nothing I could do to save her, we were both going to die and she was going to die first, but I wanted her to die knowing I was there, that I was trying to save her.'

'Did you tell Chris you were injured?'

'No – I knew she'd panic even more. I kept trying to get her up, but I just couldn't do it. Eventually I told her to drop all the hardware from her harness, then I told her to drop her rucksack. She knew then... just how bad things were. You don't dump your gear if you think you're going to survive. She asked me if I was injured... I told her. She cracked then and started sobbing... I tried to calm her down... I don't know what I said – there was nothing I could say... Then she tried to get something out of her rucksack. She was trying to reach inside the top of her rucksack with her good hand, the one that wasn't frozen. She wanted her knife...'

Calum grinds the heels of his hands into his wet eyes. I want to touch him, hold him, but know if I do, he will stop talking; I know too that he shouldn't.

'I lost it then. I started yelling at her, screaming, telling her not to give up, that I'd get her up *somehow*. But it was almost dark, we were facing a night on the mountain. She knew my only chance of survival was if she cut me free... But she couldn't find her knife. Or maybe she got it out, then dropped it, I don't know. She didn't say anything more... I kept yelling down to her but there was no answer. Maybe she lost consciousness again... I dug a kind of snow-hole for myself and sat and waited to die.' He shakes his head slowly. 'I still don't know how I didn't...

'When the sun came up there was no movement on the end of the rope. No sound. I knew she couldn't have survived a night out in the open. I steeled myself to look over the edge, to look down at her body...' He swallows several times. 'She'd taken down her hood... removed her balaclava. She'd thrown away her other glove... Her face and hands were frozen. Black. She'd done that so that I would know she was dead, so that I would cut the rope, save myself. So I did. She fell five hundred feet... then her body hit some rocks and bounced... then she disappeared into a crevasse... I set off down the mountainside and was found half-dead by another party of climbers.' He reaches for the bottle, pours himself another whisky and drinks it straight down. 'I should have died with her.'

'You nearly did, Calum. But that isn't what she wanted. Her death was tragic and pointless – why make it two?'

'So that she wouldn't have to die alone.'

'Chris didn't die alone. You stayed with her till the end and she knew that. She knew right up until the moment that she died that you were there, attached to her by a rope. She knew when she died that you loved her.'

He turns his head slowly and looks at me, puzzled almost, as if I have said something that he hadn't thought of, something that has never occurred to him in all his nightmare reconstructions of the accident. For a fleeting moment he looks pitifully grateful, then his face darkens and his hollow eyes are pleading with me.

'What should I have done, Rose? Tell her parents she died very slowly of hypothermia, in pain, alone, terrified, dangling on the end of a rope? That when she died, I cut the rope and dumped her body so that I could get down the mountain and save my own life? Should I have told them that? Because whatever I told Christina's parents is what I had to tell everybody – our climbing mates, Shona, the bairns… There could only be one story and I didn't know how to face Chris's parents with the truth. I couldn't see any *point* in telling the truth, causing them even more pain. But maybe that was just me protecting myself.'

'You did all you could – nobody could have done any more. And some people would have done less.'

'But I *lied*. I've lied for years. To *everyone*.'

'You had your reasons. Good reasons. No one has been harmed by the lie. Except you, Calum.'

'What would you have wanted, Rose? Megan and I told you the truth about Gavin's death but we didn't need to. You could have gone on for years, you could have died not knowing what happened to him. But now you do – are you glad you know? Does it help to know how *messy* a death Gavin died?'

'No, of course it doesn't, it's horrible. I'm glad I know that he's dead, that it's... all over, but I'm not glad to know how he died. I can't bear to think of him lying smashed on a rock, in dreadful pain, probably knowing he was going to die. I wish I didn't know all that... But I don't think you or Megan were wrong to tell me.'

His face twists into a derisive smile. 'But you think I was right to lie about Chris.'

'Yes, I do. It's different for me. What was it you said to me once, about your climbing friends who'd died? They knew the score. I knew the score, Calum. I'm of that world. I know about the types of injury, the accidents, the mistakes, the appalling bad luck. Chris's parents probably didn't. I spent all the years I lived with Gavin trying to prepare myself mentally for his death. But no parent expects to bury their child.'

'They didn't even get to bury her.'

I want to scream for having chosen the wrong words. Instead I take hold of his hand. One of us is shaking. I think it's Calum. 'You did the right thing. The kindest thing.'

'Kind to whom? Me?'

'To her parents, her family. And they were the ones who mattered. If you were the only witness to what happened then you had a choice about telling the truth. You didn't have a choice about Gavin. He was rescued by a team. Dave survived. I could always have found out what happened to Gavin. You couldn't have lied to me... But I rather wish you had.' I stroke his unresponsive hand. 'I think we both need some coffee, don't you? Will you drink some if I make it?' Eventually he nods. 'Good. I'll be right back.'

I wait for the kettle to boil and stare at a scruffy pin-board decorated with dog-eared postcards and fading photographs, some of Calum, some of his family, but most of climbers and mountains. In all the photos men and women are laughing. They are young, fit and happy. I wonder how many of the people pictured on the board are still alive. My eye rests on a photo of Christina taken at the foot of an Alpine mountain. I recognise the unmistakeable outline of the Eiger and wonder with a shudder if this was the last photo Calum ever took of her.

I make two mugs of strong coffee and return to Calum who hasn't moved. He sits slumped on the sofa, staring at his clasped hands. I hand him a mug and he takes it without speaking.

'Chris is why you drink, isn't she?'

'One of the reasons.'

'Does it help?'

'Aye... But not in the way you might think. It doesn't help me forget. It doesn't even really dull the pain, but drinking to excess generates a fair amount of self-disgust – not to mention quite a few debilitating hangovers – all of which allows me to simultaneously despise and pity myself.' He sips his coffee. 'And it's easier for my family and friends to think that wee Calum has a drink problem rather than a life problem – or should that be *death* problem? Drinking's the norm here – it's manly, it's Highland. Grieving isn't.'

'Does anything dull the pain?'

'Writing... sometimes.' He looks at me wearily. 'And you, Rose. *You* dull the pain. You're the only thing I've ever found that is bigger, stronger than all the fucking grief and guilt... Just being with you. You colonise my brain, like a new poem when it's taking root. I can't stop thinking about you, talking to you in my head, wondering what you're going to say next, do next...' His eyes wander over my body, then he looks away, into his coffee mug. 'And I can't stop thinking about making love to you... It wasn't so bad before we slept together, but now... now I think about you, your body, all the time.' He looks back at me and holds my eyes for a moment. A muscle flickers at the corner of his mouth and his lips thin into a tense, hard line. When I can bear the silence no longer I lay a hand gently on his forearm, but he pulls away from me and stands abruptly. He walks over to the window and stares out into the darkness in the direction of my house.

'One of us has to go, Rose and I'm quite happy for it to be me. I want a nice, quiet, *dead* life – just like yours – living inside my whisky-addled head. My family loves me and I love them – hell, that ought to be enough! I've lived without sex for years – it should get easier, I reckon, now I'm forty...' He turns and looks back at me, his head on one side. 'Does it get easier, Rose? You should know. Do you have any tips, any words of encouragement? Will you not extol the virtues of the celibate life you're so keen to pursue?'

'I'm a fake, Calum and you know it – that's why you're taunting me now. As you so rightly pointed out the night we didn't quite make love, I wanted you from the moment I first met you.'

'In Shona's kitchen...' He smiles then. The transformation of his face takes my breath away, as well as the last remnants of my resolution. 'You hardly even looked at me.'

'I didn't need to. I knew.'

'I tried to get you talking.'

'I know. You cracked some very funny jokes at poor Shona's expense and I kept laughing at them. I remember it felt... unfamiliar. As if I was using muscles in my face that I hadn't used for a long time. You don't laugh much when you live alone.'

'I was just showing off, like a big kid, trying to make you laugh. You have such a beautiful face when you're happy, Rose. You're so *alive*.'

'Probably because I've had so much to do with death. You're the same. Even when you're stupid with drink, being with you is like being on one of my highs, like breathing pure oxygen. All your words, your ideas, all the laughter... I was actually rather hoping you'd be crap in bed so that I could walk away disillusioned... But no such luck.'

Calum folds his arms across his chest. 'Och, you women are *awfu'* hard to please... There was I thinking I had to outshine himself, when what you really wanted from me was impotence.'

'Like hell I did.'

His crooked smile dies, his lips part and I sense his breathing change. As his chest rises and falls, I see the pale ridge of scar, remember the other scars and I am on my feet, moving towards him.

His hands shoot out to ward me off. 'You're going to have to leave, Rose. Go home now.'

'Calum – '

'Rose, don't *do* this to me! Not again! I've told you what you wanted to know, now go. If you don't, I'll kiss you – and the look in your eye tells me you're not about to fight me off. I'll not be *used* like that! Look, this may sound weird coming from a man – ' He looks down at his crotch and sighs, exasperated. 'Especially one with a semi-permanent hard-on – but I don't want sex, I want *love*. And that's all I'm offering. Take it or leave it.'

I stand in front of him, within arm's reach. On a precipice. 'You really think you love me, Calum?'

'Aye... Heart, body and soul.'

'I don't know if I love you.'

He shrugs. 'It's enough for me that you might.'

'You'll settle for so little?'

'You want me. You need me. I think maybe you do love me, you just won't admit it. You won't let me look after you.'

'What makes you think you can?'

'I understand just being alive isn't enough for you. Gavin just wanted to keep you alive, didn't he? He wanted you to take the drugs, stop working so hard, stop doing the things that sent you into over-drive – am I right?' I nod. 'I don't think he understood about your work, about your senses, the way you perceive the world. God knows, he should have done. He was a climber and prepared to risk his life on a regular basis in order to live life on his own terms, but I don't think he realised that you were the *same*, that mere existence wasn't enough... Maybe he loved you too much to take risks with your life.'

'Are you saying you don't love me as much as Gavin did?'

'Maybe – who knows? I'm saying I love you enough to let you do things your way. And if you fall, I'll catch you. If you break, I'll stick you back together again.'

'All the King's horses and all the King's men?'

'Aye... And I'll be around, Rose, I'll be there all the time. When you're working I'll ring you up from school and remind you to take your medication. I won't go away for weeks and months at a time. You'll know where I am and it will never be far away. Things will be... *steady*. And that will be good for you.'

'You'll die of boredom.'

'Two creative artists living and working together, arguing and having brilliant sex? How bad can that be? I think living with you will be all the excitement I can handle, Rose.'

'There'd be no children.'

He shakes his head. 'I don't want them, never have. It drove a wedge between me and Alison and I still feel the same way. Children are my work, a huge part of my life, but I'd have nothing left to give my own. Being able to write is what matters to me most. That's who I am. Bairns and poetry have never seemed compatible to me.'

'I'll drive you mad.'

'We'll see. If you can't beat them, join them.'

'Don't joke about it, Calum – it wears people out! It wears them *down*. All my friends walked away.'

'What wears folk out is the wanting, Rose – wanting things to be different. *Better*. I don't want that. I don't want to change you. I don't want you "cured". I love you the way you are. It won't wear me out. I know there's a price to be paid for what I want. Maybe it's a high price, but I'm prepared to pay it. Seems like a bargain to me.'

'I wanted to do it on my own... It seemed the only way. The safest way.'

'Maybe you could go it alone, but it will be so much harder. And riskier. If I support you emotionally I know you'll find things easier.'

'And if you let me down it could kill me.'

'Aye... which is why I never *will* you let you down. I'm not having any more folk dying on me...' There is a long silence in which we both stand quite still and wait, conscious of the space between us, the gulf. Calum does not take his eyes from mine. 'Well?'

'Well... it's the best offer I've had this year... *ever*, in fact... so I feel inclined to accept. And it will make two men very happy.'

'Who's the other?'

'My psychiatrist.'

Calum lunges and pulls me into his arms. As we kiss we are laughing, crying, both unsteady on our feet. I take his face in my hands and spread my fingers over his parted lips to stem the flow of kisses.

'Calum, will you take me home? And... will you please stay?'

'I'm no' wearing those fancy pyjamas again.'

'You looked very nice in them.'

'How would *you* know? You were out of your head.'

'Anyway you need have no worries on that score. I shall require you to take off all your clothes this time. And mine.'

He strokes my throat and moves his hand downwards inside my shirt, caressing my bare shoulder. His long fingers hover above my breasts as he rapidly undoes my shirt buttons. 'Do we have to go to yours? I'm not sure I can walk in this state of excitement.'

I grasp both his hands. 'It's bloody symbolic! I can't actually carry you over the threshold, but I'm inviting you into my home. Into my bed. Into my life... God, I must be stark, staring mad.'

'Probably. The funny thing is – I don't actually mind if you *are*.'

When we arrive at my house Calum steps in front of me and opens the front door. He reaches in and switches on the hall light, then turns back to me, lifts me as easily as if I were a rucksack and carries me over the threshold. He kicks the door shut behind him and begins to climb the stairs. I cling on round his neck, remembering the quantity of whisky he has drunk.

'Be careful, Calum... Hadn't you better put me down?'

'No. Not till we get to the bedroom.'

'It's in a terrible mess... I haven't tidied for a week. You'll have to plough through heaps of my dirty underwear.'

'Ploughing through your underwear was *exactly* what I had in mind...'

CHAPTER EIGHTEEN

Grenitote
North Uist
Western Isles

March 28th

My dear Megan,

Thanks for your postcard. I can't tell you how pleased I am you've decided to go back to college. I'm sure you won't regret it. Qualifications are bound to lead to more job opportunities for you.

I have some news I think you might be pleased to hear. Calum has moved in with me and we're very happy together. Most of his possessions are still in the caravan and that may be where they'll stay for the moment as we're now rather cramped in my little house. But he's now based here with me and we hope this will be a permanent arrangement. With his job I have to keep fairly regular hours now, so we take it in turns to cook proper meals. All in all I think Calum being around will be good for me. (For him too – he's drinking a lot less.)

Shona and Donald are both well and send their love. Last week poor Aly fell and broke his wrist playing football. He's livid because it was his left wrist so he still has to do homework. In her quest for fitness Shona has abandoned ceilidh-robics and taken up line dancing. She's a sight to behold in her cowgirl outfit! As she herself would say, 'A blind man would be glad to see it.'

I enclose your invitation to the exhibition in Lochmaddy. It will be nice if you can come but don't worry if you can't manage it. Someone from the local radio station is going to interview us (I hope not in Gaelic!) and Calum's publisher is talking about bringing out a book of the new poems using one of my quilts on the cover which is very exciting. A local photographer is taking photos of the quilts and I'm having some postcards made to sell at the exhibition.

I've decided to make a sort of pilgrimage to Skye to pay my respects to Gavin. I want to stand at the foot of the Cuillin again and see where his ashes were scattered. Calum insists on coming with me. We're going at the end of term and staying for a few days. Calum will introduce me to the rest of the team who brought Gavin down. I know this all sounds rather grim but after a lot of thought I decided it's something I want to do – need to do – before getting on with the rest of my life.

I hope to see you in June if you can make it. Take good care of yourself.

Much love,

Mum.

xxx

PS Calum was pleased to hear you're going back to college and sends his love.

Calum and I set off for Skye on an April morning. He says he will drive as he knows the Skye roads better than me and his car is more comfortable than mine. What he really means is, I will have enough to think about when we get there. Yet another example of the invisible care to which I am gradually – and gratefully – becoming accustomed.

The *MV Hebrides* leaves Lochmaddy bathed in sunshine and sails due east across the Little Minch for nearly two hours, towards Uig on the north-west coast of Skye. It is only when you leave the Western Isles and try to get somewhere else that you realise – in UK terms – you're living at the edge of the world. Uig is still a good hour's drive from mainland Scotland, now connected to the Isle of Skye by a controversial bridge. On the other side of the bridge we still have but a toehold on civilisation, since it would take another two hours to drive to the nearest Marks and Spencer's in Inverness, at a latitude north of Moscow.

Nevertheless I prepare myself for the culture shock of Skye where, most noticeably, there will be traffic going in both directions – a novelty after our sedate single-track roads on Uist – and Calum will have to try to remember the procedure for overtaking. I'm looking forward to the luxury of a supermarket larger than a corner shop, a choice of cafés and – oh joy! – a *bookshop*.

And of course the mountains... My feelings as the *Hebrides* sails into the gigantic amphitheatre of Uig Bay are mixed but among them is a fizzing excitement at the thought of seeing the Cuillin at close quarters again.

As the vessel approaches the village of Uig the odd contours of Skye strike me once more – the strange angularity after the gentle slopes and curves of Uist. Once again the landscape seems to me somehow male: the sudden corners of escarpments, the steep drops of sea-cliffs, the projecting grassy knolls seem to me to suggest the limbs and joints of a giant recumbent body – shoulders, elbows, knees. These topographical features jar an eye accustomed to the graceful undulations of Uist, but they are none the less beautiful and stirring for that.

Rain falls on Uig and the pewter sea churns sickeningly as we disembark. On the steep green slopes white houses are scattered randomly, like sheep grazing on a hillside. They look tiny, clean and bright, a Toy Town village. As Calum's car crawls out of the belly of the ship and we clank over the metal ramp onto the Isle of Skye, he asks, 'Straight to Sligachan? Or a spot of retail therapy in Portree?' That consideration again. He wants to give me time to prepare.

'No... Straight to Sligachan, please. Let's get it over with...'

The road climbs up out of Uig and skirts the west coast of Skye's Trotternish peninsula. Despite their height of three thousand feet the Cuillin are not immediately visible, even when good weather conditions prevail. Soon, on our right, we can see Macleod's Tables, twin hills, weirdly flat-topped, one larger than the other: *Healabhal Mhor* and *Healabhal Bheag* – Big and Little Healabhal in Gaelic.

Calum turns to me. 'You know the story? About Macleod's Tables?'

'Vaguely... Some nocturnal picnic wasn't it?'

'Aye... Alasdair Crotach – that's Aly the Hunchback to you – seventh Chief of the Clan MacLeod was entertained to dinner by some Edinburgh big shots. He'd scrubbed up well for a Teuchter and they were impressed by his fine manners, but they decided to give him a hard time anyway... They scoffed at his supposedly primitive living arrangements on

299

Skye and boasted that nothing on Skye could compete with the civilised elegance of Edinburgh.'

'A sentiment still echoed by many,' I add, smiling, as Calum gets into his stride.

'The clan chief replied that, on the contrary, on Skye he had a larger table, a more beautifully decorated ceiling and *much* more impressive lighting. He invited the sceptical Lowlanders to dine with him at his ancestral home. On the evening in question the fine gentlemen were escorted to the summit of *Healabhal Mhor* where, under a starry night sky, the hill's flat top was laid with food and wine while Macleod retainers stood about with flaming torches to illuminate the scene. History does not relate, but I've no doubt the menu included humble pie.'

The Cuillin aren't visible until we reach the Kingsburgh turn-off, then looking south, we see the entire jagged holly-leaf ridge, miraculously visible on this wet April day. (Unlucky tourists can spend a week on Skye and remain unaware that it possesses a world-class mountain range. Not for nothing is Skye known as *Eilean a' Cheo* – The Misty Isle.)

'There's the ridge,' Calum remarks.

'Yes.' My eyes fill and I look away. The first of the new lambs gambol ridiculously in the fields, undaunted by the rain. 'Keep talking, Calum. Please. Anything. I don't want to think. . .'

With no hesitation – perhaps he has prepared a speech for just such an eventuality? – Calum launches into a lecture on the Cuillin, somehow avoiding any reference to mountaineering. The man is a wonder.

'The name "Cuillin" is very interesting, etymologically speaking... The locals like to believe it derives from the Gaelic *cuilionn* meaning "holly" but the name is more than likely derived from the Norse *kjölen* meaning "high mountain ridge" It's a freak landscape, there's nothing else like it in Britain. It was formed when the Earth's crust ruptured and billions of cubic feet of magma were spewed up from below. The magma formed a gigantic mountain massif several miles high. It's hard to believe, but what we're looking at now is just the remnants of a system of volcanoes, originally ten thousand feet high. Seven thousand feet have been eroded... Which just goes to show how bloody *terrible* the weather is on Skye.'

'What's it like Calum – being up there? Up on the ridge?'

He pauses before answering. 'In my impressionable youth I used to think it was better than sex...' He shakes his head, then turns and grins at me. 'Now I think I must have been sleeping with the wrong women.'

At the Sligachan Inn we park in the shadow of the mountains. The tops are swathed in cloud now and as I get out of the car I look up to where I know *Sgurr nan Gillean* is hidden. As Calum takes our luggage out of the boot he looks at me. 'You're sure about this now?'

'Yes, I'm fine. It's not the mountains bothering me, actually... I didn't think – the last time I stayed here I was with Gavin...'

Calum says nothing but takes my hand and we present ourselves at Reception. A young girl leads us upstairs to our room. As she puts a key in the door, Calum turns to let me enter first. I hesitate, then cast my eyes down, at a loss.

'Rose?'

I look up at him in mute appeal. Calum meets my eyes and frowns. Then he turns back to the receptionist. 'Do you have another room?'

'Aye, but this one's the best. You'll have a grand view of the ridge.'

'We'll take another, please.'

'No bother... If you'll just wait here, I'll get another key.' She sets off down the stairs at a trot and I wait till she is out of earshot.

'Thanks... Gavin and I – '

'No need to explain – I'm not sharing any more beds with that guy.'

Supper at the inn is a strangely sober affair. In the bar we are surrounded by hikers and climbers in various stages of hilarious inebriation, comparing notes on the day's climbing and swapping travellers' tales. Calum and I sit by the fire, mostly silent. I remember sitting next to him in front of Shona's fire, having an altogether better time and I think how far we have come in just a couple of months. Calum doesn't try to make conversation, for which I am grateful. Several men in the bar know him and he introduces me without explanation, which leads to a few speculative glances. He then fields most of the conversation so that I don't have to explain why I am at Sligachan.

After dinner, Calum asks if I feel like a walk. I have sensed the physical tension in him all evening. He has been drinking beer when I know he needed whisky. His edginess is palpable and understandable. Mountains hold as many memories for him as they do for me. He stands now with his shoulders hunched, his shaggy head slightly bowed, in that way he has of looking like a coiled spring, as if he is braced, preparing to do something difficult on a rockface. It suddenly occurs to me that I have never watched Calum climb. I wonder if I ever will. If I ever could.

'Yes, let's walk. I could do with some fresh air. It might help me sleep.'

We wrap up, step outside the inn and walk over to the old disused bridge, the one that appears on the postcards and countless tourists' photographs, encircled as it is by one of the most scenic and dramatic views in the world. The night is clear and cold and the navy sky is prodigal with stars. The mountains are still snow-capped and a nail-paring of moon picks out their ghostly, glittering peaks. The river Sligachan splashes and gurgles soothingly over smooth stones and I feel some of my tension begin to seep away. I place my hands on the rough, lichened stones of the bridge, try to draw strength from their antiquity.

Calum stands behind me and encloses me in his arms. I lean back and rest my head on his chest, looking up towards *Sgurr nan Gillean*, the Peak of the Young Men, where Simon and Andy scattered Gavin's ashes.

Calum knows where I am looking. 'Rose, if you're wanting me to take you up there, I can't do it. Not after Chris... You're too precious to me.'

'No, I don't want to go, Calum. I'm sure I'm not nearly fit enough anyway. No, it's bad enough down here on the ground, thinking about Gavin being up there... I just wanted to see... see where his ashes were scattered. I wanted to see his final resting place. Hard to imagine Gavin at rest... I'm not sure I ever witnessed that particular phenomenon.'

Shouts and coarse laughter shatter the peace as men leave the bar arguing and weave their unsteady way over to the campsite. As Dave and Gavin must have done last summer.

I talk to forestall tears. 'I'm glad they cremated him... I mean, I'm sorry that there isn't a grave, somewhere I could go, but I couldn't have borne the thought of his body... *decaying*. That is so horrible – and so *not* Gavin! He was always fit and healthy – he never even got colds... Sorry Calum, this isn't really fair on you.'

'That's okay...' He buries his face in my hair and mumbles, 'I'm alive. I can afford to be magnanimous.' He tightens his arms around me. 'This is a good place to end up, Rose. The best. It's what I'd have wanted if I'd died on the hill... Or in a car accident or of old age, for that matter. I'd want to be here. To have my bones mixed in with these stones. I envy the bastard in a way – he's part of it now.' After a moment's silence Calum begins to recite softly in Gaelic.

'*Thar truaighe, eu-dòchas, gamhlas, cuilbheart,*
thar ciont is truaillidheachd, gu furachair,
gu treunmhor chithear an Cuilithionn
's e'g éirigh air taobh eile duilghe.'
'What is that?'
'It's from a poem by Sorley Maclean.'
'*The Cuillin?*'

'Aye.'

I turn in his arms to face him. 'Would you translate for me?'

'Beyond misery, despair, hatred, treachery,
beyond guilt and defilement; watchful,
heroic, the Cuillin is seen
rising on the other side of sorrow.'

I swallow hard and try to smile. 'Gavin's on the other side of sorrow now.'

Calum nods, his face pale, uncertain in the moonlight. 'Aye... So are we.'

EPILOGUE

I FEEL I BELONG NOW. A trite phrase, but how else can you describe the sense of being not an observer, but a component part of your surroundings? I do not feel separate from the land, from the sea, I feel a part of it all – albeit a tiny part. When I see a spectacular sunset here now, I feel no need to record the event with sketchbook or camera because I know I will see another and then another. Put like that, it sounds as if I take the beauty of my surroundings for granted. I don't, but it has become an everyday miracle, like Calum's love, like life itself. Each day when I wake up I am faintly surprised to find that I am still alive and not alone, to find that the sun has risen, the tide has come in and gone out again. And then I feel the connection once more, a visceral tug, a sense of belonging to the earth, being a part of its rhythms and power.

There is a place I go to when I walk, a bare outcrop of rock to which one tree clings obliquely. The tree is wind-warped, encrusted with pale grey lichen, its gnarled branches bent and splayed at unnatural angles, like broken limbs. I love that tree. I love its quirky ugliness, its tenacity, its solitariness. My tree is a survivor and what that survival has cost is eloquently graven into every straining bough.

After one of our gales Calum checks slates on the roof and I walk up the hill to my rock, my tree. When I see that it still stands, leaning at its familiar rakish angle, my heart leaps. The day will come no doubt when that tree yields but until that time I will honour my tree and its improbable affirmation of life.